THE
LYING
TONGUE

THE
LYING
TONGUE

Andrew Wilson

ATRIA BOOKS

NEW YORK LONDON TORONTO SYDNEY

ATRIA BOOKS
1230 Avenue of the Americas
New York, NY 10020

Library of Congress Cataloging-in-Publication Data

Wilson, Andrew, date.
   The lying tongue / Andrew Wilson. — 1st Atria Books hardcover ed.
    p. cm.
   1. English—Italy—Fiction. 2. Authors—Fiction. 3. Venice (Italy)—Fiction.
  I. Title.

PR6123.I565L95 2007
823'.92—dc22   2006051877

ISBN-13: 978-0-7432-9397-6
ISBN-10:   0-7432-9397-5

First Atria Books hardcover edition February 2007

10 9 8 7 6 5 4 3 2 1

ATRIA BOOKS is a trademark of Simon & Schuster, Inc.

Manufactured in the United States of America

Designed by Jaime Putorti

For information about special discounts for bulk purchases,
please contact Simon & Schuster Special Sales at
1-800-456-6798 or business@simonandschuster.com.

This is not the book I wanted to write.
This is not how it was supposed to be at all.

THE LYING TONGUE

Wherever I went I saw a question mark at the heart of the city. The first time was at the airport while waiting by the baggage carousel. I took out my guidebook, flicked to the map at the back, and the form seemed to jump off the page: the Grand Canal snaking its way through the saturated land, a constant interrogator.

I looked around and wondered what brought these people to Venice. A young Chinese man concentrated as he eased a new SIM card into his mobile. A pretty, dark-skinned woman took off her glasses, retrieved a small mirror from her jacket pocket and proceeded to drop fish-scale-thin contact lenses into her eyes. A bald man, his shaved head reflecting the harsh yellow glow of the airport lights, waited impatiently for his luggage, his eyes nervous.

I knew what I was here for. I smiled to myself as I compared my position with that of my friends back in London, preparing to start dull postgraduate courses or earning less than the minimum wage in one of the so-called creative industries. My best mate, Jake, had just taken a job as a junior on the diary page of a newspaper and was so poor he was forced to subsist on cheap wine and free canapés. I wanted something better.

In my final term at university I had told people, perhaps rather foolishly, that I was going to write a novel. London held too many distractions. All I needed was the time to write. And now I would have it.

A couple of months back, Jake had told me that one of his father's friends, an Italian investor, was looking for someone to go out to Venice to help his sixteen-year-old son with his English. It was the perfect opportunity. The plan was to teach Antonio in the mornings, which would leave me the rest of the day to work on my book, which I had decided to set in Venice. After a half-hour conversation over the phone and a scurry of emails, I was offered the job. The money wasn't great—around three hundred euros a month—but it came with a free room. I was due to start in a couple of days. I couldn't believe my luck.

After retrieving my bags and slinging them onto a trolley, I walked out into the hot night. A pink moon shimmered in the sky. I followed the trail of people heading toward the water launch through a series of makeshift plastic tunnels that trapped the heat, so the air I breathed seemed to burn the inside of my throat. As I neared the Alilaguna stop, I could hear the lapping of the tide against the side of the dock. I imagined clear, refreshing water. What I saw shocked me: a liquid that looked more like tar, thick and viscous and covered with a slimy film brimming with debris. A dead pigeon floated on top of the water, its body undulating with the gentle ebb of the tide. A current swept its body toward the dock. It had no eyes.

I didn't have to wait that long before a launch arrived. I bought a ticket on board and spent the next hour traveling through the dark lagoon. At the stop nearest St. Mark's, I lugged my bags off the boat and stopped to study my map. That question mark again. I found the tiny street just behind the piazza and made a mental note of its location. I started to walk across the square. All around me I heard the constant clapping of pigeons; there was something faintly mocking about their tone.

The hotel was small and dingy. It smelt of stale tobacco and bad drains. The proprietor, a tiny, pasty-faced man with translucent skin, limp black hair and a large, overhanging top lip fixed me with his mean bead of an eye. He stretched out his right hand, covered by a black leather glove, and gave me the key to my room, number 23 at the top of the building. I smiled, climbed the stairs and opened the door. Old wooden beams crossed the ceiling of the room. Damp stains mottled the peach wallpaper. The bed linen looked like it hadn't been washed. There was a cockroach in the miniature washbasin. But it would only be for a night. Tomorrow I would move into the Gondolinis' flat near the Arsenale. And the day after, I would start work on my novel.

+≒══≒+

As my appointment with Signore and Signora Gondolini wasn't until four in the afternoon, I had more or less the whole day to explore the city. After breakfast, I checked out of the hotel and arranged to pick up my luggage later. Although I had never been to Venice before I had a clear picture of it in my mind: an elaborate stage set floating on water, an architectural dreamscape. Yet the undeniable beauty of the city—the Venice I had seen in guidebooks and in films—was bleached out by the white-hot sun and eclipsed by the sheer mass of tourists. Tour leaders thrusting colored umbrellas high into the air tried to make their voices heard above the multilingual throng. The overweight wept sweat from every pore. Women clutching jaunty gold handbags and wearing their best costume jewelry attempted to maintain their composure while coming face-to-face with cloned versions of themselves. Many of the husbands looked unseeing, dead-eyed.

I pushed my way out onto the Riva and battled along the front. Map in hand, I crossed over the Rio del Vin and took a turn to my left, leaving the crowds behind me. I headed toward Campo San Zaccaria, where legend has it that one Michaelmas the devil appeared, and was about to take hold of a young bride and cart her off to hell when her husband scared him away by roaring like the lion of St. Mark. I didn't know whether it was true, but I had read that each year young men came to the square to reenact the ritual in an attempt to guarantee the constancy of their future wives. I thought about Eliza back in London. I pictured her in bed with Kirkby. He had a broken arm, and I imagined him fucking her with his sling held close to his chest as if he were nursing a newborn baby.

I pushed open the wooden door of the church and stepped inside the darkened, cool interior. An elderly woman, head bent, eyes closed, kneeling beside a pew, mouthed a prayer to herself. Her paper-thin eyelids fluttered and twitched as if she had just stumbled from her bed, still dreaming. I walked around and stopped in front of Bellini's *Sacra Conversazione,* or, as it was sometimes called, *Madonna and Four Saints.* While I was studying for my art history degree I had often gazed at this altarpiece in my textbooks. Now I took out a coin and placed it in the slot. Artificial light flooded the painting, illuminating the angel playing a stringed instrument at the feet of the enthroned Virgin and the infant Jesus, his little palm raised to bless the four saints below him. There was St. Peter with his keys and book, St. Catherine with the broken wheel, the scholar St. Jerome swathed in red, holding another thick book, and St. Lucy with a little jar that was supposed to contain her eyes, wrenched from their sockets by Diocletian. I imagined the little globes bobbing about in salty water, pupils dilating in confusion and fear.

When the light timed out, I walked past the altar that was said to contain the body of St. Zacharias, the father of St. John the Baptist, and down the right aisle toward the chapel of St. Athanasius. A man wearing large, dark glasses—bluebottle like—sat behind a desk. In Italian, I asked how much it would be to enter, but he did not reply; instead he gestured toward a sign that informed me that the fee was one euro. I gave him a coin and he waved me by. Ranged around the walls, above the fifteenth-century choir stalls, were a number of paintings, including a depiction of the birth of St. John the Baptist, an early work by Tintoretto; a scene of David with the head of Goliath by Jacopo Palma the younger; and, above the door, an image of a martyr being tortured, the saint's eyes gouged out by a man holding what appeared to be a poker.

I wandered into the next chapel and admired the golden altarpieces by Vivarini and d'Alemagna and the frescoes of the Florentine artist Andrea del Castagno. Through a glass square in the floor I saw, at a lower level, some mosaics that had survived from the ninth century, and, walking down some stairs, I came to the crypt, now flooded by a couple of inches of water. The dank-smelling space, with its series of columns and arches reflected in the water below, felt oppressive, claustrophobic. I had to get out. I traced my steps through the chapels back to the main church and down the central aisle toward the front door.

I stopped for an espresso and studied my guidebook. I wanted to see St. Mark's and the Palazzo Ducale, but I couldn't face the crowds that gathered around the piazza so I decided to walk across to the Accademia. I took a series of backstreets, away from the main thoroughfares, down calles so narrow they never saw the sun, before I finally emerged near Campo Santo Stefano. I crossed the Accademia Bridge, pausing to take in the view of the Grand Canal, but as I came down the steps I saw a long queue curling its way out of the gallery's door. I didn't want to wait and couldn't bear the thought of standing near all those people, so I opted to go to Santa Maria Gloriosa dei Frari, another of the churches I had studied in my course, which was situated in San Polo, just to the north. As I walked through Campo Santa Margherita, I smelt the delicious aroma of frying garlic, fresh tomatoes and chopped basil. I checked my watch. It was nearly one o'clock—time for lunch. I sat down at an outside table of one of the cafés in the square, and after a cheap meal of spaghetti al pomodoro, I looked around me, relishing every detail. Two small boys squealed with delight as they played football in the square, the sound of the ball hitting the ground, an exact echo of my heartbeat. Housewives chatted with men in aprons selling octopus, prawns, spider crabs and fish from a series of canopied stalls. Young couples strolled hand in hand, feeding each other extravagantly colored ice cream, their lips mixing the flavors when they kissed. Everything seemed so alive, so new. And I could be part of it.

I had another coffee, paid my bill and made my way to the Frari. Inside the enormous, T-shaped church I heard the whisper of shoes across the marble floor and the muted murmur of a tour guide in the distance. I walked past the neoclassical monument to Canova, a pyramidal structure that contains the sculptor's heart, to Titian's *Ca' Pesaro Madonna*, a portrait of Jacopo Pesaro waiting to be presented to the Virgin and child. The image, I had been taught, had revolutionized altar painting in Venice because of the artist's decision to shift the Virgin from the traditional central position over to one side and also because of its humanity, the way Titian had invested the figures with a tender reality. As I studied the painting, moving back and forth to admire the rich blue of St. Peter's robes and the harmonious nature of the composition, I felt unnerved by the image of a boy dressed in white satin situated at the bottom right-hand corner of the picture. No matter where I moved, the curious, accusatory eyes of the youth followed me, as if to tell me not to forget that one day, like him, I would be dead. Although I tried to appreciate Titian's other masterpiece, *Assumption of the Virgin,* that dominated the high altar and the rest of the church's treasures, tombs and monuments, I couldn't concentrate. The face of that boy wouldn't leave me.

Just after three o'clock, I started to make my way to the Gondolinis'. I walked down to the San Toma vaporetto stop on the Grand Canal and pushed my way onto a crowded water bus. I fought my way to the back of the boat and, just after the Accademia, I managed to find a seat at the stern. Sunlight turned the water to mercury and cast the buildings in a dreamlike hue. As the boat sailed away from the San Zaccaria stop, in the glass panels of the doors that separated the outside seating area from inside, I saw the reflected images of the Campanile and the dome of Santa Maria della Salute. The motion of the boat was beginning to make me feel a little nauseous, and as I stepped onto terra firma at Arsenale, I felt as though I was still on water.

I had been told that the family had a series of rooms in a renovated warehouse building just around the corner from the Corderia, the former rope factory. As I approached my new neighborhood, I noticed that the number of tourists started to decrease. I looked at my map to check the exact location of the street and then walked until I found the home of the Gondolinis, an enormous redbrick structure that overlooked a small canal. I pressed a buzzer and waited. There was no answer. I pressed again. Still nothing. I searched through my bag to find the email from Niccolò Gondolini. It was the right address. Perhaps the family was out. I held my finger on the buzzer and then pressed it a couple of times again in quick succession. There was a click and the door opened.

The staircase was dark. I reached out to find a light switch. As I did so, a man's voice echoed from above.

"Adam Woods? Is that you, Adam? We are . . . up here."

Niccolò Gondolini, I assumed. Perhaps he had been in the bath or on the telephone.

I climbed the wooden steps, occasionally stopping to feel my way along the wall until my eyes adjusted to the gloom. As I reached the second floor I saw a door that had been left open. I paused for a moment before stepping in. A man with his back to me stood by a far window, his form surrounded by blindingly bright light. I shielded my eyes from the glare.

Before I could say anything, I heard the click of high heels on marble behind me. I turned around to face a woman. Everything about her was doll-like, petite and perfect. She was middle-aged, but her alabaster face was curiously free of lines.

"Adam, I am . . . pleased that . . . you have come," she said. Her English was heavily accented, and she pronounced the words as if she were trying to navigate her way across a stretch of slippery stepping stones. "Niccolò is pleased, also, that you have come."

As we shook hands, she gestured to her husband, the man by the window. He turned and walked toward me. Like his wife, Niccolò Gondolini was immaculately presented, but deeply tanned with oil-black hair swept off his forehead. On his wrist he wore a chunky watch, its face circled by diamonds.

"Please, this way," he said, gesturing toward a room off the hallway. He frowned, perhaps because he was not comfortable speaking English. I told them that I understood basic Italian and that if they spoke slowly I would be able to follow them. From then on they spoke in their own language.

The three of us entered a white cube of a room. The only furniture was a low-lying, gray sofa and one high-backed chair. The walls were completely free of paintings and bookcases.

"You can sit here," said Signor Gondolini, pointing toward the sofa. His wife smiled reassuringly at me, but I could tell there was something wrong. Niccolò looked down at the floor.

"I'm afraid we have ... something ... of a ... a ... a difficulty," said Signor Gondolini.

"Yes," said his wife. "It's best we get straight to the point: it seems that we cannot offer you a job after all, Mr. Woods."

"I'm sorry?" I said.

Signora Gondolini turned toward her husband, expecting him to provide an explanation. He wouldn't meet my eyes.

"What is the problem?" I asked.

The man remained silent.

"It's like this," said his wife. "It's rather—how shall I put it?—embarrassing. Everything was ready for you and Antonio; well, he was really looking forward to you coming here. But then we discovered something. It's a little ... delicate."

There was another pause as they looked at one another. Niccolò seemed to nod in her direction as if giving his wife permission to carry on.

"It seems our son has done something rather stupid," she continued. "Late last night we received a call from the husband of our maid. As soon as I picked up the phone, he started shouting and screaming. I told him to calm down, to slow down. He was calling Antonio all these names—filthy, dirty names that I don't need to repeat to you. But he said that ... that Antonio had been seeing his daughter, Isola. That morning she hadn't gotten out of bed. Her mother went in to see what was wrong. She was crying, you see. At first she refused to tell her what was wrong. But then she blurted it out—she is pregnant. Pregnant with what she said is Antonio's child."

Her voice dropped down to a whisper, so I had to lean a little closer to her. She smelt faintly of honeysuckle.

"Adam, she is only fourteen years old and—"

"So you can imagine what we did," Niccolò interrupted. "We questioned him, asked him whether it was true. Yes, he had been with Isola, they had had . . . some kind of relations. Finally he said that he would stand by her—a ridiculous idea. The stupid boy! He is just sixteen. His life is ahead of him. A nonsense!"

"There was a real commotion—you can imagine, Adam, can't you?" said his wife. "But there was no way we could allow him to throw his life away. So this morning we arranged for him to fly to New York to stay with my sister. It's all still rather messy with Isola's parents, of course—God only knows, it's going to be impossible to carry on employing Maria—but we'll have to sort something out. But I'm afraid that's really no good for you, is it?"

My new world had just collapsed and anger coursed through me, but I found myself nodding sympathetically. "Of course it can't be helped," I said. "I'll find something else. Like you say, you had to do what was best for Antonio. And I suppose he can improve his English in New York just as well as if he were stuck here with me."

"I'm pleased that you understand, Adam," she said. "It's so kind of you. Niccolò and I were so worried about what to say to you. We felt so responsible."

Niccolò's large hand reached inside his jacket and pulled out his wallet. "We will pay you your first month—that's the least we can do," he said. "And if there's anything else you need, just let us know."

I took the three hundred euros. I knew that wouldn't get me very far, but I smiled anyway and thanked him.

"What will you do?" asked Signora Gondolini. "Will you go back to London? We could also pay your flight, don't you think, Niccolò?"

"*Sì, sì,* of course," he replied. "Have a little holiday and then just tell us when you are ready. We'll get the ticket for you."

But what had Britain to offer? A broken relationship and the prospect of a summer at home with my parents in Hertfordshire. And I had to write my novel. When I had told my father of my ambitions to write, he had just sneered at me. No, I had to stay.

"I think I'll stick around in Venice a little while," I said. "I suppose I'll try and find another job. I'm not in the mood to go back home just yet and—"

Signora Gondolini jumped up from the chair, her perfect black bob swinging around her face as she did so. As she spoke, her tiny hands flapped in the air like a pair of butterflies. "Niccolò—Niccolò—," she said with delight. "I've got it!"

"*Cosa?*" Her husband looked at her with slight irritation.

"The perfect job—for Adam," she said, turning toward me. "I can't believe I didn't think of it before." She took a couple of breaths and started again. "You remember the old English gentleman Maria used to do errands for?"

Her husband looked at her blankly.

"You know—the one who never goes out. The writer—what is he called?—Gordon, Gordon . . . Crace. That's it. The one who wrote that book years ago and then—nothing."

I could see that Niccolò still didn't really understand what his excitable wife was twittering about and that as far as he was concerned, he had fulfilled his side of the bargain. He was a rich man who had eased his conscience by paying me and offering me a flight. Now he just wanted to get rid of me. No doubt my shabbiness was beginning to annoy him in his elegant surroundings.

"Have we ever met him?" he asked.

"No—I told you, he hasn't been out for years," she replied. "But Maria had said that he's getting a little . . . old . . . and needs a companion. Someone who will get his shopping, do the odd errand for him, tidy the place up. Is that something you might do, Adam?"

To be honest, anything that would let me stay in Venice would have appealed, and I was intrigued.

"Yes, of course. That sounds great," I said.

But then her expression changed.

"Is there a problem?" I asked.

"Well, there could be," she said. "The best way to get hold of him would, of course, be through Maria. But now it's a little awkward between us. She's not so friendly to us, as you can imagine, and I doubt she'll come back."

"Yes, I see."

"But I'll give you his address. Maria wrote it down for me once as a reference, although do you remember if we ever received a reply?"

Niccolò shook his head.

"Maybe you should write to him anyway. I don't think he has a telephone."

She walked across the room and into the hallway and came back with a piece of paper and a fountain pen. Ink flowed onto the blank sheet in great big loops. She passed it to me and I read the address. Palazzo Pellico, Calle delle Celle. I must have looked confused because the next thing I knew, Signora Gondolini took out a map.

"Let's see if we can find it for you," she said.

Perhaps it was just my imagination, but I was convinced that as her finger moved over the map, it traced the form of a question mark across the city.

⊢⊱══⊰⊣

I couldn't bear to check back into that dive of a hotel, so, on the Gondolinis' recommendation, I walked to a cheap but clean pensione in Castello. They had a room—nothing special, but at least I didn't feel as though my skin was creeping off me. After unpacking, I asked for a sheet of writing paper and an envelope and, in the small bar, I wrote a letter asking the reclusive Gordon Crace for a job.

Before leaving the Gondolinis', the Signora had filled me in on his short-lived but nevertheless quite spectacular literary career. His first and only novel, *The Debating Society,* published in the sixties, was a sensation. It had been greeted with enormous critical acclaim and translated into all the major languages. His publishers and readers all around the world had waited for another book—he was nothing less than *una stella,* she said—but he had never produced, or at least never published, another novel. Apparently, with the money from the film rights Crace was rich enough never to need to write again, but for someone of such passion, of such drive, it was strange never to want to see your name in print again. Perhaps he had nothing else to write about, she surmised. Maybe he was burned out. Or could it have something to do with affairs of the heart? Signora Gondolini's black eyes twinkled as she said this; her husband turned his head and pretended not to hear.

I had already heard enough to be intrigued. In the letter I told him how I had heard about the job and went on to outline my background—my degree in art history at London University (results pending), a basic grounding in Italian, and a need to stay for at least three to six months so I could start writing my novel. I said that although I liked to think I could be good company, noting what Signora Gondolini had told me about Crace, I also added that I appreciated silence and the need for privacy. It wasn't a masterpiece of a letter by any means, but it was succinct and, I hoped, without pretension. I folded it carefully, eased it into the envelope and sealed it. I wrote the address of the hotel on the back and checked my map. Crace's palazzo was only a ten- or fifteen-minute walk away. I decided that instead of posting it, I'd deliver the letter personally. I gathered my things together and walked out into the night.

Although teeming with tourists during the day, when the sun dipped over the lagoon, Venice transformed itself into another city altogether. As I wandered down unmarked streets, catching fragments of the moon's reflection in the waters, I felt myself slipping away. I had no thoughts about finding a job, Eliza or the situation back home. No one knew me here and I was free.

I walked through Campo Santa Maria Formosa, where the Virgin, in a shapely guise, was supposed to have appeared to St. Magnus, past the church built in her name, and carried on down one of the calles off the square. I wandered around the tangle of alleyways that all seemed to lead down to the same dark canal, but I still couldn't find the address. Then, near the Calle degli Orbi, I passed a narrow passageway that didn't seem to have a name.

At the end of the gloomy alleyway, I came to a slightly wider calle—Calle delle Celle, "the street of the cells"—at the bottom of which stood Crace's palazzo. The only entrance was a tiny bridge that ran from the street over the water to an imposing doorway that was illuminated by an outside light. Behind the door it looked as though there was a courtyard. Running down the center of the large, three-story, perfectly symmetrical building, like a spine of a long-dead monster, was a series of arched windows, four on each level, the extrados sculpted out of white marble. In one of the rooms on the first floor, candles flickered, illuminating patches of the darkened interior and casting strange shadows onto the ceiling. There was no sound except for the gentle lapping of the water.

I took the envelope out of my bag and walked as quietly as possible across the bridge. The letter box was on the left side of the door, carved into the marble gate in the shape of a dragon's head. As I pushed the letter into the creature's mouth, my hand brushing against its worn-down teeth, I stepped into a circle of light. Back over the bridge, I looked up once more to see a shadow crossing the room before melting into the dark.

The next afternoon I returned from a day of sightseeing to find a letter waiting for me at the pensione. The man at the front desk told me that it had been delivered by messenger just after lunch. I ran up to my room and ripped open the envelope.

Palazzo Pellico
Calle delle Celle
30122 Venezia

Dear Mr. Woods,

Thank you so much for your letter. I cannot tell you how pleased I was to receive it, coming as it did at so opportune a time. My previous employee, whom I had just taken on, left only a few days ago, and I've been at a loss as to what to do.

As a result, I wondered whether you might be interested in coming here to discuss the matter further. Of course, at this stage I cannot promise you the job. Cer-

tain aspects of my life will need to be discussed, and your suitability for the position will have to be investigated. However, your qualifications do seem, on the surface at least, quite impressive.

If you do wish to take this further, please write to me to arrange a suitable date and time. I do not have a telephone, and I dislike stepping outside my home.

Yours sincerely,
Gordon Crace

I wrote back to Crace suggesting a day and time and, again, hand-delivered the note so as to speed up the process. Crace sent a letter back to the pensione by messenger to say that was acceptable and that he looked forward to our meeting. My future was being mapped out before me.

⊹══⊹

I stood outside Crace's palazzo. It was the morning of my interview and my palms were damp with sweat. I had dressed in the only smart clothes I had—a cream-colored linen suit and a white shirt. Just before I left the hotel I checked myself in the mirror. Sunlight streamed through the window, bleaching out my blond hair, making it so difficult to see my features that I had to draw the blind and examine myself in the room's half light.

I was a couple of minutes early for my appointment with Crace, but I didn't feel like strolling around in the heat any longer. I took a deep breath and walked across the bridge. As I pushed the bell on the side of the door, I stared into the unseeing eyes of the marble dragon that guarded the letter box and smiled to myself. It was obvious that Crace had a sense of humor, even if it

was a black one. I knew that from reading his book, which I'd finished in the early hours of that morning.

The Debating Society centers on a group of sixth-form boys
at a minor English public school who meet each week to discuss
a certain pressing issue or topic. After talking about the usual
subjects—capital punishment, animal rights, the advantages and
disadvantages of socialism, oligarchy versus democracy—the
leader of the society, Charles Jennings, puts forward a motion to
debate, in secret, the merits of murdering their respectable classics master, Mr. Dudley Reeve. The boys pass the motion, thinking it all a hoot until one day Jennings lures the teacher into a
forest and bludgeons him to death. There is no reason given for
the murder—the master is neither an abuser nor a sadist; in fact,
he is a rather gentle and kind man—and it seems the only motivation lies with the passing of the motion in the debating society.
At the end of the book, Jennings is not caught and he, together
with the rest of the boys in the debating society, leave school, go
to university, and take up respectable professions with the secret
buried in their past. On the back of my paperback edition, which
I had found in a second-hand bookshop in Dorsoduro, there were
a selection of quotes from critics raving about the novel's sar-
donic humor, how it cleverly used the framework of the crime to
expose the dark heart of British society. There was a lot Crace
could teach me.

I pressed the bell again. Crace was in his early seventies and
perhaps it took him a while to get down the stairs to the door. But
then, just as I released my finger, the door edged open.

In front of me stood a man who seemed much, much older
than I had imagined. He was stooped, nearly bent double, and as
he slowly raised his head upward to look at me, I saw that the
flesh on his neck had lost all definition. His tiny gray-green eyes

narrowed as he squinted into the sunlight, and instead of moving forward to greet me, he took one step back into the shade.

"Adam Woods?" he said. His voice was crisp and sharp, distinctly upper class and authoritative.

"Yes. Sorry I'm a little early," I said.

"Never mind," he said, slowly lifting his right hand to shake mine. It felt like the lifeless body of a tiny bird.

"Come on in. This way," he said, leading the way into a portico-lined courtyard.

The walls of the yard were crawling with vines, snaking up the columns and the staircase that led to the entrance on the first floor. Dotted around the outside space were a number of large pots containing overgrown bay trees or pink hydrangeas. In the center of the courtyard there was what looked like the top of a Corinthian column, its capital decorated with acanthus leaves, on which stood the figure of a naked cherub, darkened by green-black moss.

"As you can see, I've let things get a little out of hand," said Crace. "That's one of the reasons I'm obliged to employ someone such as yourself, Mr. Woods. Now, let's go upstairs and have a drink."

As he slowly climbed the stone steps, his right hand grasped the metal banister for support, a tendril of a vine caressing his fingers. I noticed that his yellowing skin, discolored and speckled with liver spots, looked like thinning, ancient parchment. The linen suit that hung from his emaciated frame, once cream, now sallow and jaundiced, seemed like the loose, decaying flesh of a dead man.

At the top of the stairs, he stepped directly into the portego, a grand central hall that ran the length of the building. The mullioned windows at each end of the vast space were so dirty that they not only obscured the light, but forced me to question whether I had really seen a form walk across the room when I had delivered my letter the other night. The etchings and prints that lined the walls were thick with cobwebs; the elaborate stucco work and the decorative touches of the ceiling and cornices had long lost any touch of splendor, and the cloudy white marble floor was covered with balls of dust and fluff. Behind me I noticed that there was another staircase, an internal one, that led to a door secured by a padlock.

"Oh, I never go up there," he said, meeting my gaze. "I haven't in years. It's completely empty. I never bother with the floor below either, as it's damp and always flooding out. Follow me."

He led me down the central hall, with its wonderful display of drawings, etchings and prints, and through some double doors into the drawing room. Its walls were covered with a rich red fabric across which were displayed an array of Renaissance paintings in elaborate gilt frames. The windows on the street side of the palazzo were shrouded in heavy red velvet curtains, and the only light came from the two lamps that stood on either side of the marble fireplace, over which was a large antique mirror. An enormous chandelier hung from the ceiling, its shards of glass occasionally ringing above us.

Crace shuffled across a large Persian rug and eased himself down into one of the two red velvet chairs by the fireplace and gestured for me to sit in the other.

"Oh what a silly fool," he said, just as he was settling down into the chair. "I've forgotten to get you a drink."

"Don't worry," I said. "Please, let me."

"That's really very kind of you, Mr. Woods. What would you like? Gin? Whiskey? Dry sherry?"

Although it was only eleven in the morning, coffee, water or other nonalcoholic drinks did not seem to be on the menu.

"A sherry would be lovely, but I'll get it," I said. "And you?"

"Yes, I'll join you. You can find everything in that cabinet over there." He raised a bony finger and pointed toward a side of the room that was in shadow. "Most kind of you, most kind."

I spotted another lamp positioned near the drinks cabinet, but as I was about to switch it on, Crace barked, "No—no more light. I think we have enough."

I withdrew my hand from the switch and bent down to get the drinks. Crace had already set aside two glasses, both of which were exquisite—one a cristallo funnel-shaped glass with a baluster stem, the other a goblet with a fine *vetro a retorti* filigree decoration—yet sticky to the touch, covered with dust and coated with smudges, perhaps even hair. I poured the clear, sweet-smelling liquid into the two glasses, handed one to Crace, placed the other on a little side table by my chair, and sat down.

"Now, Mr. Woods, I know something about you from your letter, but can you tell me a little more about yourself?"

Rather like a reptile, Crace fixed me with his eyes. They were small and seemed to flit about the room while at the same time never leaving mine. I cleared my throat.

"Yes, of course," I said. "I've been in Venice now for just over a week, and as I'd said, I'm here to try and write."

Crace nodded but remained silent.

"I've just finished an art history degree at London University, and before I get distracted, I think it would be a good idea to try, to give it a go, at least."

"Have you written anything before?"

"Nothing you would call proper writing—a couple of fragments of short stories. Nothing that I could show anybody, if that's what you mean."

"Have you always wanted to be a writer?"

"Well, yes, for as long as I can remember," I said. "But I haven't really had very much encouragement from my family. My father is a banker—I grew up in Hertfordshire—and he wanted me to do something useful. I think he thought art history a decadent choice for a degree. But I want to prove to him, and to myself, that I can actually write. I want to set the novel in Venice, which is why it's so important for me to stay here."

"Yes, I see," Crace replied.

Another pause.

"And which is why I think this job, working with you, would be perfect for me," I continued. "I can help you around the house, do your shopping, a bit of cooking, some cleaning. I can sort out your post and settle bills and such like. It looks as though your courtyard might need a bit of a clear out, and I could do that, if you like. Really, anything to make your life more comfortable, to give you more time to write."

He grimaced as if steeling himself against some kind of inner pain.

"I don't write, Mr. Woods, in fact, I wish I had never done so," he said. "If you were to take on this position, it is something I would expect you never to refer to. And I mean that most sincerely. It is a part of my life I wish I had never lived. Of course, you would be able to talk about your writing—to deny that would be cruel—but I really could not abide you discussing mine—with me or anyone else. Do you understand, Mr. Woods?"

I didn't understand at all, but nevertheless I said that I did.

"There is also one other thing you should know about me," he continued. "I never set foot outside this palazzo and I never expect to do so. You may think it odd—people have called me worse things, I imagine—but although I have lived in Venice for thirty or so years now, I have never desired to see it."

"You mean you've never been outside?"

"There really is no need, no need at all. As we all know, it is the easiest city to visit without ever going there. Anyway, the Venice in here," he said, tapping his head, "is so much richer and stranger than anything I could ever experience out there. The so-called *real world* is vastly overestimated, don't you think?"

I answered with another question. "How have you managed, I mean, in the past?"

"Previously, when I was in much better health, I relied on local women to do my shopping and various errands," he said. "The last one, Maria, she was all very well, but somewhat prone to nervous hysteria. Made me feel on edge—no good, no good for my constitution at all. And the girl I used to organize sending those letters to you is not particularly reliable. Now I realize that in order to carry on, I need to employ someone such as you. As I had said in my letter, the boy I recently employed did not work out, and that's why you are here today."

I nodded and waited. Crace took a sip of sherry and seemed to compose himself.

"Mr. Woods, I am an intensely private person. What I'm sure you have already gathered is that whatever you witness within these walls is for you and for you alone. It's not as if I have anything to hide, but you must guarantee total confidentiality. If I found out that you had so much as whispered something as trivial as, I don't know, what I had for breakfast or how much milk I like in my morning coffee, you would have to go. And go straightaway. I really could not abide that." He paused. "Do you have any questions, Mr. Woods?"

"Could I just ask about the conditions? Hours and—"

"Of course. Sorry not to have brought that up sooner," he said. "Your duties would include making my breakfast, doing

the shopping, and buying food and wine; I have a few good bottles set aside, but I like to keep them for special occasions. You
would also be responsible for making a light lunch and supper—
don't worry; I don't eat very much, so that shouldn't be too difficult—and any other little jobs that might crop up. You would
have your own room, which I'll show you, and as much free
time, as is reasonable, for you to pursue whatever you want. But
only here—only within this palazzo. This is important. I cannot
abide being left alone. Of course, you need to be able to get the
shopping, but if it's done every day, then that shouldn't take you
long. And in any case, I should imagine you want to get on with
your book."

"Yes, that's right."

"Of course, many young men would reject such a notion
straightaway. I'm sure you're about to tell me you couldn't live
under such a draconian system. Don't worry—it won't offend me.
In fact, I would totally understand if—"

"No."

"Sorry?"

"I mean, that would not bother me in the least. I'm sure it
would help me focus my mind, get on with the book. So that's not
a problem."

"Really?"

"Yes, a little self-discipline is exactly what I need."

"Oh, good. And as for money—one always has to talk of it
even though it's terribly vulgar—I could pay you something
like . . . let's see . . . how does five hundred euros a month sound?
That would be just for you, of course. You would stay here free,
and I would provide your food and such like. Is that sum what
you would have expected?"

To be honest, it was much more than I had thought would be

offered, and I said that it would be a very generous amount indeed.

"And if you were to take up the position, when could you conceivably start?"

"More or less straightaway," I replied. I thought of my hotel bill stacking up. "In fact, probably the sooner the better."

Crace smiled for an instant, his thin lips stretching back to reveal a row of surprisingly white teeth.

"Would you like to see the room in which you might sleep?"

Crace pushed himself out of the chair, took a few moments to steady himself and then walked not toward the double doors that opened out into the portego, but another door that led into a dark corridor.

"There's the kitchen," he said, pointing to the room opposite. I noticed that dishes were piled high in the sink and a rotten smell lingered in the air. "Nothing special, but adequate, I'm sure." At the end of the corridor, he stopped. "And this would be your room, here."

He opened the door into a sparse, simply furnished room with a white-painted wooden floor, a single iron-frame bed, a built-in wardrobe and a desk by a shuttered window that looked out over the canal. The starkness suited me perfectly, and in contrast to the rest of the palazzo, this room looked relatively clean, as if its last occupier had made an effort to wipe out all evidence of his own existence. I wondered about the boy who had slept here before me and why he had been forced to leave.

"That's fine. It's all I need, or would need," I said, remembering that I still had not been offered the job.

Crace must have sensed my eagerness because as he led me out of the room and back down the corridor toward the portego, he stopped and turned to me.

"So, Mr. Woods, if you are happy with the situation, I don't see why you can't start immediately."

"You mean you're offering me the job?" I felt infused by happiness.

"Yes, if you would like it," he said.

"Thank you. That's wonderful," I said. "I'm sure I won't let you down."

As we walked down the portego, I noticed that off the other side of the central hall there was another corridor that presumably led to his quarters. Intuiting my interest, he nodded in that direction and told me that yes, his bedroom and study were located off that corridor.

"As well as the bathroom—a shared bathroom," he added. "I hope that's all right with you?"

"Yes, yes, that's completely fine," I said.

"I would show you the rest of the palazzo now, but—"

"No, don't worry; that's fine. There's no rush," I said.

Passing one of the many etchings, prints and drawings that lined the walls of the portego, I said the first thing that came into my head. "I hope you don't mind me saying, but you've got a wonderful art collection, Mr. Crace."

He smiled, obviously pleased that I had congratulated him on his fine aesthetic taste.

"Oh, do you think so? I've had these works for years. A mix of originals and copies, but I'm rather fond of them, yes."

We stopped by a pair of elaborately decorated but dusty *cassoni*, each chest located on either side of the double doors that led into the drawing room. On the wall facing me, in a simple ebony frame, there was what looked like the frontispiece of an old book. Printed on thick ochered paper, the woodcut showed an elderly man named "Il Griti" wearing flowing robes and a curiously shaped hat sitting on an impressive throne, holding out his left hand to receive a book from a younger man who was kneeling before him. Above the younger man, who was bearded and named as Il Lodovici, there was a symbol of a sun, inside of which was the face of a woman, her rays shining directly down on him.

"Yes, quite a sweet piece," said Crace, noting my interest. "From *Triomphi di Carlo* by Francesco de' Lodovici. It shows the writer presenting a copy of his book, his romance on Charlemagne, to his patron, the Doge Andrea Gritti. It's thought that as the portrait of Il Griti is definitely that of the Doge, then the bearded chap must be Lodovici and the lady in the sun there, giving him inspiration—ugly little thing that she is—must be Lodovici's muse. Not sure where I picked that up from, but quite charming in its own way."

Next to this was a small sketch of a boy with curly hair wearing a loose tunic, raising his hands in alarm, his eyes stretched wide with terror. The drawing of black chalk on quite discolored paper was very fine indeed and looked like a fragment of a cartoon done in preparation for a larger work.

"Do you know what this is a study for?" I asked.

"Yes, as a matter of fact, I do," he said. "It's one that Battista Franco did for *The Martyrdom of St. Lawrence*. Do you know it?"

"No, I don't, I'm afraid."

"Oh, it's wonderful, wonderful. Look here," he said, directing me to the opposite wall. "I've got a rather fuller version of it done by Cornelis Cort."

He pointed out an engraving that documented the whole terrible scene of St. Lawrence being roasted alive on a gridiron, a torturer skewering his skin with a pitched fork, another assailant stoking the fire beneath him, the martyr raising his hand toward two angels in the heavens, the sky full of fire and smoke.

"As you can see, inscribed on the gridiron, 'Titian, the imperial knight, invented this,'" he said, pointing toward the writing beneath the martyr's body. "And, of course, one would really like to own one of his two paintings of the scene. But as one is in the church of the Gesuiti here in Venice and the other in the Escorial, it's impossible."

I knew from my first impressions that Crace's collection was a fine one, but until that moment I had not quite realized its importance. He owned some serious—and very valuable—works of art. As I looked around the portego, its walls covered by prints and engravings, remembered the paintings that I had seen earlier in the drawing room, and imagined the undoubtedly exquisite pieces that hung in the rooms I had not yet entered, I tried to estimate how much it all must be worth.

"Yes, a really wonderful collection," I said, gazing around me.

"Oh, nothing more than the vain collection of a silly old fool," said Crace, waving his hand in the air in a dismissive gesture.

We carried on walking down the hall toward the stairs, where I stopped and turned to him.

"Do you have a record of your artwork? I mean, an inventory?"

"No, I don't think I do. Why?"

"I just wondered if you would let me—after I've done all the cleaning and tidying and what needs to be done—make a record of everything you've got. It's just that your collection is really one of the best in private hands I've ever seen. Of course, I'm no expert, but I think it might be useful for you, perhaps for insurance purposes."

"Would you not find that a terrible bore?"

"No, not at all. Rather the opposite. It would give me a great deal of pleasure."

"Very well, if you like."

"Thank you."

He accompanied me back down the stairs and into the shady courtyard.

"So, see you tomorrow then," he said, lifting up his hand.

"Yes, and thank you again," I said. "Is there anything you want me to bring? Anything you need?"

"Maybe just a few groceries—bread, milk, some fruit—and," he said, looking around him, "what about a pair of secateurs? I'm convinced these dreadful vines are about to choke me to death."

✦

I woke early, impatient to start my new life. I didn't have to think about the past. Everything was going to be different now. I packed my things into my rucksack, paid my hotel bill, and enjoyed an espresso and a croissant in a little café by a side canal. I did some shopping for Crace and arrived at his palazzo a little after ten. When he opened the door, I noticed that he had an amused glint in his rheumy eyes and that his thin skin stretched across his sharp cheekbones as he laughed. It took him a few moments before he could speak.

"Sorry, Mr. Woods," he said. "I've just read the funniest thing. Come in, come in."

We traced the same route as the day before, past the mass of vines, up the staircase, down the portego and into what he called the red room. He continued to laugh to himself.

"Something has obviously amused you," I said.

"Oh yes, it has . . . indeed, indeed," he said, sitting in his chair.

He took a series of deep breaths and composed himself. A couple of books lay on the table beside him. I squinted to see the titles of the two musty-looking volumes covered in red leather with gold writing embossed on their spines.

"As you can see," he said, picking up one of the books, "I've been reading Thomas Coryat."

I looked blankly at him.

"Coryat? You know, he wrote this most splendid book, *Coryat's Crudities*," he said. "He was born in Somerset, came to Venice in the early seventeenth century and was by all accounts a bit of a buffoon. Said to have brought the fork to England. Anyway, in this book, he talks about the wonderfully gory goings on in the Sala del Tormento, the torture room in the Ducal Palace."

"Oh, I see," I said, wanting to hear more.

"It's really good stuff. Just listen to this." He brought the book farther down onto his lap, was about to read and then said, "Let me first tell you the context. A prisoner was brought to the torture chamber where he must have seen this terribly basic equipment, simply a rope and a pulley that were fastened to the ceiling. But then his arms were pushed behind his back and bound, and he was hauled up on the rope until he was left dangling from the ceiling where he—listen—'sustaineth so great torments that his joints are for the time loosed and pulled asunder.' That's what I love about Venice: it may look like a beauty, but its appetite for violence is insatiable, don't you agree?"

Crace didn't give me time to speak.

"Of course it used to be," he continued. "I mean, the murders in the old days were just spectacular. All that blood and gore. And what do you reckon we have now? The best it can do, it seems, is the odd stabbing—two men fighting over a woman usually. Yes, that old cliché, I'm afraid. Or, if really pushed, a wife beater a bit hot under the collar who one day hits his missus a trifle too hard. Where's the entertainment value in that?"

I laughed at Crace's impassioned little speech. So this was how he was going to welcome me into his house.

"Actually, talking about Coryat, have you heard the theory of how the rise of the knife and fork resulted in the reduction of the murder rate?" he said.

I shook my head, baffled.

"Oh, it's quite interesting, if a little simplistic," Crace continued. "In 1939 a Swiss sociologist published a book that took this as its central argument: that the gradual introduction of 'courtly' manners—actions such as wiping one's nose with a handkerchief and using a knife and fork instead of the fingers—was responsible for the change in society between the medieval and the modern."

He enunciated each word with the utmost clarity, and I could tell that he was enjoying his lecturing me.

"Just after it was published, Germany invaded Poland and these ideas were forgotten. It wasn't until the late seventies, I think, that the book was republished in America, and recently crime statisticians have started to take this idea a little more seriously. It's true that in the seventeenth century murder rates dropped, but the question is why? Standard theories about why people commit crime, such as the growth of cities, the gap between rich and poor, did not apply in the seventeenth century. The growth of cities and the rise of industrialization came much later, after the drop in the murder rates."

I tried to follow his argument.

"Could the drop in murders therefore be traced to a psychological transformation, a view of ourselves as somehow more refined, more civilized? And if this is true, then I blame Coryat himself for the lack of juicy murders today. If history could be repeated, I'd have him stabbed to death with his own fucking fork."

Crace looked at me with an intense, serious stare. Was this

some kind of test? For a couple of seconds I didn't know what to say. Then I took a gamble.

"I think there's only one answer," I said, meeting his gaze with an equally earnest demeanor. "We should ban cutlery—it's the only way."

Crace doubled up with laughter, the loose skin of his neck swinging from side to side. I laughed along with him—it was the right answer—but as I did so I suddenly felt the need to go to the bathroom. I tried to think of other things to take my mind off it and looked at some of the wonderful paintings on the walls of the drawing room, but it was no good. I cleared my throat.

"Excuse me, Mr. Crace, I'm sorry, but could I use your loo?"

"Oh, of course. How silly and thoughtless of me," he said, shaking his head. "I haven't even shown you around properly. Disgraceful. Come on, come."

He led the way out of the drawing room into the portego and turned right down another narrow corridor, opposite the one that led past the kitchen and down toward my room.

"This door here," he said, pointing to a door on his left, "leads into my bedroom and study, and this door is the one for the bathroom. When you're finished, come and find me in my room."

I pushed open the door and stepped into the large white room, which smelt strongly of the sewers. The floor was covered in hair and what looked like slivers of shredded toilet paper, some of which appeared to be blood-stained. I walked past the bath, which was deeply ringed with grime and ocher-yellow with age, to the toilet, which had its lid down. Tentatively, using my forefinger I lifted up the lid and seat. The bowl was coated in black-brown smears. This would have to be my first job, I told myself, quickly flushing the loo without looking down again. I moved over to the sink to wash my hands, but the soap, once creamy white, looked so encrusted with dirt that I opted to just rinse my fingers instead, bypassing altogether the musty towel that hung from the nearby rail.

As I came out, feeling slightly soiled, I made a plan in my head detailing everything that needed to be done and in what order. People at university, Eliza even, had always thought it odd that I was interested in keeping things neat and tidy. Obsessive, they had said. But they should have thanked me. I could never understand how people could exist surrounded by mess. If you lived somewhere, it was your duty to keep it clean.

I was sure Crace would be grateful for the help I could give him. After all, it couldn't have been much fun for him living like this. The bathroom—cleaning the toilet, bath and basin—would have to be tackled first of all, followed by the kitchen. Then I would dust everywhere, get rid of all the cobwebs that had accumulated around Crace's paintings and drawings, sweep the floors, polish the furniture and cut back the vines in the courtyard. How long would it take me to get the palazzo into some kind of shape? And then what about the upper floor that Crace had said was no longer used? Did he expect me to clean that as well? I dreaded to think what kind of condition that was in.

I knocked on Crace's bedroom door and heard his voice telling me to come in. I entered the large room, which had windows overlooking the canal. Clothes—jackets, trousers, socks, underpants and vests—were strewn all across the floor. Crace was nowhere to be seen. I walked across the terrazzo in the central part of the room, and then onto wine-dark parquet that had been laid in each of a series of alcoves that ranged around the edge. In one of the alcoves, situated between elaborately decorated buttermilk-colored columns, was a bed complete with a carved ivory headboard boasting a tempera painting of the Virgin and Child flanked by a couple of saints. Above this, Crace had hung another beautiful Madonna; I couldn't discern the artist but it was of exquisite quality. The walls of the alcove were lined with a rich fabric covered by a pattern of broken columns and capitals. The bed itself was surrounded by thick burgundy curtains. As I brushed past it, a cloud of dust spores mushroomed by my knees.

"There you are," he said from behind me.

I turned to see Crace walking out of a room I presumed must be his study.

"I thought I might get started—on the cleaning front," I said.

"Yes, yes, good idea. I hope you don't find me too feral. I have let things slip rather, I'm afraid."

"Where do you want me to start? I thought maybe the bathroom and the kitchen first, followed by the rest."

"Are you sure? I was rather looking forward to a drink."

"Well, it won't take me long," I said.

"If you're certain. It's not really the nicest way to welcome a guest into my home, though, is it?"

"The sooner it's done, the nicer it will be for all of us," I said quite firmly.

"If you insist."

We walked out of the bedroom, down the corridor and out into the portego.

"I'll give those windows a wash as well, to let some light in," I said, gesturing toward the end of the grand hall that overlooked the canal. "And then at some point, after I've done down here, you can tell me what to do about upstairs."

"Oh, no, there's no need to bother with that," he said. "I haven't been up there in years. I think it's probably so dirty up there that it's started to clean itself."

Smiling, he accompanied me through the double doors that

led directly into the kitchen and showed me the cupboard under the sink where he thought I could find cleaning materials. I bent down and took out an old green bucket full of dried cloths and dirt-smeared bottles of bleach, scouring fluids and detergent, all of which were empty.

"That's decided the matter for us, hasn't it?" said Crace, his eyes twinkling.

"How do you mean?"

"Well, you've got nothing to clean with, and I can't possibly let you go out and leave me. After all, you've only just arrived. It would be terribly bad manners."

"But it will only take—"

"No arguments. We'll have a drink and then we can talk about it. Now, what will you have?"

After a couple of drinks—dark, sickly sweet sherry, this time in glasses I had quickly washed out—I finally managed to extract myself from Crace and go in search of a shop. He insisted that I should be gone for no longer than fifteen minutes. I knew he didn't like to be left by himself, but I didn't think he was that serious. When I arrived back at the palazzo with two plastic bags full of bleach bottles, detergent, lime scale remover, wax polish, rubber gloves, a new toilet brush and a couple of packets of scourers and cloths, he was standing at the top of the stairs in the courtyard with a pained expression on his face, looking at his watch.

"Another minute and I'm afraid it would have been all over," he said quietly.

"Sorry?" I said, breezing up the stairs toward him.

"Oh, never mind," he sighed. "Never mind."

After making sure Crace was settled in the drawing room, reading and with a glass full of sherry within easy reach, I set to work. In the bathroom, I raised the blinds, sending clouds of dust into the room, and then let some fresh air into the space. I put on my rubber gloves and attacked the toilet first, blasting it with half a bottle of bleach, which I let stand while I cleaned the sink. I took down the shower curtain, which was so badly mildewed that I would need to buy another, and scrubbed the bath, but while I managed to clean away a good deal of dirt, it was impossible to erase the oval of grime that ringed around its upper edge, a visual echo of its top lip. Using the shower attachment, I rinsed away the dirty water, extracted a handful of gray and yellow hairs from the plug hole and wiped the surface once more. I swept the floor, cleaning up the hair balls and strips of toilet paper, and emptied a waste bin full of even more loo paper, old plasters and worms of dental floss. I cleaned the mirror on the front of the small medicine cabinet above the sink, sorted out the shelves inside (which seemed to contain a great many plasters as well as some sleeping pills) and wiped all around it. Before opening the toilet, I flushed it a couple of times and then started to scrub, using even more bleach to try and shift the buildup.

Disposing of the rubber gloves I had used to clean the bathroom, I put on another pair and started on the kitchen. I slowly dismantled the tower of dirty dishes in the sink, careful not to break anything. After running out of space on the work surface, I placed the rest of the plates, pots and bowls on sheets of old newspaper on the floor. Bits of food—old pieces of half-chewed meat, disintegrating vegetables, a few splintered bones and a mass of flaccid green fibers—coagulated at the bottom of the sink, giving off a rank, rotten smell. I fingered my way around the rim of the plug and gathered it all up, shaping it into a ball in my hand and disposing of it in a black bin liner, and then started to wash the dishes.

How long had Crace been living like this, I wondered. From the evidence all around me—the dirt, the neglect, the mess—it seemed like he had lost the ability to cope some months ago. But most probably he was the type to resist employing someone, out of pride more than anything, for as long as reasonably possible. He had obviously reached a point where he realized he could no longer carry on living like he was. But what of his former employee, the boy who had lived in my room before me? From the state of things—he couldn't have spent much time here at all. That, or he had only bothered to clean his room and nowhere else in the palazzo.

By late afternoon I had managed to clean the bathroom and the kitchen and had started to dust the cobwebs from the drawings in the grand hall. One of the etchings depicted an angel blowing a trumpet, holding a wreath and standing on a sphere, flanked by two figures beneath, one a male satyr, the other a woman surrounded by scientific and military instruments. As I leaned closer to the etching, I felt someone watching me. I looked up. Crace was standing outside the double doors of the drawing room, looking down the portego at me, smiling.

"*Io son colei che ognuno al mondo brama, perché per me dopo la morte vive,*" he said in perfect Italian. "'I am she whom everyone in the world longs for, because through me they live after death.' The inscription underneath."

I squinted as I tried to make out the Italian verse at the bottom of the etching.

"*An Allegory of Fame,*" said Crace, walking toward me, repeating the first two lines and then continuing, "and if vice or virtue operates so as to obtain plunder or honorable empire, I am infamy for the former and for the latter fame. Vice has only blame from me while virtue has glory, palms and crown."

"I didn't realize you had such good Italian," I said.

"Oh, just a little. It's rather beautiful, though, this etching, isn't it?"

"Yes, it is. Who is it by?" I asked, trying to see if it was signed.

"Battista del Moro, thought to be done around 1560. But I think it's interesting that despite the rather moralizing verse underneath it, the figure of fame is looking not toward the personification of all that is good, but toward the satyr, the symbol of evil. And, if I'm not mistaken, I think she's rather enamored of him, wouldn't you say?"

I had to admit that yes, in the etching, she did seem more attracted to vice than to virtue.

⊹⊱─━─⊰⊹

At the end of that first day I fell into my bed, exhausted. As I lay there listening to the gentle ebbing of the water, with the moonlight shining through the slats in the shutters, I felt that I was in some kind of dream, a character in a surreal vision. I'd never met anyone like Crace before, and I could tell it would take me a while to get used to his strangeness. Over a simple supper of spaghetti with tomatoes, basil and Parmigiano, which we had at the table in the kitchen, I asked him why he had decided to come to Venice and how he had chosen this palazzo. Although he told me not to be offended, and from his manner he was far from rude, he refused to answer, saying that those kind of details were extraneous to my needs. The fact that he existed in the here and now, he said, should be enough for me.

I learned that it was better to wait for him to introduce a subject into the conversation. He adored talking about his art, and I enjoyed listening to him—and that night he told me about how he had amassed a great deal of his collection, buying pieces twenty or thirty years ago for next to nothing. The names he recited were certainly impressive. In addition to the works he had already described to me, he owned drawings and etchings by Palma Giovane, Domenico Brusasorci, Benedetto Caliari, and Domenico Tintoretto; and paintings by Paolo Veronese, Paris Bordon, Moretto da Brescia and Lorenzo Lotto, as well as a good deal of quite exquisite glassware by some of Venice's finest craftsmen.

Over coffee he asked me about my art history degree, and I sketched out the arc of the course and its structure, chronology and theoretical stance. I tried to impress him by showing off my knowledge of Vasari, but he dismissed the writer of *Lives of the Artists* with a wave of his hand and a comment about how he had introduced biographical vulgarity into art history. He agreed, he said, with Cellini, who thought Vasari nothing better than a coward and a liar. By the way, had I read Cellini's autobiography? I replied that I had not. It was great fun, he said, his eyes gleaming. He summarized it for me before outlining Cellini's seemingly insatiable appetite for violence and how he had committed a series of murders in cold blood, events that he related in the book with unadulterated glee. He described an incident in which Cellini had tried to knife a man in the face, but after his victim suddenly turned around, he stabbed him under the ear instead. Crace thought this story hilarious, and as he laughed, his little reptilian eyes disappeared into the folds of flesh in his face.

"Cellini said that artists, unique in their profession, should stand above the law," Crace said, finally catching his breath and studying me closely. "Free of responsibility and able to disregard the rules. Do you think the same thing, Mr. Woods? Please say that you do."

Although I wasn't quite sure what to say, I thought it best to agree with him. As I nodded my assent, he looked at me with what can only be described as an expression of affection.

"I can see that we're going to get on splendidly," he said.

+>===<+

It took me a week to clean the palazzo, and during that time I frequently felt as though, no matter how much effort I put into it, the apartments refused to relinquish their patina of dirt. It was like some kind of protective shell, a barrier that resisted any attempt to penetrate or invade it.

The ingrained dirt on the mullioned windows at the two ends of the portego seemed particularly stubborn, almost acting as a shield to distance Crace from the outside world. Using a rickety set of stepladders I had found in a cupboard in the kitchen I climbed to the top of the windows, took hold of my cloth and cleaning spray and started to attack the grime. Although my cloth got darker and darker, nothing seemed to be coming off the surface of the glass. But finally a small coin-shaped pocket of light shone through the window, growing and growing until the glass had cleared and I could see outside.

One side of the palazzo looked onto a street, separated only by a narrow stretch of water and a bridge, the other onto a much wider canal. A boat laden with oranges, grapefruits, limes and lemons glided by. A gondola, steered by a proud, haughty-looking man and seating a kissing couple, lolling about in the back with honeymoon happiness, slowly made its way past me before it disappeared around a corner. Across the other side of the water, an elegant dark-haired woman stood on her balcony smoking a cigarette. Everywhere I looked people were getting on with their lives, having an existence, while Crace immured himself in his palazzo, a self-imposed prisoner. But at least after I had cleaned the windows, Crace could see out of his gaol.

The vines in the courtyard, which were planted in a small patch of ground near the gate, had a life of their own, their tendrils weaving up and around the staircase in a determined attempt to invade the interior. It was almost as if they wanted to asphyxiate the palazzo, squeezing the life out of everything inside. As I cut through the woody stems that grew up and around the columns and the metal latticework, the whole organism seemed to shift and move in a stubborn effort to survive. The only way to defeat it, I found, was to cut it into as many small pieces as possible and then deposit them into black refuse bags, but even then the tendrils tried to snake and slip away.

Similarly the moss growing on the Corinthian column and the naked cherub in the center of the courtyard was stubborn and hard to shift. After I had tried, and failed, to remove it using a cloth, I had to resort to using an old chisel, which I had found under the sink, but the job was still laborious and time consuming.

I spent those first few days in a permanent sweat, stripping down to my vest and shorts as I tried to make the place look decent again. As I cleaned the interior, I disturbed ancient dust, flakes of skin and strands of hair, which I imagined belonged to those who were long dead. The dirt had a smooth, almost powdery texture to it, pulverized and softened by the process of time. I moved piles of books, cleaned Crace's soiled clothes, carried pieces of furniture, swept, dusted, scrubbed and exterminated. Spiders had made their homes behind exquisite artwork, the frames being used as miniature proscenium arches on which to drape their webs, their own spectacular sets. In the kitchen, by the rubbish bin, I discovered a colony of ants that regularly feasted on the packet of sugar that Crace often left on the work surface. And in his bedroom, living between the dark, damp folds of his bed curtain, a few small toadstools had started to grow. Cockroaches lived in the bathroom, and wood lice often crawled out from under the Persian rug in the drawing room.

As I neared the end of the heavy-duty cleaning, I realized that not only had I not touched Crace's study but I had not even seen it. By this point I had learned enough about him to realize he had a highly developed, if not obsessional, sense of privacy, and I thought it only best to seek his permission to enter the room. I put down my cleaning materials and, still wearing my vest that was now stained and mottled, walked down the portego and through the double doors into the drawing room, where Crace sat reading.

"Mr. Crace, I wondered whether I might be able to ask you something."

"Yes?"

"I've nearly finished the cleaning now, but I realized I haven't done your study. Do you want me to?"

He looked thoughtful for a moment and then resigned, defeated. "I suppose you'd better. It is rather a state. There is a good deal of correspondence on the desk, which does need sorting out at some point."

He sighed, put his book down on the table, slowly stood up and shuffled toward me. As he passed, his bony hand brushed against my skin.

"Come with me," he said.

I followed him out of the drawing room, down the portego into his bedroom and through the door at the end of that room, which led into his dark, windowless study.

"Is there a light in here?" I asked.

"Yes, just over there," said Crace, pointing toward the outline of a desk by the far wall.

As I switched on the light, I saw that the desk was piled high with letters, some of which had fallen down onto the Persian rug below. Underneath the mass of correspondence was a mug covered in mold, a rotten apple core, a few screwed-up yellowed tissues and an ink pen. On a low wooden stand near the desk was an earthenware ink pot in the shape of a terrapin; underneath the layer of dust I could see that it boasted a fine yellow, green and beige sgraffito decoration. In addition to the bookshelves that lined the room, there was an open display case, a sort of cabinet of curiosities, full of *objets,* including a slipware flask in the form of a scallop shell; a blue and yellow bowl that showed a young shepherd boy on a mountainside being abducted by an eagle; a number of exquisite vases; a few miniatures, some surrounded by frames of silver or black velvet; a white marble relief featuring a young boy placing his left hand into a bowl of fire, which I think was a representation of Mucius Scaevola; an ornate pair of brass candlesticks and a triangular box with winged figures at each of its ends, which I took to be a perfume burner. Everything in the cabinet was covered in a thick layer of dust.

On the walls, papered in a blood-red fabric, there were a few old architectural plans of Palladian villas, their frames hanging at odd, tangential angles, and in every corner of the room stood towers of books, so unstable they looked like they might collapse at any moment. By the door there was a chest, similar to the ones in the portego, on which stood a bronze statue of a kneeling satyr holding a shell and, near it, a highly decorated, beautifully fluted marble urn.

"I don't know where you'll begin," he said, gesturing with despair. "But I suppose you'll have to start somewhere."

"Don't worry, I'll soon have it sorted for you."

"But as I said, ignore the correspondence until I've decided the best way to approach it," said Crace, drifting out of the room. "It's gotten so out of hand, I'm not sure what to do about it. I'm going to do some reading on the bed. Just shout if you need me."

Leaving the letters to one side, I got to work straightaway, consigning the mug, apple core and tissues straight to the bin. I dusted each of the objects in the cabinet, taking care over each one, cleaned the Persian rug, swept the marble floor, tidied up the books and straightened the frames hanging on the walls. As I worked, I wondered how and when Crace had managed to do all his collecting; I presumed it must have been before he had confined himself; that or he had authorized a dealer to search for things on his behalf.

As I started to clean the chest by the door I noticed that its wood was fissured, dry and scarred. I fetched a tub of wax polish from the kitchen and carefully started to apply the sticky dark substance to the chest, massaging the mixture, which was the color of burnt sienna, deep into the wood. The polish stained the ends of my fingers a gangrenous black-brown, and for a moment it was as though my hands were those of a dead man.

I picked up the figure of the satyr, with its horns, pointed ears, beard, hairy legs and cloven hoofs, and examined it closely. The shell, which the creature held in its right hand, would, I guessed, most likely have functioned as an ink well, and although it was grotesque, there was something quite intriguing about it. I placed it back on the chest and reached for the urn, which I thought was most probably funereal, when I heard Crace's voice.

"Don't touch that. Leave it."

"Sorry . . . so sorry," I said, moving away, but not quite sure what I was supposed to have done.

Crace shuffled toward me, his head shaking with fury.

"Oh, I suppose it was my fault. I should have told you," he said, trying to compose himself.

"Excuse me?"

"Oh, very well. I'd better tell you. There's a gun—there—loaded—in that urn."

"What?"

"It's just for my own protection. Tiny little thing, so small you'd think it wouldn't kill a fly. Never used it, of course."

"I see."

"So, I'm telling you just so you know it's there."

"Don't you think it might be better if you kept it somewhere else, somewhere a little more secure?"

"What? Like a safe, you mean? I'm not going to wait around messing with a fucking combination lock while a team of burglars work their way through the palazzo and steal everything I've got."

Crace sensed my anxiety and smiled.

"Look, don't worry. It's nothing."

He lifted the lid of the run and reached into the vessel. His fingers had molded themselves around the gun, its surface decorated with mother-of-pearl.

"See? It's nothing," he said. "But if you want me to move it, I will."

"It's probably fine where it is."

"Why don't you go and make of us both a nice drink?" he said, sighing. "Look, it's nearly six o'clock, and I think we both deserve a little tonic, don't you?"

"What would you like?" I asked.

"Let's see . . . what about a Campari soda or even . . . a Negroni. Do you know how to make a Negroni?"

I told him I did.

"Well, that's what it will be then," he said, putting the gun back into the urn and ushering me out of the room. "Cocktail hour approaches."

I poured equal measures of Campari, gin and sweet vermouth into the cocktail shaker, mixed them together, strained the alcohol into glasses filled with cracked ice and a slice of orange and passed one of the tumblers to him. As I drank down a draft of the bitter-tasting pink liquid, I noticed Crace staring at me with a curious expression on his face.

"Salute!" he said, looking away.

"Salute!" I repeated.

+≻══≺+

Despite my employer's eccentricities, we settled into our respective roles quite easily. Although Crace loathed the idea of venturing over his little bridge that linked his house to the alleys, streets and squares, I could tell that he enjoyed my company. Perhaps I was a little flattered that he took such a keen interest in me and felt relaxed in my presence. He was, or at least had been, a famous writer, and I was on the very lowest rung of the literary ladder looking up at him. He was genuinely grateful that I was helping him and he cheered up a good deal after he realized it was much more pleasant to live in clean rather than dirty surroundings.

After I had done everything I could to make the place look superficially respectable and had taken an inventory of his art collection, I asked him if there was anything else that needed to be done. I was finding it difficult to get down to writing the novel and was looking for an excuse not to work. What about the letters in his study? Did he want me to tackle those? He decided that would be, after all, a good idea and so one morning, after breakfast, about a month after I had first started, we walked into his study to see what could be done.

Although the desk had been cleaned and the room looked much tidier, the letters were still sprawled across the surface in a chaotic heap, piled high in the middle like a paper pyramid.

"When did you last open a letter?" I asked.

"Apart from yours, which you took the trouble to deliver by hand, it was some time ago, I'm afraid," said Crace. "But I do hope you'll be able to sort them out for me. I got so bored of reading the same letter over and over again, so I stopped opening them."

His face flushed as he grew angrier and angrier.

"Always probing, always wanting answers to why I wrote the first book and why I stopped writing. Graduate students, mostly, dreadful creatures. Looking for significances where there aren't any—at all. However, aspiring, overly curious biographers, it has to be said, are much, much worse. Vultures circling around me, waiting for me to die, eager to get the first bite at the wizened flesh on my corpse. Asking to come and look at my papers, my journals, my diaries. Wondering whether I had, during all this time, actually carried on writing but refused to have my work published. I mean, what an idea! Inquiring whether they can come and talk for an hour or so, completely off the record, of course. Bloodsuckers and vampires and ghouls, jumped-up vulgarians no better than those who stand by and gawp at the scene of an accident. They make me sick, the lot of them."

Crace looked at the pile of mail with disgust and then realized the violence of his outburst.

"Sorry. I—"

"Would you rather I weed out such inquiries?"

"Oh, would you? That would be marvellous," he said. "In fact, you could probably throw most of them away."

He paused.

"Although I'm sure it's mostly rubbish, you'll probably find the occasional check from my publisher, which I suppose will come in useful. To be honest, if I didn't need the money, I'd rather burn the checks. Damned royalties keep rolling in, a constant reminder."

Crace's eyes misted over. Silence.

"Of what?" I asked quietly.

He pursed his lips, was about to speak and then decided against it.

"Oh, nothing, nothing," he said, trying to smile. "A reminder of my previous foolishness, that's all."

"I'll start on these right away," I said, gesturing toward the letters. "Don't worry, I'll soon have it sorted out."

Before disappearing to read, Crace had given me a paper knife and, slowly, I started on the mass of correspondence. I began at the top of the pile, working my way downward, looking for both checks and requests of a biographical nature. I was also curious to find out more about Crace.

I sliced into the letters, scanning them quickly to see whether they contained anything of importance. Although they were mostly the usual, predictable dross that Crace had suggested, one of the letters, in an expensive buttermilk-colored vellum envelope, stood out. The handwritten note was written on headed notepaper, and the name—Lavinia Maddon—and the address and telephone number were embossed in black ink at the top.

47a Eaton Square
London
SW1

Dear Gordon Crace,

I am so sorry to have to write to you once again, but perhaps you didn't receive my letter of 12 February. In case that letter went astray, let me outline what I had written.

First of all, I must apologize for having to write to you without an introduction. I realize that you may dislike such an effrontery—I can hardly blame you—but it is important that I get in touch with you.

I am sure that you have been approached many times before, but I am extremely keen to write your biography. Well, not so much a straightforward biography, but a book looking at the phenomenon of literary success and literary silence, using you as a central figure, an organizing metaphor, if you like. Obviously as this would make use of biographical material—for example, letters and interviews and such like—I would like to come to an understanding with you about this.

I realize, from what I have heard, that you may not be keen on such an enterprise. But please let me assure you that the book—commissioned by Pieria Publishing, which, as you know, is one of the top literary houses in Britain—will not be sensational in any way. Of course, I would have to refer to the incident back in 1967, but perhaps in the book you would be able to put forward your side of the story. That is only a suggestion, so please do not take offense if you would rather not. I totally understand how sensitive a subject it is.

For your reference, my previous books have included biographies of Jean Stafford, Constance Fenimore Woolson, J. M. Barrie and Virginia Woolf, and my work has been published in many respected journals, including the <u>London Review of Books</u> and the <u>New Yorker</u>.

I do beg you to get in touch so that we can talk about this further and put to rest any anxieties you may have. I can easily travel to Venice to meet you at your convenience.

Yours sincerely,
Lavinia Maddon

I read through it once more. A letter from an aspiring biographer, one of the so-called vultures that Crace had described. I felt pleased with myself at having found it and hoped that Crace would be appreciative of my work. But this incident in 1967 intrigued me. What was Lavinia Maddon referring to? She seemed serious and respectable, so I set the letter aside, intending to show it to Crace at the end of the day. I continued to rip open the envelopes, tossing most of the letters into the bin, but I still couldn't find any checks. They were probably at the bottom of the pile, knowing my luck. I pushed my hand deep into the pile's papery heart, fished around with my fingers, and pulled out a clutch of letters. One, a request for Crace to appear at a literary festival, was postmarked 12 April 1998—four years ago.

I stood up and stretched, yawning. The small study was hot and airless. I couldn't breathe. I needed a drink. I'd do a few more and then I'd have a break. I took another one from the pile and was immediately struck by the messy, almost indecipherable scrawl on the envelope. You could hardly make out Crace's name, let alone the address of his publisher. It was amazing it ever got to them. The short note was written in blue Biro, the ink smudged in places, and spelling mistakes littered the page.

23 Church View
Winterborne
Dorset
DT11 0GF

Dear Mr. Crace,
I have written to you before, but I did not get no anser. Have you forgetten him? You couldn't have. He was so special to you. Is his memory not worth the money? You know were we live. Please send it. We need it, you don't.
                    Mrs. M. Shaw

How odd. Crace would have to see this. Perhaps it was black-mail. There was no date on the letter itself, but it was postmarked Dorset, 17 May—two months ago.

I grabbed the two letters—Lavinia Maddon's and the one from the mysterious Mrs. M. Shaw—and walked through the palazzo to find Crace.

"Mr. Crace? Mr. Crace?"

My voice echoed down the portego. There was no answer. I entered the drawing room, where I found Crace in his chair, his chin resting on his shirt collar, snoring. I backed out of the room quietly and tiptoed down the hall and into the kitchen. I'd show him the letters later. I'd use the afternoon, or as long as it would take, to try and find the other letters sent by these two very different women and show him the lot. That way the matter could be settled easily and with the minimum of fuss. He could decide whether to proceed with the project suggested by Lavinia Maddon and what should be done about the suspicious-sounding Mrs. Shaw. I would try to do as much groundwork as possible before talking to him about both subjects. My diligence, I was sure, would please him.

+≒≒+

I left Crace dozing and enjoyed a lunch of salami, bread and tomatoes, reading Aretino's *Selected Letters* as I ate. Afterward, I went back to the study and worked on the correspondence. I sifted through the pile looking for the telltale handwriting on the envelopes—one style elegant and learned, the other childlike and primitive. As I sorted, placing the letters that I had examined to my left, I thought about Crace and the mysteries of his past.

For all his oddness—well, perhaps, precisely because of it—he was a fascinating man. No wonder there was so much interest in him. Despite what Lavinia Maddon said about using Crace's story as a metaphor for fame and failure or whatever it was, it was clear she was interested in the story of his life, especially this incident in 1967. And what kind of hold did this half-educated woman from Dorset have over him? Crace had told me that he no longer wrote, but I had no idea why he had decided to stop.

Before I went any further, I thought it was probably worthwhile to try and find out a little more so that when I did take the letters to Crace, I would understand what he told me. I stood up and looked around the room, listening for Crace's approach. It was all part of my job, it was research. He'd thank me for it once he knew the circumstances. To be on the safe side, I left the study, walked through his bedroom, back down the portego toward the drawing room and peeked around the double doors. Crace was still in his chair, asleep, his eyes fluttering like butterflies on a pair of withered leaves.

Back in the study, I started to check the shelves of his book-case. Many of the books—dusty volumes with red spines, Dante, Petrarch, Spenser, Donne, Byron—looked as if they had been published a couple of centuries ago. I couldn't see a single title dated later than the 1920s or 1930s and certainly no copies of Crace's own novel.

I turned back to the desk and started to search the small drawers situated in its upper section. In one there were a couple of tiny gold keys that looked like they might unlock a suitcase or a valise. In another there was an envelope, held together by string twined around a button fastening. I looked at the door. No one there. I slowly uncurled the string, winding it out in an ever-increasing circle until the envelope opened. Inside was a smaller square, buff-colored envelope, the kind young boys used to keep stamps or coins in. It looked as though it had been sealed, al-though one of its corners curled back, revealing its underlip. I hesitated for no more than a second before delicately easing it apart. At first I thought there was nothing in it, but then I real-ized that there was something camouflaged, nestling at the bottom. A crescent-moon-shaped locket of hair, flaxen. I pushed my fingers into the envelope and pulled it out. It felt brittle and old, as if it had been snatched from the head of a porcelain-faced, Victorian doll.

Over the course of the next few days, whenever I had a spare moment, I searched the palazzo for a copy of *The Debating Soci-ety*. I scanned the shelves, pulling out volumes hidden two or three deep, but still nothing. It was if he had tried to erase every trace of his past success.

I was forbidden to ask about his writing, yet I needed a little background so as to know how best to respond to those two let-ters, how best to protect him. If I could just find out a few hard facts that would help fill in the blanks about his life, then I would feel more confident about knowing what to do and what to say. I would then be in a better position to help.

The opportunity came one day when I realized we were running out of coffee. Just after starting the job, I had done an enormous shop, buying, on Crace's instructions, excessive quantities of food for the store cupboard. Crace hated me leaving him for any length of time—the few minutes it took to nip around the corner to buy our fresh brioche each morning was just about acceptable—yet obviously supplies were down once more. I would have to venture out and stock up. I knew it would be unwise if I missed Crace's breakfast, and so I set aside the few grains of fresh coffee for him and made do with instant for myself. Then I went through the ritual of preparing breakfast.

I filled the espresso maker with water, spooned in the last of the coffee, screwed on the top and placed it on the gas ring. The flames licked the bottom of the espresso maker, spitting as they came in contact with a glob of tomato sauce spilled on the hob from the previous evening's supper. I turned down the gas, grabbed my keys, and ran down the portego to the staircase and into the courtyard. I crossed the little bridge that led me to the outside world and snaked my way through the tangle of alleyways to the pasticceria around the corner. Crace, I was sure, knew exactly how long the trip should take me, because whenever I returned, clutching my bagful of brioches, he had taken his position at the breakfast table just as the espresso had started to hiss.

"Buon giorno," I said as I returned into the kitchen.

"Oh, good morning, Adam," said Crace.

"I thought we'd try something different today rather than brioche," I said. "The pasticceria had the most lovely baicoli. Look."

I slipped the little biscuits, named after the tiny lagoon fish that they were supposed to resemble, onto a plate and displayed them proudly before Crace.

"Quite adorable, yes. What a treat."

I poured his coffee into a cup and made myself another instant.

"What's wrong with you? Gone all prole on me now, have you?"

I laughed, looking at my cup.

"No, it's just that we're out of coffee. The pasticceria didn't have the blend you like. Actually we're down on most things. I'm going to have to do another big shop."

"How can that be?" said Crace. "I thought we still had a cupboard full of provisions. Surely we don't need more."

I talked him through the list of what we needed, adding how awful it would be if we ran out of something essential during the long afternoons when all the local shops were closed. Would he really want me disappearing for hours at time searching for a shop, not knowing when I would return? Surely it would be better if I got everything we needed today.

"But you promise you won't be very long?" he pleaded.

"I'll try and be as quick as I can."

"That's no good," he snapped. "You need to tell me exactly. You don't understand—I have to know. I need to know when you are coming back."

I looked at my watch. It was nine in the morning. The shopping usually took me an hour or so, but that day I planned on incorporating something else into my trip.

"Three hours?" I said.

Crace looked taken aback, almost as if I had insulted him.

"No, that's far too long. An hour and a half."

I felt like I was in an auction, competing in a bid for myself.

"Let's compromise. Two hours."

Crace paused before nodding his head.

"Very well—but not a minute longer."

After breakfast, he shuffled into his study and came back with a handful of notes. Although he measured out his time, he was certainly more than generous with his money. I wondered where he kept what must be quite a considerable stash.

"Here is three hundred euros," he said. "If there's too much to carry, take a water taxi back to the bridge. And what you don't spend, you may keep."

"Thank you," I said, taking the cash, feeling his finger linger just a moment too long on the palm of my hand.

"So I'll see you back here at eleven," said Crace as he closed the door and I walked across the bridge.

As soon as I was out of sight, I quickened my pace and took my guidebook from my rucksack. I flicked to the blue pages at the back. Getting Around. Resources A–Z—accommodation, banks and money, business, crime and safety . . . drugs . . . health and hospitals . . . internet and email. I worked out which of the internet cafés was nearest, found its location on the map and started to walk as quickly as I could. After the claustrophobia of being stuck inside Crace's palazzo with only a wizened old man for company, I found walking through the crowds intensely enjoyable and liberating. I smiled at a couple of Italian shop girls as they walked by and even turned around to watch them strut down the street. I caught a whiff of coffee as I strode by a bar, and even though it was only 9:30 and I had plenty of time, I had to fight the urge to sit down at a table and just watch the world go by.

A few minutes later I found the street, past a bank, a fruit shop, two pasticcerias and another bar. I walked back up again. I began to panic. There was no sign of it. It must be here. I would simply have to ask. I walked into the bar. Five or six men stood at the marble counter enjoying their morning wine—un'ombra, "a shade," Venetians called a glass of wine, because traditionally wine used to be stored in parts of the city that were not exposed to the sun; the digging of cellars, of course, was completely out of the question.

I bought a bottle of water and asked the barman—a man with a leathery, contour-lined face—about the location of the Network House.

"It's next to the bank, down some stairs," he said. "But it's closed."

"What time does it open?"

He puffed on a cigarette.

"It will not open," he said. "Closed for good."

"Are you sure?"

He inhaled again, as if that was answer enough, and turned away.

I retrieved my map from my bag and found another internet café—a twenty minutes' walk away. I checked my watch. I would not have as much time as I had hoped, but it wouldn't take me long to do the shopping. I downed my water, left some coins on the counter and walked toward Dorsoduro. As I snaked my way across the city, over the Accademia bridge and through the narrow calles, I tried to enjoy the two hours out of captivity. But with each snatched glimpse of a yet another church that housed spectacular art, I felt increasingly resentful and angry.

I arrived at the internet café feeling like I had bathed in a warm, sticky liquid. The physical relief on entering the air-conditioned space was immense, but I knew I hadn't time to relax. I went to the reception desk, where I was assigned a computer, logged on and typed in the address of a search engine. I entered

Crace's name. Over five thousand hits. Why hadn't I heard much about him before? I clicked on the first entry on the list.

The potted synopsis of his life told me that he had been born in 1931 in Edinburgh, where his father worked as a science master at a public school. He went to Oxford in 1949, where he read English, and graduated in 1952. Crace decided to follow his father into teaching and took a job at a little known fee-paying school in Dorset. It was while he was a teacher that he wrote his first novel, *The Debating Society,* published in 1962. "A clever conceit that rises above the drive for mere novelty, *The Debating Society* unmasks the pretence of our so-called modern civilised society to reveal the darkness lurking beneath," was how a critic from the *Times* had described it. I wondered how the teachers and the parents of the boys at Crace's school had reacted to one of the masters writing such a novel. The report also said the book, to date, had sold over three million copies. But although there were reports that Crace was at work on another novel, he never published anything else. In 1967 he told a journalist, "I am giving up writing because I have nothing relevant left to say. I have enjoyed enormous success with my first novel, and I thank all my readers for their support and encouragement. However, I am sure they would not thank me if I carried on publishing. Why spoil such a perfect, beautiful relationship?"

I clicked back to the five thousand hits and scanned down the list for clues. More bibliographies, more potted outlines of Crace's life, but nothing deeper, nothing more detailed. What about that woman, Mrs. M. Shaw? A surge of adrenaline flowed through me as I tapped in her name and Crace's in the search engine. I bit into my left thumbnail as I waited for the results. I was sure I was onto something. The tiny circular computer icon whizzed around the screen for what seemed like several seconds too long before it

flashed up the message, "No search results." I repeated the process
using the surnames only but just got some useless genealogical information about a family in Fort Worth that happened to have the
two names in their conjoined history. I was about to tap in Lavinia Maddon's name when I looked at the clock at the top right-
hand corner of the screen. It read 10:14 AM. I only had
three-quarters of an hour to do the shopping and get back to the
palazzo.

Just before I was about to end my session, I clicked back to
my initial search results and scrolled down one more time. Buried
amidst all the extraneous material—the duplicate entries, the
posted discussions about the merits of the film versus the book,
and gossip about various cast members of the movie—was one
entry that began with the words, "Writer Gordon Crace finds
tenant dead—suicide." I double-clicked on it, my heart beginning
to beat faster. The details were sketchy, but it was obvious someone had posted the information culled from a newspaper report
back in August 1967. I scanned the story for a name of the dead
person, but nothing came up. I terminated my internet session,
paid at reception and rushed out. Thankfully, Billa, one of the few
proper supermarkets in the whole of Venice, was nearby in Zattere.

I shopped manically, throwing groceries—fresh fruit and vegetables, bread, olive oil, coffee, cold meats and cheese—and more
cleaning materials into the trolley as I steered my way through the
supermarket. After queuing up and paying for the shopping, I realized that I still had enough money left to get a water taxi back
to the palazzo—I would have to as it was already 10:45. Using my
mobile, I called the central water taxi office, but I was told they
didn't have one free for another half hour, which was far too late
for me. The longer I waited at Zattere, gazing across the waters at

the Mulino Stucky building on Giudecca, the more anxious I became. Every one of the little speedboats that motored past was full, and my attempts to hail one were dismissed by their drivers with arrogant turns of the hand and supercilious expressions. Just as I was about to give up hope, a vaporetto surrounded by clouds of fumes chugged down the Canale di Fusina and stopped. It was an 82, which would take me to San Zaccaria. I didn't have time to get a ticket, but would have to risk it. The journey down the canal, between the two islands and past the baroque splendor of Santa Maria della Salute, was probably one of the most sublime experiences in the world, yet I paid no attention to the famous sights; I was too worried about what I would say to Crace when I got back. It was as if traces of guilt were smeared across my face and I was sure he would see them.

At San Zaccaria I found—just as it was too late to really make a difference, of course—a free water taxi. After negotiating the price, the driver, a handsome muscular man with a tanned face, took hold of the shopping and helped me into the boat. It was clear he was friendly and wanted to chat; as he guided the taxi through the narrow canals toward Castello, he kept turning around and smiling, but I wasn't in the mood. No matter how much I told myself not to worry, that I had done nothing wrong, the more uneasy I became. As we approached the side canal that led to Crace's palazzo, I saw a flotilla of gondolas bobbing up and down in the dark water. What was it that Crace had said the other night about gondolas? "'Like coffins clapt in a canoe'—Byron," he said. It was an old observation, now something of a cliché, but the image had unsettled me.

I arrived back at the palazzo at 11:30. I crossed the bridge and let myself in. It was quiet.

"Gordon? Gordon?" I shouted as I opened the door. "Sorry I'm so late. You wouldn't believe it—I couldn't find a water taxi anywhere."

There was no response.

I walked into the drawing room, but Crace wasn't there, nor was he in the kitchen. I knocked on the door of his bedroom.

"Gordon? Are you there?"

I opened the door and saw him lying on his bed. Was he asleep? The parquet floor creaked as I walked toward him.

"Don't come near me," he said, still with his eyes closed.

"Sorry?"

"You promised you'd be back by eleven. And look what time it is. It's just unacceptable behavior. Completely unacceptable."

"But it was just impossible to find a water taxi. At Zattere—"

"So what did you come back in? What was it that dropped you off down there—a giant water rat?"

Crace had obviously been watching from a window and had seen me get out.

"Yes, I did get one—finally—but not until San Zaccaria. Honestly, Gordon, I—"

"You'll find an excuse, but it's no use." The rhyme sounded odd, sinister even.

I realized there was no point in arguing. "I'll let you calm down a little and then perhaps we can talk," I said, turning to go.

Crace slowly eased himself up on the bed and opened his eyes. "It's just that you know I simply cannot bear it."

"What?"

I waited for an explanation.

"I cannot endure it, being left like that. You've no idea how much it pains me."

I didn't say any more, hoping my silence would prompt some further insight into his peculiar character, but none was forthcoming.

"I know I've made you promise before and it didn't make much difference," he said, pursing his lips. "But you must tell me now whether you are prepared to do what I say. Otherwise I will have to let you go just like I did with that other unfortunate boy."

"The one before me?"

"Indeed."

"What happened to him?"

"He reneged on his promises and he had to be dismissed." I sensed that Crace's anger was subsiding. "But I really would rather not go through the whole process of finding another."

He obviously needed me. I could understand why my predecessor did not last long in Crace's employment, but I realized I needed Crace too.

"I'm sorry I didn't get back in time. But it was completely out of my hands. I probably should have set out sooner, but honestly I didn't do it on purpose. And yes, I'll try to make sure it doesn't happen again."

"Very well. Very well." He paused. "So what's for lunch?"

+>=<+

I cannot say how—or exactly when—the idea first occurred to me. It was one of those thoughts that seemed like it had been floating at the back of my brain for days, just waiting to take shape.

Crace's biography. *I* was going to write it.

I was the perfect person. I had the access—the subject was under my nose. I had the time. And I doubted whether the novel I was planning would ever take shape. Surely it was better to make my name with this project—an in-depth portrait of a once-successful author, now so reclusive that he hadn't stepped out of his crumbling palazzo for the last twenty years—and then present the publisher with my novel. I was certain that his was an extraordinary story, one I was sure I could make work. Why should some stranger—this Lavinia Maddon—cash in on Crace? For all her vestiges of seriousness, her *New Yorker* bylines and her flashy address, she had no inside knowledge of the man. She didn't know him as I did.

I realized that it would probably be quite impossible to publish the book while Crace was alive. But surely it was only a matter of time before he keeled over and died. Even though he was not yet seventy, from my own eyes I could tell he was not in good health. He was as frail as an old, starved dog. I would do the research, get as close to him as I possibly could, and then publish as soon as reasonably possible after his death. And although Crace had said he loathed the idea of biography and biographers—nothing but "publishing scoundrels" he called them—I was sure that he would appreciate such a tribute to his life. It was only fitting that it should be done by someone who understood him, someone who cared.

In search of more letters from Lavinia Maddon, I tackled the pile of correspondence once again. But now, inspired by my new plan, I looked for anything of interest—snippets of biographical detail, postcards from old acquaintances, publishing returns. If a letter intrigued me, I either set it to one side to read later or copied it down into a new notebook I had bought for the purpose. To Crace, who sometimes walked in as I worked, it looked as though I was doing a particularly thorough job. He stood behind me, laying a hand lightly on my shoulder, uttered a couple of approving phrases and then shuffled out.

One of the first letters I came across in my quest for the heart and soul of Crace was the original approach from Lavinia Maddon, dated 12 February. My God, she was good. You had to admire her determination, her seductive way with words. No wonder she had attracted so much praise. The note was charm itself, shrouding her real intention—to expose and exploit her subject—with fancy phrasing and elegant expressions. She did not want to cause offense; she had Crace's best interests at heart; if he agreed, she promised to show him his quotes for approval; she was not concerned so much with biographical fact as with literary form. Reading it almost persuaded me that she was the best person for the job. I slipped the letter into the sleeve at the back of my notebook; I would deal with her later.

That morning I also finally came across a couple of royalty checks. It was incredible that Crace's novel was not only still in print, but that it sold in more than respectable quantities. I thought I'd present Crace with the checks over lunch. It would be interesting to see his reaction. After all, everything now was research.

Just after preparing a lunch of bread, Parma ham, figs and cheese, I told Crace to close his eyes.

"For what purpose, may I ask?"

"I've got something to show you"

"What?"

"Wait and see," I said.

"It seems extremely tiresome. Why can't you show me now?"

He pretended to be irritated, but I could tell he was as excited as a schoolboy faced with the prospect of an unexpected gift.

"Come on now."

"Oh, very well."

As the thinning skin drooped down over his lids, I imagined him dead and placing two coins on his eyes.

"Hold out your hands."

He reached toward me, his hands cupped like a supplicant. I placed the two statements from his publishers into his palms.

"You can open up now."

Crace blinked and looked down, his weak eyes first twinkling in anticipation and then recoiling in horror. He dropped the statements. His throat quivered, a gobbet of spit appeared at the corner of his mouth.

"What? What's wrong?"

He was so perplexed he couldn't talk.

"I thought you'd be pleased to see them—they're your checks. You're still selling quite well."

Crace struggled to catch his breath as he reached out for his glass of water.

"The title—" he spat out. "Get rid of the name."

"Sorry?"

"On that statement . . . I don't want to see it. I can't bear to. I thought I'd told you—no mention, no mention at all."

I picked up the pieces of paper, ripped off the checks and then threw the accompanying statements, which bore the name of the offending novel, into the bin.

"Look—they're gone now."

"What were you trying to do? Kill me?"

"I'm sorry, Gordon. I just didn't think."

"That's right, you didn't, you never do. Do I really have to go through it all again?"

"But I don't understand. Why do they upset you so much? Even though you don't write now, I would have thought that you might at least be proud of your past achievements."

I knew I was pushing Crace further than he really wanted to go. But it was important. I had to know.

"As I said, it's a different life to me. What I am now and what I was then are two separate entities. I don't really want to say any more."

"Of course. I understand," I said, nodding my head and trying to look as sympathetic as possible.

Could I risk another question? "But do you not miss it? Writing, I mean."

The weak muscles on the right hand side of his mouth twitched, and for a second I thought that Crace would explode, that he might dismiss me on the spot for trying to probe into a territory that he had told me, many times, was definitely off-limits. But then his face relaxed and he looked at me with sad eyes.

"I made a decision to stop. It was just no good."

I wanted to pursue the line of inquiry and try to get him talking while he was in the mood.

"Do you mean the writing? That you thought it was no longer up to your usual standard? Is that why?"

"No, that was not it at all. I mean it was no good for me, no good for those around me."

"Oh, I see," I said.

He was going to be a difficult subject to crack, but the secrecy with which he surrounded himself made the prospect so much more alluring. And I was determined. I was confident that this could be the making of me.

+─══─══─+

I wrote back to Lavinia Maddon that afternoon, telling her that Crace was not interested. I thanked her for her inquiry, but informed her that unfortunately Crace was an intensely private man and couldn't abide the idea of a biography, no matter how literary. He would write to his publishers to tell them not to cooperate in any way, and if she continued to pursue the matter, he would consult his lawyer to see what further steps could be taken to prevent her writing such a book. Of course, he would deny use of his copyright material, and without that he was sure that any such book could not be written. I signed the letter in my own name and added, in parentheses, "personal assistant to Gordon Crace." I was also careful not to give away the address of the palazzo. I didn't want my competition to come sniffing around here.

There was no need to tell Crace any of this. After all, he had told me to weed out such inquiries and deal with them as I saw fit. I was just following orders. He would be pleased by my actions.

But what should I do about the other letter, the one from Mrs. Shaw? I searched through the correspondence to find previous letters from her but came up with nothing. I knew I had to be careful. If the situation ever got out of control, if she really was blackmailing Crace and the police became involved, I had to make sure that whatever I wrote could not be used against me. But I needed to find out more and I felt that this woman knew a great deal. Perhaps she was a way to understand Crace better. I decided on a simple, straightforward approach.

Palazzo Pellico
Calle delle Celle
30122 Venezia

Dear Mrs. Shaw,
 I am writing to you on behalf of Gordon Crace, to whom you wrote on a couple of occasions. In order for Mr. Crace to consider your request, could you please supply me with more details? I am confident that if you state your case as fully as possible, you will stand a better chance of gaining what you wish for.

*I can understand if you do not want to put all this
down in writing. But if you send your telephone number
to the above address in Venice, I could ring you and talk
through the options. Please be assured that whatever
you say will be treated confidentially.*

*As Mr. Crace's personal assistant, I am the best person
to deal with in this matter. If I talk to you, perhaps we
can come to a suitable arrangement.*

Yours sincerely,
Adam Woods

I nipped out to post the letter as Crace was having his afternoon nap, making sure I left a note saying I had gone to buy some
wine. From the palazzo it was only a ten-minute walk to the
Fondaco dei Tedeschi, the former German merchants' building
that was now the central post office. As I approached, I saw the
crowds traipsing up and around the Rialto Bridge and wondered
if any of them knew the glorious history of the building that faced
them, that the simple, plain facade of the Fondaco dei Tedeschi
was once covered in elaborate frescoes by Giorgione and the
young Titian, faded portraits now in the Ca' d'Oro. And that the
"scourge of princes" Pietro Aretino, every day for the twenty-two
years that he had lived in his house on the Grand Canal, had
gazed out of his windows at this building, a view he thought was
the loveliest in all the world. I doubted it. All anyone seemed interested in was fake designer tat on sale at the canal-side stalls.

After being cooped up inside Crace's palazzo, I was tempted
to walk around and explore. Apart from that first day in the city, I
hadn't had the chance to really see and do the things I had always
dreamed of—St. Mark's, the Palazzo Ducale, the Scuola di San
Giorgio degli Schiavoni, the Tintorettos in the Scuola Grande di

San Rocco and in the churches of San Polo and the Madonna dell'Orto, or even just an afternoon sunbathing at the Lido. I resented the fact that I had to rush back to Crace, but comforted myself with the knowledge that I had embarked on a new project, one that had the potential to transform my life. Around the corner from the palazzo, I bought a couple of cakes and a bottle of Fragolino, and when I entered the drawing room, I found Crace still in the same position in his chair, his head gently tipping forward onto his chest as he slept.

+══─═══+

I started to get up earlier and earlier, rising as the weak sun of the dawn filtered through the shuttered windows of my room. As I washed and dressed, I felt driven by a new purpose, an overwhelming curiosity—a desire to know. I used those early mornings to write in my notebook and scour the palazzo for signs of Crace's past. I took it upon myself to look a little deeper, searching through drawers and cabinets. Their dark, secret spaces looked like they should hold clues to Crace's character, but they contained nothing but the meaningless detritus of life—receipts, bills and circulars. The only real, tangible object I had found that looked like it might be something of significance was the lock of flaxen hair hidden away in Crace's desk. I was keen to have another look at it, but as it was cosseted away in the study next to the bedroom, I couldn't risk Crace finding me.

Each morning, as I heard my subject getting ready and my time alone was about to come to an end, I was left feeling increasingly dissatisfied, frustrated and angry, wondering why Crace's presence wasn't more substantial and visible.

Just as I was about to lose confidence in the validity of my project, something happened that boosted my spirits. One Wednesday morning, I was sitting on the top step of the stairs that led down into the courtyard, sipping an espresso, when I heard something fall into the letter box. Crace was already up but not dressed. After drinking a macchiato, he had decided to retire to his bedroom, where he said he would do a spot of reading and then proceed to get ready. He said he would return for breakfast in about a quarter of an hour and that he rather fancied scrambled eggs on toast.

"You do know that I like my eggs hardly cooked at all," he said. "So you mustn't put them on until you see me sit down at the table. You won't forget now, will you?"

The first time I had cooked the dish for him, he had screwed up his face in disgust and made me throw it all away. "Like little coolie clumps of shit," he had barked at me then. He insisted on standing by me as I whipped up the eggs once more and stirred them in the pan. Just as the yellow mixture began to solidify, he tapped me on the shoulder and told me to turn the heat off. The slimy mass looked like something premature. As he spooned the viscous, formless eggs into his mouth, he made a series of appreciative slurping noises that turned my stomach. I wasn't going to forget.

The sound of the letter falling into the box reminded me of the time when I had pushed my application through the dragon's mouth. I remembered the sensation of my fingers brushing against the cold marble.

I ran down the steps, past the Corinthian column with its naked cherub, to the door. Fixed to the back of the wooden door, immediately behind the dragon's head, was a gray metal box. Using my thumb and forefinger, I tried to flick open its lid, but nothing moved. Thinking it was merely jammed, I pressed harder into the metal rim. A sharp edge cut cleanly into my thumb, leaving an inch-long gash. As I pushed my thumb into my mouth and tasted the metallic tang of blood, I noticed a tiny lock at the side of the box. How could I have been so stupid as not to have seen it?

Crace had told me that all the mail forwarded from his publisher would be hand-delivered by courier and, as a result, I had never needed to open the letter box before. When I had written to Mrs. Shaw asking her to write to me at the palazzo, I had assumed I would be able to intercept the letter before Crace even knew it had arrived. I had never seen him check the letter box. I never thought that it would be locked.

I bent down and studied the tiny lock. I rimmed it with my finger, somehow thinking that feeling its contours and indentations would succeed in teasing it open. I considered smashing it. I looked around the courtyard for a rock and even thought about using the sculpture of the cherub as a weapon, but knew that such an action was impossible as it would raise Crace's suspicions. The only way was to find the key, a very small key.

I ran back up the courtyard stairs and down the hall. I heard Crace in his bedroom, walking toward me. A couple more seconds and we would be face-to-face.

I slowed down and turned my back on him. I couldn't let him see the panic in my eyes.

"I'm nearly ready," I heard him shout. "You can get the eggs on in a minute."

He wanted breakfast.

"As I was reading, I started to feel hungry." His voice was coming closer.

I walked into the kitchen and started to crack open the eggs. As I poured a dash of milk into the mixing bowl and began to whisk up the mixture, I noticed that my hands were shaking.

"You can put the pan on now."

Crace was outside the door.

"And the toast."

I looked up.

"What's wrong with you?"

As I dropped a spoonful of butter into the pan and placed it on the gas, I felt his eyes on me. "What do you mean?" I said, pretending to concentrate on the breakfast so as not to meet his gaze.

"You're not your usual cheery self, that's all. Has something happened?" I noticed a slight note of panic in his voice. I had to keep him calm.

"Oh, just a little preoccupied. The novel isn't going so well, that's all."

"You know I can't give you any advice on that front, I'm afraid," he said as he eased himself into his chair.

I stirred the eggs, buttered the toast, served the dish on a plate and took it over to Crace.

"What happened to your thumb?"

"I cut it on that knife over there," I said, pointing to the counter. "The one I used to crack open the eggs. I must have been miles away. But I was careful to wipe my hands before making your breakfast."

"Even if a few drops of blood did fall into the eggs, who cares?" he said, shoveling the amorphous mixture into his mouth and smacking his lips. "They would taste delicious with a little of you in them."

His voice was flirtatious, creepily so. But perhaps now was a good time to try and ask about the key.

I sat down next to him and moved my chair a little closer. The proximity brought a slight flush to his cheeks and his little eyes glinted mischievously.

"Gordon?"

"Yes?"

"I think someone pushed something into the letter box this morning. I'm sure it's just rubbish—a flyer or something like that—but I thought I should probably try and clean it out for you. After all, when was the last time you looked inside it?"

Crace put down his knife and fork as he thought.

"It must have been a few weeks. Why, not since you dropped off your last letter. But what's the point? And as you say, there'll be nothing of any great import inside."

"But if I don't clear it out, surely all the letters will start spilling out of the dragon's mouth onto the street."

"So?" Crace said, resuming his breakfast. "Who cares? It will teach the little fuckers a lesson, don't you think? Show them we don't even read their crap they shove into the box."

I had to try again, this time another tack. I took a deep breath. "I'm afraid I've got a confession to make."

Crace stopped eating again and looked at me. I licked my lips and swallowed nervously.

"I know you told me not to give out this address"—as Crace's face contorted with anger, little globs of half-eaten egg flew out of his mouth—"but I'm afraid I had to write to my girlfriend back in London—Eliza. We split up just before I came out here, and there were lots of things we hadn't sorted out. She started sleeping with one of our lecturers, and I suppose I still had feelings for her. I said some awful things before I left, did some things I regret. And so I just had to write to her to tell her how I feel. I was desperate for some contact, the kind that only letters can bring, when you can express emotions that are impossible to communicate over the telephone."

"I see, yes," said Crace, his features softening. I was, after all, speaking the truth. Well, at least my emotions were genuine.

"I know I went against your rules, but if you could just let me retrieve the letter and read it, that's all I'm asking."

"You didn't tell her my name, did you?"

"Yes, I mean, no—I didn't tell her. Or anyone else. I just said I was staying at this address, trying to write my novel, looking after it while the owner was traveling abroad."

Crace's eyes narrowed, squinting as if trying to see inside me. "Very well, very well," he said. "But just on this occasion." He paused as he finished off his breakfast. "But what happened between you? Between you and—"

"Eliza."

"Yes, between you and Eliza."

He seemed interested, so I told him a little about her, how we'd met and how much I had liked her. After I had finished talking, he pushed himself out of his chair and told me to wait in the kitchen while he went to fetch the key. I tried to map out his route around the palazzo from the sound of his footsteps so as to visualize the location of the key if I needed it again. From what I could make out, it seemed he walked down the portego and through the corridor that led into his bedroom or study. I remembered the keys I had seen in the desk that housed that lock of hair.

"Here we are," he said, returning to the kitchen and stretching out his right palm to reveal a key so tiny it looked like it would only unlock a dollhouse. "The key to all mythologies—well, of the miniature variety anyway."

He giggled at his own feeble little joke, and to keep him in good humor, I laughed along with him.

"So, let's go down and see what's inside the box, shall we?"

As he turned away from me and started to move toward the door, I realized I had to think of something quick.

"Gordon? Gordon, please wait. There's something else I need to tell you."

"Yes?"

"It's a rather sensitive subject, I'm afraid."

I made an effort to look worried and somehow slightly ashamed. I dropped my head forward and stared at the floor like a schoolboy caught in the midst of some terrible misdemeanor.

"Adam, what on earth is the matter?" Crace's voice was soft and gentle. "Come on, let's sit down."

As we resumed our positions at the kitchen table, I watched as Crace placed the little key at the side of his empty plate, near the edge of the table.

"It's terribly embarrassing and very p-personal," I began, deliberately stumbling over my words, "and I'm not sure how much you might be able to help me. But I can't keep it to myself any longer."

Crace looked at me intently, his eyes burning into me. I could tell he was intrigued.

"I'll try and help in any way I can. Please feel free to tell me anything you like."

I took a deep breath and started my story. "Well, for as long as I can remember, I always felt a strong connection, a liking for . . . for . . . other boys."

Crace's narrow, slit eyes widened, his nostrils flared and he leaned closer toward me.

"At school, I suppose I had terrible crushes on a series of slightly older boys, which everyone says is perfectly natural, but then there was something else. There was a sort of longing. I never did anything, you understand, but it was always there, like a shadow in the background."

"I see."

"I remember one lunchtime when I was in the fifth form, I was sitting by myself in a classroom reading a book when one of the boys, one of the boys I liked, came in. I can hardly describe what I felt. He swaggered into the room—he was built like a rugby player—and sat on the desk in front of me. Then, without looking at me, he lay across the neighboring desk and stretched himself out."

Crace swallowed and ran a moist tongue over his thin lips. His eyelids had started to droop and it looked as though he was slipping into some kind of hypnosis. I continued with my story.

"He raised his arms above his head and then he ran one of his hands across his shirt, so that he exposed his stomach. I couldn't bear it any longer, I wanted to reach out and touch him, but I felt confused. His head faced the blackboard, turned away from me so I couldn't look into his eyes and perhaps he was completely unaware of my presence or at least regarded me as so insignificant as to not worry about. I stretched out my hand and"—I reached across the table as if to imitate the action, maintaining eye contact with Crace as I did so. I checked the position of the key, still lying by his plate at the edge of the table and then grabbed Crace's left hand—"touched him."

Crace woke up from the somnambulistic state with a start. His hand jumped, displacing my own. Exaggerating the force of the movement, I brought the top of my hand down on the key and brushed it off the table so that it landed near my foot. I quickly moved my shoe, trapping it underneath. I was certain that Crace, with his poor eyesight, had not seen.

"Oh God, how stupid of me," I said. "I'm so sorry, but I'm sure it's around here somewhere. I just hope it hasn't gone down one of the cracks in the floor."

Crace was silent.

"I can't believe I told you all that nonsense," I said as I continued to pretend to scan the floor. "Sorry to burden you with all that."

Crace turned and looked down at me. I felt my face reddening.

"No, not at all. Obviously it's something you needed to get off your chest, so to speak. Never mind about the key—you can look for it later. You may as well continue telling me the rest of the story."

"Well," I said, clearing my throat, "these things never end how you want them to, do they? Just as I reached out, another boy burst into the room. I think he saw what I was about to do but didn't say anything. Nothing happened after that—we never had the opportunity, he left to go to university and we never met again. But it's funny that hardly a week goes past that I don't think about him."

"And how did this affect your relationship, may I ask?"

"Eliza always suspected that I might have had those kind of feelings. I told her I had never done anything about it, and she was so supportive and understanding. She even suggested that I try it; she said she wouldn't mind. Of course, now in retrospect, I realize why she had said that—she would feel less guilty about her own secrets."

"Yes, I see," said Crace, nodding sympathetically. "And how do you feel now?"

"Confused," I said. "I'm not sure what I want—and I still have feelings for Eliza."

"Do you mind if I give you one piece of advice?" said Crace, clearing his throat.

"No, please do. I'd be really grateful. I am in a bit of a state about all this."

"Of course, I don't know the whole situation, by any means," he said, overemphasizing the last three words of the sentence. "But if I were you, I would make a clean break of it with your girlfriend and tell her the truth—that you are uncertain about your preferences and need some time to explore various options. There's no point suppressing anything at your age. You need to experiment."

"But I feel apprehensive; it seems so wrong somehow. A bit seedy—do you know what I mean?"

Crace paused.

"It's far from wrong or dirty, Adam. In fact, the love between two men can be one of the most beautiful things on earth."

He didn't say anything for a few moments. Then his eyes started to dance nervously around the room. Clearly, his confession had embarrassed him and he wanted to retreat into the safety of our previous conversation.

"Where is it? It must be on the floor somewhere," said Crace, shifting in his chair to turn around.

"I'm sure I'll find it," I said, taking the opportunity to quickly bend down and pocket the key.

I stood up and walked across the kitchen. I crouched down to pretend to look for the key, but as I ran my hands across the floor, something caught the cut on my thumb.

"Oh, for God's sake, Adam, watch what you're doing. You're bleeding all over the place. Go into the bathroom and wash it off."

I pushed my thumb into my mouth and sucked the blood away. Yet as soon as I pulled it out again, a bright red bead bubbled up to the surface of the skin.

"Just let me clean this up first," I said, getting a cloth from under the kitchen sink. But as I bent down to wipe up the smear, more blood trickled out of me.

"Give it here," said Crace. "You'd better go and find a plaster before you bleed to death."

"Okay, you're right," I said, knowing that if I was quick, this was my opportunity to retrieve the letter.

I walked down to the bathroom, opened the mirrored cabinet above the washbasin, and took out the tin box that housed various creams, lotions and pills. The medicinal smell reminded me of school. I fingered around in it, careful not to spill any drops of blood into the tin, and fished out a plaster. After applying it to my thumb, I switched on the taps, dashed back through the hall, careful that Crace didn't see me, down the steps and into the courtyard, sunlight blinding me as I moved out of the shadows. I dug deep into my pockets to retrieve the tiny key, but as I brought it out, ready to insert into the letter box, it seemed to slip about like a little fish out of water. I looked up at the top of the staircase to make sure Crace wasn't watching me before pushing it into the lock. With one click, it opened.

I lifted the metal lid and dropped my hand inside. I heard a rustling of paper and pulled out a thin, airmail envelope covered with scrappy handwriting. It was from her. I desperately wanted to tear it open and read its contents, but I had to get back upstairs. I shoved it into my pocket, dropped the lid of the letter box and turned the lock. Then I ran back upstairs, down the portego to the bathroom, switched off the taps and into the kitchen. Crace was struggling to get up from his kneeling position.

"I'm sorry. The damned thing just wouldn't stop bleeding, so I had to keep it under the tap," I said as I helped him to his feet.

"Let's see," said Crace, grasping my hand and bringing the cut digit closer to his face. "Your hand is still hot."

He eyed me with suspicion.

"What do you mean?" I asked, trying to buy time to think.

"You can't have put your hand under the tap to stop the bleeding because your hand is not cold."

I didn't know what to say. Had he guessed? Had he seen me?

"Let me explain—"

Crace cut me off. "You fool, you're supposed to put it under the cold, not the hot tap. Didn't your parents teach you anything?"

I had to disguise my relief.

"I just hope I never have to depend on you for first aid."

We both laughed.

"Now, let's find that fucking key, shall we?"

Needless to say, it didn't take us long to find it. When I thought Crace wasn't looking, I simply took it out of my pocket and quietly placed it on the floor, behind one of the legs of the dining table.

"There it is," I said, pointing. You could just see the end of it sticking out from the shadows. I stretched out and grabbed it, bringing it up to show Crace as proudly as a boy diver brandishing an oyster containing a fat pearl.

"Well done, Adam, well done," he said, patting me lightly on the arm. "So let's go and see what secrets the box holds, shall we? You don't mind, do you?"

He seemed unusually keen to accompany me downstairs, and I couldn't fob him off any more. Perhaps my story had been so compelling that he now felt unusually involved, curious to know more about Eliza and the situation back home. Maybe he even felt like part of me in a funny sort of way. It didn't matter. Who cared? Now there was nothing to fear. I had retrieved the letter from the box. I was on his trail. I was in control.

We walked slowly together down the portego. I supported him as he lowered himself down one stair at a time into the courtyard, his skeletal hands cupping themselves around my shoulders, occasionally touching my neck as we descended. Crace stopped for a moment as we passed the Cupid sculpture in the center of the courtyard and mumbled something about love not looking with the eyes but the mind. He turned to me and smiled.

"Go on then, Adam. Let's see what's inside." He gestured to the box.

As I pushed the key into the lock, a bloody fingerprint on the lid looked back at me like an unblinking, dark red eye.

"Found anything?" asked Crace.

I lifted the lid, trying to smudge away the print as I did so. I reached inside.

"There's nothing here," I said.

"Now, isn't that strange?"

All I wanted to do was escape into my bedroom where I could read the letter. But as I helped Crace into his chair in the drawing room, he patted the neighboring chair and gestured for me to sit by him. He looked at me with a serious, concerned expression.

"I think we need to talk a little more about what we were discussing earlier," he said.

There was no way out of this one. I sat down beside him. I could feel my face beginning to burn.

"But before we do, I feel it only fair that I tell you a little about myself," Crace said, his tongue flicking over his thin, dry lips. "I've deliberately given you very little information or insight into my life, and please don't think that is a reflection on you. In fact, it has nothing to do with you whatsoever. I have to be careful, you see. Well, I suppose I feel I have to be careful. Oh, I'm afraid I'm making very little sense." His face seemed to crease and crumple like an old sheet of paper. "Of course, I know what you must think of me, living here without stepping outside—"

I tried to speak, to come to his defense out of a spirit of politeness, but he raised his hand and brushed aside whatever I was going to say.

"And I do think that to the outside world I must appear rather an eccentric, indeed quite a sad creature—never engaging with anyone, never experiencing anything, forever locked into my own little world, surrounded by my books and my art, remnants of another age. But I'm happy, whatever that really means. Well, as happy as I'm sure I could ever be."

He paused and took a deep breath before he shifted in his seat.

"Listen to me, circumnavigating the main issue as usual. Sorry, Adam, it's just that I haven't talked like this for such a long time. You'll have to forgive me if I digress or wander off down some conversational pathway that looks like it's leading to nowhere. But the only reason I'm doing this—the only reason at all—is because I feel it might help you. There was a time in my life when I felt confused and unhappy and . . . uncertain about what and who I wanted."

I waited for him to continue.

"I was young, like you. After Oxford I started work as an English master, and one of my first jobs was at this school in Dorset. Again like you, I had ambitions to write. I had an idea for a novel, and I worked on it when I wasn't teaching. It all seems so long ago now. In a way, I can't believe it's me I'm talking about. Anyway, soon after starting at the school, I became very friendly with another teacher, Ruth Chaning, who taught art on a part-time basis. She was about my age, in her early twenties, and as both of us were new to the school and did not know many people in the area, it was only right and proper that we should spend time together. Throughout our friendship I waited for the right moment to tell her that ... that I was not attracted to women. But when, one night, walking back from the village pub, she reached out and pulled me toward her and kissed me, I felt like it was too late. The right moment had passed. It wasn't that I felt sorry for her, but looking back it was terribly immature of me not to say anything."

He roused himself as if suddenly waking from a dream. "Sorry. This is far too much. You don't need to know all this. I don't know why I'm telling you. All I meant to say was that I know what it's like to be in your situation."

It was the first time I had heard Crace say anything in detail about his own personal life. And I made sure to memorize every single word.

I wanted to know more. I steeled myself to ask a question. "Did you feel attracted to any other members of staff, besides her, besides this Ruth?"

"I did feel drawn to another, but he ... they ... were not members of the faculty," he said.

"Someone who worked in the village? Someone you met outside the school?"

The question was too much for Crace. It was as if the conversation we had been having had never taken place.

"I thought I told you never to probe into my life, my personal life. That was one of the areas we went over and over in the interview, and you said that you would abide by my rules—"

I had to interrupt him, to make him see sense. "But, Gordon, it was of your bidding. I didn't ask you to talk about the past. You initiated it, don't you remember? You said it might help me ... with my dilemma ... my attraction to other boys."

I stared hard at him. His lips worked silently, as if trying to form ghost words, phrases and expressions he would have used if he had continued in his attack on me.

"Sorry. I didn't mean to raise my voice," I said. "It's just that you started it all off. Talking, I mean."

He frowned and his eyelids flickered. He concentrated so hard that it looked as though he was trying to untangle a piece of memory tape that had knotted itself inside his head.

"Oh, yes, so it was. How silly of me."

"Obviously I wouldn't have asked you anything, but I thought you wanted me to. I thought you wanted to help me . . . help me understand."

Surely there was no harm in trying. After all, a little self-pity might elicit some more information.

"You're right. You're perfectly right," Crace said. "Perhaps it's time I got it off my chest. What is there to be afraid of?"

He paused.

"I'm not sure where to start."

The lines from his face seemed to melt away and he looked, for a moment, like a lost little boy.

"What about at the school?" I suggested. "Your time there?"

"Ah, yes, the school—Winterborne Abbey, a truly splendid place. Really quite magical. Surrounded by woods, in a hidden valley. Named after the medieval abbey next to it, now used as the school chapel. In fact, the abbey is full of fine sculpture and fascinating pieces, relics and such like."

He was beginning to waffle. But I felt that I couldn't interrupt him. Anything he said was material.

"You know that for years Winterborne had been a private house. But before then a village once stood on the land. A proper settlement, you know, with three public houses, a high street,

common land. But then around 1780, this chap—something of an
upstart, I should imagine—bought the land, decided he didn't like
the view or the smell or the people and cleared it all out. He
shifted the village a mile or so away and had it rebuilt for his
estate workers. Then he employed Capability Brown to landscape
the valley and had a house built for himself. Quite an achievement, I suppose."

"So you had a happy time there?"

"Oh yes, the boys were a delight to teach. So full of curiosity,
eager to learn, a great sense of intellectual freedom about them.
They sucked up information like little sponges, the dear things."

"You must have had your favorites."

"You're right there, Adam. I did, yes."

"So you say you felt similar to me? Didn't your relationship
with the other teacher—the woman—work out?"

"No, it didn't, for one reason or another. And then I fell in
love." As he said this the muscles in his face seemed to go into a
kind of spasm. "Oh, for God's sake, man, spit it out," he said to
himself. "It's only Adam, that's all. He wouldn't say anything,
would you Adam?"

He turned to look at me. "I fell in love . . . with a pupil, with
one of my boys . . . his name was Chris—Christopher Davidson.
He was not one of the younger boys, so please don't think I'm like
that."

"What did he look like?"

Crace narrowed his eyes as if by doing so he could conjure
forth an image of the boy.

"Blond hair, a beautiful color, like ripened corn."

"How did you meet? I mean, how did you, you know—"

"Become intimate?"

"Yes."

"He was a scholarship boy, only there because his father got a job as the school's organist. Parents didn't have a bean. But he had a natural aptitude for poetry and language, almost an instinctive ability to read underneath the words, if you know what I mean. I recommended that he read English and try for either Oxford or Cambridge, and we met up after school for regular tutorials. His parents did not have any books in the house and yet they produced this angel of a son."

"So what happened?"

"I still find this terribly difficult to talk about, Adam. I'm not sure—"

"Look, I find what you are saying really helpful to me. It may even—"

"I'll try, but I'm just warning you—"

"Don't worry. It might even help you to—"

"Perhaps you're right."

He took another deep breath.

"We spent more and more time together—it was totally above board. I was intrigued by him, and I suppose he must have looked up to me. Dreadful thing happened with his father, lost him, poor thing."

"And then?"

"Surely, Adam, you've got the gist of it, haven't you? For God's sake, boy, what do you want? Blood? The next thing I know, you'll be getting a tape recorder out or taking a sworn statement from me."

Do not blush, I told myself. Don't laugh awkwardly. Just look as normal as possible.

"What happened then is that we fell in love. Okay? That's what happened, Adam. We left the school soon after Chris turned eighteen. We moved to London, and Chris enrolled in an English literature course. But, encouraged by me, the stupid fool I was, I told him to drop out of university after only one term. He had had amazing A-level results and showed a lot of potential, but after a great deal of thought, I believed that his talent was such that he should really start creating something of his own. Looking back, I'm sure I was jealous of his youth, his beauty. I was afraid that if he stayed on at university, he might meet someone of his own age.

"So I kept him. Kept him with me where I could see him. Both of us wrote, or at least tried to write, every day. He became more and more frustrated. He started drinking—both of us did. A case of a little drink to put us in the mood for writing—you know, accessing the subconscious and all that bollocks. A whiskey and soda after breakfast to help harness the muse—what utter crap! I tried to help; I went over his work, but it seemed as though he didn't have . . . well, he didn't have much to say. Of course, he didn't have anything to say. He had barely begun to live."

Crace snorted with self-hatred. "What was I thinking of? Chris, my beautiful boy. I should have let him go. I should have forced him from me. That life was no good for him, and it was obvious he was unhappy. I wouldn't let him out of the house. I wanted him there, you see, with me. Do you understand?"

As he looked at me, his eyes pleading with me to say something, I almost felt sorry for him. I filed the words away in my head, ready to transcribe them as soon as I got to my room. My notebook was filling up gradually as I gathered the raw material for my book. Crace in his own words, his own pitiful, miserable, sordid little words.

After this outburst, Crace said no more. His head drooped forward onto his chest and he resumed that position of fatigued defeat I had seen him adopt so many times before. It was as if all the life had been sucked out of him, his corporeal body reduced to a shell. I stood up to leave the room, and he waved me away with a skinny hand.

In my room I took out my notebook from my rucksack, which I had stashed away out of sight under my bed, and wrote down our conversation as quickly, but as accurately, as possible. Then I fished out the letter from my pocket and tore open the envelope. It was written in the same scrappy hand as before. The paper was thin and cheap, and black Biro smudges covered the page like squashed flies. A dirty fingerprint marked the top right-hand corner.

23 Church View
Winterborne
Dorset
DT11 0GF

Dear Mr. Woods,
Thank you for your letter. It is much appreciated. Please call me on 01258 893489 and we can discus the matter further. Mr. Crace will be curios to find out more, I guarante that. You see we now know how Chris died.
I also have some more surprises for you.
Yours,
Mrs. M. Shaw

I was beginning to see the pieces fall into place. I now knew that Chris was much more than Crace's "tenant." And the implication from this shabby blackmail attempt was that there was something suspicious about the way he had died. No wonder Crace felt so damned guilty. No wonder he couldn't write.

I was certain I wasn't going to find the answers by simply asking Crace. He had already told me much more than he had ever wanted to say. If I pushed him any harder, even if I did use the excuse that his words helped me cope with my sexual confusion, I doubt I would get much further with him. I suppose his reticence on the subject spoke for itself; if there were something suspicious about how Chris had died, Crace wouldn't want to talk about it, would he?

A phone call to Mrs. Shaw—that was the obvious first step.

I shoved the letter in my pocket, found my phone card in my wallet—I didn't want to use my mobile in case Mrs. Shaw kept a note of my number—and walked back down the portego. I peeked into the drawing room; Crace stared ahead in an unseeing daze, blind to the world.

"I'm just going to pop out to get a bottle of wine for supper," I said. "I think both of us could do with a drink."

Crace nodded. "Very well." His voice sounded distant, sad, as if talking about the past had infected the present. "Don't be long now."

As soon as I was outside, I took out the letter and read it once more. I was filled with excitement. This latest twist was a biographer's dream. Subject as potential murderer—I couldn't get better than that. I walked down the calle and through the meandering streets imagining my future. Jake had filled me in on the often ridiculous amounts of money paid by some British newspapers for serialization rights of certain newsworthy books. How much would they pay me? More than enough money to buy time so I could then get down and write the novel. I would make my name, perhaps even do a deal with a publisher for two books, first a biography and then my novel. That would show my father. That would show all those people back home who never had any trust in me, Eliza and Kirby. Better revenge than a mere broken arm.

I stopped at a phone outside a bar and dialed the number. There was a slight delay before a connection was made and then it seemed to ring forever. I was on the point of replacing the receiver when I heard a crackle on the line.

"Hello?" The voice was that of a man's, old and rasping.

"Can I speak to Mrs. Shaw, please?"

The man cleared his throat. "There's no Mrs. Shaw here," he snapped.

"Oh, I'm sorry," I said. "Is this 01258 893489?"

"Who's speaking?"

"It's Adam Woods. Mrs. Shaw wrote me a letter—about the writer Gordon Crace? She said that I should telephone this number."

"Oh, I see," The man's voice suddenly took on an ingratiating, weaselly tone. "Yes, of course, of course, Mr. Woods. Very nice of you to call."

"Can I speak to Mrs. Shaw, please?"

"I'm afraid you can't. I'm afraid Mrs. Shaw is no longer with us," he said.

I was beginning to have my suspicions that the whole thing was a setup, that it was all some kind of hoax. What was going on?

"It was me who wrote you that letter. I'm, or I was, the nearest thing to what you might say was Chris's stepfather. Mrs. Shaw—Maureen—died in February. Cancer ate her away. Nothing but skin and bone at the end. She got so weak—"

"I'm sorry to hear that Mr. . . . Mr.—"

"William, William Shaw. After her husband died, Maureen took my name, but we never married, you see."

"Do you have something that might interest Mr. Crace?"

"Yes, you might say that, you might indeed," he said, his asthmatic rasp whistling down the line.

"Can I ask, first of all, why you didn't write using your own name?"

"At one stage Maureen and Mr. Crace knew one another. Not very well, of course. But she looked up to him. She did then, before she found out what was going on, you know. I thought writing as Maureen would grab Mr. Crace's attention. A name from the past, if you like. Sounds like it did the trick, didn't it? Rattled him right and proper, I should think."

"Mr. Crace has assured me that he wants to settle this matter. He's told me he wants it cleared up, but of course you must give me something to go on. I'll have to report back to him with as much detail as possible. You do understand that?"

"Yes, indeed," he said. "Maureen knew there was something odd from the beginning. She never believed her son could do that . . . you know . . . kill himself the way he did. When I asked why, how she could be so certain, she just said that she knew. She didn't want to go into it, but she said it was as near to murder as you could get. If she was so sure, why didn't she go to the police, I asked. But she felt sick at the thought. The shame of it, was all she would say. Of course, she was never the same after it happened. But now that she's dead, everything has changed. Circumstances are different. Things have come to light, Mr. Woods."

As he finished the sentence the words seemed to degenerate into one long wheeze. I imagined him yellowed by cigarette smoke, fingers stained, lungs drowning in blackened tar.

"May I ask what exactly has come to light?"

"A book—a writing book. Found it when I was going through Maureen's things. She'd hid it away all this time, never let on to me. That's how she knew, you see. Knew that Chris didn't do it. It's all there—and, God bless us, much more besides—in that book."

"Can you tell me what kind of book, Mr. Shaw?"

"You know . . . what do you call it . . . his diary."

I knew straightaway I had to see the diary. It would be the key to Crace. If he wasn't going to reveal any more about himself, and after his recent confession it seemed unlikely, then this was the only way. I was sure that if I could only find out more about the death of Chris I could at last begin to understand Crace.

I told William Shaw I would have a word with Crace and then call him back. I wanted to elevate the matter beyond mere blackmail, give it some kind of respectable gloss. I said that it was highly likely the author would want to secure the diary and transfer it into his hands for safekeeping. Of course, Crace would insist that some kind of settlement be made; after all, he didn't want Mr. Shaw to go to all that trouble without a little remuneration. Was there a figure he had in mind? Mr. Shaw went silent on this point. A thousand pounds, I suggested.

"I find that acceptable, Mr. Woods," he replied.

So now all I had to do was to negotiate my way out of Crace's palazzo and get my hands on the money. My instinct told me that the latter task would be easy compared to trying to extricate myself from Crace's grip. I had saved up quite a large chunk from my monthly salary, but this would also have to pay for my airfare back to Britain, my travel down to Dorset and accommodation. And what would I say to Crace?

By the time I wandered from the phone booth to the wine shop and bought a couple of bottles, I had my plan. Crace hadn't moved since I had left him. I uncorked a bottle of slightly perfumed white, poured him a glass and held it out for him. He took it mutely.

I sat down beside him. "I've just heard some really bad news."

Crace raised his head and looked at me.

"While I was out, my mobile rang. It was my mother. Her mother, my grandmother, has just died."

She had, in fact, been dead several years, and my other grandmother had died before I was born. Tears began to well up in my eyes.

"I was so close to her. I can't quite believe it. Oh, gosh, look at me—"

I felt the wetness on my cheek and tasted a slight saltiness at the corner of my lip.

"I'm sorry. I didn't mean to—"

Crace raised his hand from his lap and brought it up to my face. With an exquisite tenderness, he wiped a tear from my cheek.

"You poor boy. You poor, poor boy," he said.

It was his act of kindness that did it, his gentleness that reduced me to sobs. He believed me, and I felt wretched, absolutely wretched. But now I had no choice.

"My mother wants me to go home for the funeral, but I know how much you hate to be left. I don't have to go, but—"

"Of course you must go. There's no argument, simply nothing more to be said."

"But will you be all right? I mean, who will—"

"Don't worry yourself, Adam. You can easily get one of the women from the shop to deliver the provisions. It's imperative that you go. Don't worry about me."

"But I feel so awful. Honestly, though, I'll be back as quick as I can, definitely within a week or so."

At this I thought he would explode, but he only looked at me with pity.

"Take your time. I'll be fine."

"Thank you, Gordon."

"What was she like, your grandmother? Oh, sorry—that was terribly insensitive of me. You probably don't want to—"

"No, it's fine. I'm sure it will help to talk about her." I wiped my eyes and nose, sniffing a couple of times. I actually felt genuinely upset.

"She was a wonderful woman, really unique. Sara, she was called. Born before her time. Incredibly spirited and lively, always game for a glass of champagne, even though she was, oh, ninety-two or something like that. I think she could even do the splits well into her seventies."

The memory, which was real enough, made me laugh. Crace smiled back.

"I'm sure you must have been very close?"

"I was closer to her than to my parents, even to my mother."

"She must have been a wonderful woman, as you say."

"She was. I remember the way she used to stroke my hair as a boy, playing with it between her fingers, saying it was like spun gold."

"When's the funeral?" asked Crace.

"At some point next week. We're just waiting for a final date."

"So you must get back as soon as you can?"

"Yes, I suppose I must. But really, if you'd rather I stayed with you, I will. Honestly."

"Would you really do that, Adam, if I asked you?" Crace looked a little incredulous, flattered perhaps.

"Yes, of course. I know how much it means to you to have someone you trust around."

He paused for a second, as if assessing his mood. What would I say if he really asked me to stay?

"No, I'm not going to do that. Even *I* wouldn't be so selfish." He started to raise himself from his chair. "Now, come on. Let's get your things in order. You've got a plane to catch."

⊹══⊹

The trust in his eyes was the worst thing. It made me feel so shabby somehow. It would have been so much easier if Crace had behaved coldly toward me, or if he were angry or suspicious about my decision to fly back to Britain. But he seemed to understand what the death of my grandmother meant to me as if he too had once experienced similar feelings and emotions. I forgot for an instant that he might be a murderer. In fact, for a moment, it felt like I was the criminal.

The two of us chatted as I gathered together my things. Just as I was about to pack my wash bag, I looked down into the rucksack and saw my notebook, open. The wash bag I was holding fell from my hands, its contents clattering down on to the wooden floor.

"It's only natural that you're feeling jumpy, a little on edge," Crace said. "After all, you have suffered quite a shock, you know."

"Sorry, yes," I said, bending down to pick up shaving foam, toothpaste and a nail clipper. I noticed a pack of razor blades nestling next to Crace's foot.

Our eyes met.

"Here you are," he said, reaching down for them and passing them over to me. "You don't want to forget these. No, it's a perfectly common response to grief. You might even feel nauseous. Do you feel nauseous, Adam?"

"Yes, a-a little," I stuttered, dropping the razor blades back into the wash bag and placing it inside the rucksack, on top of the notebook.

"Shaking, sickness, confusion, irrational thoughts—you might experience all those in the next few hours or days. So you must look after yourself. Get plenty of rest. Take a drink—a serious drink, a glass of whiskey or cognac—if you think it might help."

He suddenly looked miserable.

"I'm not sure how we will be able to keep in touch, but that's too bad, isn't it?"

I felt soiled by guilt, almost as if Crace could see traces of my plans inscribed into my skin.

"Here, take this," I said, giving him my mobile phone in an effort to try to make myself feel better. "Just in case you need it. And I'll be able to call you on it."

"Why, I wouldn't know what to do with it."

"Just keep it on," I said, fishing in my bag for the charger. "And when the battery runs down, plug it into this. Then I'll be able to check on you."

"Are you sure?" he said, much more cheerful now.

"Yes, of course. I'll rent another one at the airport when I land."

"That is terribly kind of you. Now let me do something for

you. Let me give you this," he said, bringing out a stash of money. "At least it can cover the cost of the phone and some of your expenses. And I want to pay for your flight—your return flight."

"I couldn't possibly accept, Gordon. No, that's too much."

"No, I insist. Anyway, it's purely selfish on my part. At least then I know you'll be coming back."

He laughed a little as he said this.

"That's incredibly kind of you. Thanks. But I'm not sure which day will be best for me."

"Oh yes, I see. Of course." He looked slightly disappointed but tried to cover it up. "Then why don't you book a ticket and then if you need to change it, well, so be it."

"That's perfect. Thank you."

After calling the airline on my mobile and showing him how to use the phone, we enjoyed another drink together. I arranged for Lucia, the teenage daughter of the woman who ran the pasticceria, to drop off food for Crace in my absence and then rang for a water taxi. As Crace and I walked through the palazzo and down into the courtyard, the sun had started to set, fragmenting into hallucinogenic, bright shards that painted the stonework a surreal mix of pinks, violets and blood reds. The sound of lapping water outside added to the dreamlike effect. Everything seemed distant, somehow alien, as if I were viewing events from a distant perspective or watching myself projected onto a large screen.

"You know, I'll miss you, Adam," he said. "I feel that over the last few days—you know, with all these things we've been talking about—we've really gotten to know one another better. It did unsettle me quite a lot, uncovering all that about the past, and at one point I thought I would not be able to carry on, but in fact it really has helped me. Do you feel it's helped you as well?"

"Oh yes, definitely," I replied. "It's really helped clear my head. Get things into proportion, straighten things out, so to speak."

Crace smiled weakly. "I wouldn't be at all surprised that it even helps with your writing. I know the last time we talked about it, you said that you were having difficulties."

He stared at me, waiting for an answer.

"Erm, yes, I think it will. I know I haven't done much recently apart from take a few notes. You know the kind of thing—sketches, ideas, rough drafts."

"It's from these little germs that great infections grow. There's nothing like being possessed, taken over, swallowed up by one's own writing. Maybe you'd like to show me what you've written when you come back. Of course, if you don't want to, I'd totally—"

"No, of course I'll show you. In fact, I'd really value your opinion."

"I can't wait," he said, embracing me with his skeletal arms. "I know you have to go, but please come back just as soon as you can. We might even be able to carry on our little talks . . . "

I walked through the doorway, down the calle and saw that the water taxi was waiting in the side canal.

"It's here," I said, walking back toward him. "I'd better go. I'll see you in a week or so. I'll get back as soon as I can, I promise."

I turned to go.

"Oh, Adam," said Crace.

"Yes?"

I looked back at his thin, wasted form standing there silhouetted by the heavy wooden door.

"Nothing. It doesn't matter."

I walked toward the speedboat, and Crace closed the door.

Arriving back in England was like coming across an old scar to find the wound reopened, the flesh festering underneath. I had blocked Britain out of my mind and refused to think about Eliza and the situation. After all, I had a new life in Italy. I had plans, grand ambitions. I had my book to write.

But as the plane circled the gray skies, tipping on its side to give an occasional glimpse of the patchwork of fields below, I began to feel more and more nauseous. My mouth was dry and bitter. I closed my eyes and saw Eliza, remembered running my fingers through her glossy, sloe-black hair, and tracing the vein running down her neck with my tongue. Her eyes opened—a flash of ice blue. Another image. We were in bed. It was early morning and the weak light filtered into the room. I reached out to her, but she stiffened at my touch. I listened to her breathing, shallow, tense little breaths. She switched on the light beside the bed and turned toward me, serious-faced. There was something wrong. It wasn't going that well between us, was it? Surely I had to agree.

What was she talking about? I thought we were just fine, no, better than that. I thought we were unique, that we would be together for—I couldn't see a time when we would be apart. That's how close I thought we were.

She had felt a gap between us recently, a distance that she thought would only grow with time. She knew it wasn't my fault, that I couldn't help it, that those kind of problems, the difficulties I had communicating and—what was it she said?—empathizing with people were really hard to overcome. It probably went back to something in my childhood. Or perhaps I would never understand the root of it all. Maybe it was just the way I was.

She had found me vaguely amusing to begin with. My disconnection with the world around me. It was endearing, she said. But after a while it had become ever so slightly annoying. And now she was beginning to have doubts about the future of our relationship. No, she hadn't met anyone else, she said. No, she really hadn't, she maintained.

I remember her lying there, naked. Her flesh almost translucent, pearl-white. Her red lips beginning to tremble, her hands shaking. She told me I was hurting her, really hurting her. Stop it, she said, but I had to make her see that what she was saying was nonsensical. She wasn't talking about us, I told her. She was telling me a story, relating the problems of another couple she had met.

I think I pinned her wrists down. I know she couldn't move. She was rigid. She looked like a painting, ever so beautiful, almost dead. I felt incredibly aroused. I pushed into her, but she tried to fight me. She started to scream—thin, weak little childlike shrieks—but there was a portable CD by the bed and I simply switched it on and turned up the volume.

By the end of it, I was sure she would change her mind. She couldn't live without me. She got off the bed and went into the bathroom. I heard the shower gush water and I heard her sobs.

She would never leave me now, I was certain.

When she came out of the bathroom, her eyes looked glazed over, strange somehow. I told her how much I loved her. Her head jerked forward and she clasped her hand over her mouth. I couldn't hear what she said—her words were all muffled—but I think it was something about how much she loved me too. She walked across the room and put on her clothes. She had to go out, she said. Just to get some milk. She'd be back in a couple of minutes. It was Friday, and I was looking forward to spending the weekend with her.

I waited for Eliza to come back, naked and immobile on the edge of the bed, thinking that not moving would stop time or at the very least slow it down. Goose bumps covered my skin, turning my legs and arms into chicken flesh. With each creak of the stairs or slam of the flats' front doors, I raised my head in anticipation, confident that it was her. She had met a friend and gone for coffee. She had gone to a lecture and then made a trip to the library. She had fallen down and cut her knee and had to go to casualty. Wild surmises ran through my head like a series of hallucinations, each more believable than the last.

But Eliza did not come back that day. Sunlight faded from the room, and I was left sitting in the dark, listening to the sounds of the city.

+≻═━═≺+

I had to see her before doing anything else. Just to convince myself that she had actually existed, that I hadn't manufactured the whole thing inside my head.

After picking up another mobile phone at Stansted and changing my euros into sterling, I took a train to Liverpool Street and then a tube to North London. I emerged from the suffocating heat of the underground at Kentish Town. Drizzle fell from a greasy, yellow-black sky. Outside the station, a drunk sat in a puddle of his own piss, smiling. A woman with the face of an angelic child and the body of a prepubescent girl held out her hand for money. When I placed a pound coin into one of her tiny hands, her remarkably unlined face lit up with delight.

The route from the station to the flat was one I had taken so many times that it was indelibly marked in my brain: right at the first junction, left just after the pub, straight on past the pastel-colored houses and the corner shop, and second on the right. As I walked the last few steps down our street, my hand automatically searched my jeans pocket for the key. But, of course, I no longer had it. Things had changed since then.

I stopped by one of the trees in the road and moved into the shadows. A light was on in what used to be our bedroom in the rented flat at the top of the house. Was she there now, inside that room? Was she with him? What was he doing to her? He must have brainwashed her. Why else would Eliza want to go off with a man old enough to be her father? His tawny beard nuzzling her neck, his flabby body rubbing up against her—I still couldn't believe that she could prefer him to me.

I'm not sure exactly when I realized what was going on. Certainly not that day when Eliza walked out. I called her mobile repeatedly, but it automatically switched to answer mode. I dialed her parents' number, woke up her father who told me never to contact Eliza again. Stay away from her, he said. She doesn't want you—doesn't want you anywhere near her. If it had been up to him, he would have called the police. Had she been in trouble, I asked. He told me to fuck off and slammed the phone down.

On the Monday we were due at a lecture together, *Tarquin and Lucretia: Representations of Power and Gender in Sixteenth-Century Italian Painting.* I would see her there and ask her what was wrong. Obviously I had done something to upset her, but surely we could patch it up and sort it out—behave like adults, for goodness' sake. I washed and dressed, carefully combed my hair, and took the bus into college. I arrived at the lecture hall early and had something like fifteen minutes to kill, so I went to the coffee bar where I thought I might spot her. As I walked, I saw people eye me with suspicion. Jackie, a close friend of hers, was sitting on a low sofa with another friend, whose name I could never remember. Had she seen Eliza anywhere? She looked at me with undisguised contempt. How on earth could I show my face around here, she said, after what I'd done? If it were up to her, she'd have me locked up for life. She'd have my balls cut off as well.

I don't know what Eliza must have said, but everyone made it pretty clear that I was not their favorite person. I sat through the lecture, even took a few notes, but I couldn't really concentrate. Perhaps I had been a little rough with her. It wasn't right, I'd admit that, but that didn't mean we were through, did it? If only I could talk to her, to make her see sense.

No matter where I looked or who I asked, I couldn't find Eliza. I wandered through the corridors of the college and out into the street feeling lost, abandoned. I tried to convince myself that everything was fine, that we had just had a silly row, but deep down I think I realized it was more serious.

Memories flashed into my mind, stinging my consciousness with associations of past happiness. The first time we talked: I passed a note to her in a lecture saying how much I liked her skirt, a colorful Mexican design with little circular mirrors sewn into its seams. To frighten the devil away, she said, and then she laughed, her pale blue eyes glinting like sunlight on ice. The first time we kissed: We had been for a drink and were wandering through Covent Garden. We stopped by an old, wooden market barrow. I was nervous, but she reached out her hand and touched me. Later that night, the first time we made love. My first time with anyone. My hesitancy and her warmth and confidence.

I couldn't accept there would be no more of her.

That day when everything altered forever, I raced back to the flat, secure in the knowledge that she would be there. As I walked toward it, I rang the number. From the other side of the street, I looked up and saw a shadow move across the living room. But the phone carried on ringing and no one answered. I took out my keys, pushed the Yale into the top lock, but as I tried to turn it, something jammed. I forced it out and made sure I had the right one. As I fumbled with the keys, I noticed that green wood shavings littered the ground, slim slivers of curled wood, a nest of snakes on the doorstep. Eliza had changed the locks.

I banged on the door, desperate to see her. I called out her name. I rang her mobile again and again, but still she would not answer. I told her that I wasn't going to move until I had seen her. I waited and waited and finally I heard footsteps move down the hallway. She had changed her mind. She was going to let me in. Everything would be back to normal. She would tell me how silly and how sorry she had been, and she would plead with me to have her back.

The letter box opened, a white envelope nosed itself out. I tried to reach her, grasping through the thin aperture of the door, but her footsteps faded away and I was left with just the letter.

She wasn't going to press charges, she said. If I would leave her alone, that's all she wanted. If I tried to contact her, speak to her in any way, she would tell the authorities at the college and even ring the police. All she was asking was that I stay away, stay away for good. Finals were not far off—we only had a couple of months to go—and she didn't really plan on coming into college. She would do most of her revision at home. She would give my belongings, together with the presents I had bought her, the occasional CD and old film on video, the sweet but inexpensive gold chain, to one of her friends, who would arrange a meeting at college. After the term ended, we would probably never see one another ever again.

She really had thought of everything—efficient and as single-minded as ever.

I remember that those words seemed to fly into my eyes like shrapnel. After finishing it, I half-expected to see the letter splattered with gobs of squid-ink black blood from the backs of my eyes. The reading left me reeling, and I staggered back down the street unbalanced as if the magnetic poles of the earth had shifted under my feet. At some point on the way back to the tube, I think I vomited into someone's front garden.

As I recalled that scene from a few months ago, I stood and stared at the flat. I didn't want to hurt her—not at all. Just a glimpse of her would be enough. I was over her, of course, but it would be silly to travel all this way and not see her. I shifted the weight from foot to foot and wedged my rucksack up against the tree. Occasionally a person walked down the street, spotted me and, no doubt thinking I was a potential mugger, crossed the road and carried on walking. After I had been waiting for about a half hour (by which point I felt as much a natural part of the scene as one of the trees that lined the street), the front door to one of the houses nearest to me opened. A man—glasses, early fifties, blue V-neck jumper—walked in my direction; as I didn't recognize him, I assumed he must have moved into the street relatively recently.

"Excuse me." His voice was clipped, upper-crust. "But are you all right?"

He wasn't interested in my welfare at all; he just wanted to check out whether I was going to break into one of the houses.

"Yes. Sorry to worry you. It's just I've just come from the airport and my friend who lives over there," I said, pointing to Eliza's flat, "didn't realize what time my flight arrived. I'm just waiting for her to come back."

"Oh, I see. Well, good luck," he said, smiling, relief relaxing the muscles in his face. "Good night, then."

"Good night."

I hadn't given much thought to where I would spend the night, but as it was getting late I thought it would be best to go back to my parents'. They didn't know of my return, but I was sure that they would like to be surprised. Just as I squinted at my watch to calculate how long it would take me to get back to Hertfordshire on the Thameslink line, I heard the click of a door opening.

A chink of light slashed into the night, illuminating the area around Eliza's front door. A woman with dark hair cradling a batch of newspapers in her arms stood in the entrance. She paused for a moment, gazing into the dark as if she could almost sense my presence. I took another step back into the shadows, hoping the dark spot by the tree shielded me from her sight. She licked her pale, thin, beautiful lips, bent down and eased the lid off the green recycling box that lay outside in the front garden. She slid the papers into the plastic container, straightened up again and turned away. I wanted to call out to her, perhaps just shout her name so I could see her reaction. I opened my mouth to speak, but my throat was paralyzed. As she closed the door and the entrance returned to darkness, I said her name to myself, silently.

I couldn't waste anymore time on her. I had moved on. I had a job to do, certain things to find out.

As I walked away from the flat and down to the station, I

imagined Eliza's reaction to my biography. I saw her walking into the bookshop on the high street, browsing through the paperbacks, and then suddenly stopping as she sees my name emblazoned across the cover and spine of a big, fat book. She picks it up and turns it over and over in her hands, not quite believing what she sees. She flicks to the inside back cover, presuming that it must be some other, older Adam Woods. But she would be wrong. Her eyes widen slightly as she reads the words: "Adam Woods studied art history at London University before moving to Venice, where he met the reclusive novelist Gordon Crace. This is his first book; his novel is due out next year."

It would be the best revenge. The infliction of pain—physical violence—would be nothing compared to that sensation.

On the platform, a couple of young teenagers, their faces hidden by their hoods, kicked a plastic takeaway box. A middle-aged, besuited man nodded his head in time to a beat only he could hear. A slapper in a tight white skirt shouted into a mobile as I walked passed her.

I suddenly felt weak and unbearably tired. I knew where my parents kept their spare key—under a large cardboard box at the left-hand side of their garage—but thought I should ring them to tell them I was back. After all, it was late.

I dialed their number using my new mobile.

"Hello?" It was my mum, her voice deep, groggy.

"Hi, Mum. It's me."

"Adam? Where have you been? It's been so—"

"I'm fine, Mum. Listen, I'm home. I'm in London."

"Are you all right? What about your teaching job? What about Venice?"

"I'll tell you everything when I get home. I'm about to get a train. I'll be there in about half an hour. Is that okay?"

There was a pause. I heard a shuffling noise and then a series of muffled, unintelligible words, as if Mum had put her hand over the receiver.

"Yes, that's fine, darling. We're . . . I'm looking forward to seeing you. It's too late to go through everything when you come in. You'll be tired. But we'll have a chat tomorrow. There's an envelope for you—it looks like it's from college, your exam results."

"Oh, yeah," I said. I couldn't really care less how I had done in my degree. I had a new life now. "I'll look at it when I get in."

"I hope you've done well, you deserve it." She paused. "But, Adam, I've got to tell you that your father is still very upset and angry. Just so you know. We were hoping you'd send us a forwarding address. Not knowing how you've been, you can't imagine how—"

"Okay, okay, Mum. Got to go—the train's about to come any minute."

It wasn't quite true. I had at least five or seven minutes to spare, but I didn't want to hear it. Not those words, not again.

***

"Jake? Hi. It's Adam."

"Adam . . . hi there. Where are you? Where've you been? It's like you . . . you disappeared, man."

"I know. I'm sorry. I've been in Venice—writing. But I'm back in London—for a couple of days anyhow. Listen, I was going to go back to my folks, but things are still a bit difficult with them, you know?"

"Yeah, right. You can always crash here if you want. There's only a mangy sofa, but it's yours if you'd like it."

"Really? That's great. I'm in North London at the moment, so I'll be there in . . . what . . . half an hour?"

I rang my mum back and said that I'd changed my plans. I could hear the disappointment in her voice, but told her she could call me and gave her my new number. She had probably thought Dad and me could thrash out our differences once and for all and we could start behaving like a happy family, as if that was ever going to happen. I heard my father in the background snarling about how I never thought about anyone else except myself. But she made me promise that I would at least go and see them in the next couple of days so I could pick up my post and find out about my degree.

On the Tube down to Brixton, I suddenly felt the possibility of happiness. Of course, I would have to keep my plans to myself. There was no point in boasting to friends about the Crace book, the biography of a literary murderer. Instead, I would maintain that I was still writing the novel, which was, in a way, true. Nobody would know what I was really working on. And then people would be amazed. By the time I emerged from the escalator at Brixton and smelt the mix of burning incense, pot and beer, I felt almost indestructible, like the events of the previous few months had never happened.

I breezed up Brixton Hill and strode confidently through the maze of streets that led to Jake's estate. He lived on the ground floor of an ex-council block. I pressed the buzzer and waited.

"Hey, come on in, mystery man," Jake said, appearing at the door, arms outstretched.

"How are you?"

His flat smelt faintly musty, as if the windows hadn't been opened in months. Old papers cluttered the hallway and piles of books threatened to collapse and spill across the wooden floors, a detail that reminded me of Crace's palazzo before I had cleaned it. Jake poured me a glass of wine, but I could tell he had something serious to say.

"So what was with all the silent treatment?"

"I know," I said, running my hand through my hair. "I'm really sorry, mate. It's just that . . . it's been really difficult."

"I heard from my dad that the job, the teaching thing, fell through. When I heard that, I thought you might come back to London."

"I did think about it. Can you believe the little fucker got a girl pregnant—the maid's daughter? The family sent him off to New York."

"So you've been in Venice since then?"

I nodded and took a gulp of wine.

"Doing what?"

"Mainly just working on the book, you know." I wasn't lying. I made an effort not to lie.

"How's it going? Pleased with it?"

"Yeah, yeah, it's fine. It's coming on."

"So it must be pretty pricey—Venice, I mean. Did you get another job?"

"Yeah, sort of as a personal assistant to an old writer. Odd jobs, clearing, tidying. Gives me lots of time to do my own stuff, you know."

"Great, great," said Jake. "Anyone I would have heard of?"

"No, shouldn't think so. Not exactly a household name."

"So what brings you back to London? Thought you'd said you'd never come back. In fact, from the way you acted, I thought—"

"Yeah, I know," I interrupted. I didn't really want to be reminded about the past. "I was a little . . . overexcited, I suppose."

"You can say that again. Jesus, you were far out."

I looked at my glass and ran a finger around its rim. I felt Jake's eyes on me, as if he was trying to assess me.

"So you were about to say—what brings you back?"

"Oh, I'm just doing a spot of research for this writer. He's interested in genealogy."

"Yeah?"

"In his family history," I added. "He wants me to find his birth certificate, trace his grandparents, follow the line back into the past—"

"Okay. Sounds interesting."

"So how have you been? How's the job?"

"Madness, real madness," he said, laughing. "I get pissed every night of the week and meet the most gorgeous creatures you've ever seen. Legs up to their armpits. Blonds. Best job in the world."

I could tell Jake was fooling himself. At university, he had nurtured grand ambitions to write about politics and social change; at heart he was an idealist, and I suspected that his job on a newspaper diary sniffing around for snippets of gossip about C-list celebrities fell far short of his own expectations.

"What are you doing for lunch tomorrow?" I asked.

"Erm, have to see. Why?"

"It's just that I've never seen where you work. I'd love to see where it all happens—you in the center of things . . ."

I think that made Jake feel good.

"You can come into the building, if you like. We can go to the high-class, ultra-glamorous house restaurant, aka the canteen."

Both of us laughed weakly.

"That sounds great," I said. "Just one more thing—does your newspaper have a cuttings library?"

"Yes. Why?"

"It's just that I thought it might help me with my research."

"You're welcome to use it if you like. I can call down and tell them that you're doing some freelancing for me. No problem."

"Thanks," I said.

The cutting was as thin and yellow as Crace's skin. It was dated 8 August 1967 and was from the *London Evening News.*

WRITER FINDS TENANT DEAD

Bestselling novelist Gordon Crace, author of *The Debating Society,* discovered the body of his tenant, 20-year-old aspiring writer Christopher Davidson, in his Central London home yesterday. It appears Mr. Davidson took his own life.

"I came back from the British Library and found Chris dead in the kitchen," said Mr. Crace, whose first novel was a worldwide sensation. "It was such a shock. I knew he had been depressed but never expected this."

Mr. Davidson rented a room in the novelist's mews house in Bloomsbury. The two men met at Winterborne Abbey, the public school in Dorset where Mr. Crace taught English. Mr. Davidson was a former pupil.

It is thought that after trying his hand at novel writing, Mr. Davidson met with little success. Mr. Crace, meanwhile, is hugely successful. It's estimated *The Debating Society* has sold close to half a million copies, and a producer has recently acquired the film rights. Police have con-

firmed that the inquest will be held at
some point in the next few months.

It was obvious what the reporter was trying to imply, but I suppose the laws of libel prevented the press from talking openly about the relationship. Crace's file was not as thick as I had expected, containing only a handful of cuts. Most of them were brief news items and reviews. I searched through them, looking for the reports of the inquest, but nothing seemed to cover it. There was one announcing Crace's retirement from writing, which contained the quote I had picked up from the internet and then a brief snippet about how he had settled in Venice. It was as though for the last thirty or so years Crace had ceased to exist. As I read through them looking for clues, I felt like I was researching the life of a dead man.

I asked the librarian, who was so short that his head only just appeared over the top of the wooden counter, for the file on Christopher Davidson and waited by the notice board for it to arrive.

"There you go," I heard someone say behind me. "Excuse me, here is your—"

The librarian handed me a buff-colored envelope with the word "DEAD" stamped in red at the top right-hand corner. It was so thin that I expected it to contain nothing, but after teasing open its rim, I saw that the envelope contained two small cuts—the one I had already read and a report on the inquest, also from the *London Evening News,* dated 4 December 1967.

WRITER'S SUICIDE BLAMED ON
FAILURE

A suicide note found by the body of aspiring writer 20-year-old Christopher Davidson revealed that he took his own life

after suffering from a prolonged spell of writer's block, an inquest heard today.

The tenant of bestselling author Gordon Crace could not cope with the success of his landlord. The two men lived together at 7 Thanet Mews, Bloomsbury, where it's said that Mr. Davidson rented a room. The 20-year-old took an overdose of sleeping pills, washed down with alcohol, in the early hours of 7 August. Mr. Crace, 36, found the body and rang the police.

The coroner heard that after arriving at the scene, the police discovered a typewritten suicide note by Mr. Davidson, who had been dead for several hours, saying that he couldn't carry on any longer as his writing career had not turned out as planned.

Psychiatrist Herbert Jennings explained to the coroner the devastating effects of writer's block and how it could, in extreme circumstances, lead to suicide.

The court also heard from Gordon Crace himself, who gave evidence about his tenant's state of mind leading up to the death. Although he knew Mr. Davidson had suffered from low spirits, on the day of 6 August he appeared to be in a positive frame of mind.

"I left him at the kitchen table by the typewriter," said Mr. Crace. "He told me that he was going to try and bash out a story. He had really high hopes for it. Of course, I had always encouraged him in his writing and really had faith that he would produce a fine novel. I never expected him to do anything like this."

The two men met when Mr. Crace was a teacher at Winterborne Abbey School, Dorset. They had lived in Bloomsbury for two years.

Verdict: suicide.

I photocopied the cuts and dropped the envelopes back into the returns tray. The fragmentary shards of Crace's life were beginning to fall into some kind of shape.

At last I had something tangible to go on, something with substance. I walked down the cobbled mews, imagining myself to be Crace. He had moved into this street when he was thirty-four, only thirteen years older than I, yet it was hard to think of him as a young man. The photograph that accompanied the item on the inquest showed him to be quite a handsome figure: strong features, a fine head of brown hair, almost a Romantic face. I took out the photocopied sheet and stared at the picture once more, running my finger around the image like a curious child toying with a dead insect. I squinted at the photograph and then looked up and down the street, trying to picture his life here.

The street was undeniably pretty, with clusters of flowers and tubs sporting lush foliage outside each door. Crace's life here, I imagined, was relaxed, cultured. After a morning at his desk, he would come out onto the street and perhaps walk down to the pub at the end of the mews where he would read the paper and enjoy a beer and a sandwich. Sometimes he would chat with one of his neighbors, converse not about literature or anything like that but just local gossip. Occasionally Chris would join him for a bite of lunch, but often he told Crace that he felt he had to work through as he was finding it difficult to get anything on paper. Crace told him just to relax, not to think so hard about what he wanted to achieve, just throw any old thing down, bash anything out; he could always worry about the style later.

In the afternoons Crace usually glanced over the pages he had produced that day, correcting and rewriting. But he rarely did more than two thousand words a day. Before he went to bed, he always made sure he had the next scene in his head, yet he adored the unexpectedness of his characters, the sense that they were alive, that no matter how much he tried to get a fix on them they would always shift a little, warning him not to take them for granted, to tell him that they were independent. It was an odd feeling, like talking to the dead.

Chris often asked him how he did it, and honestly he couldn't tell him. The younger man occasionally got angry, lashed out in a silly way, accusing him of keeping back information on purpose so that he would fail. It wasn't like that at all, Crace told him. By this point Chris had usually consumed half a bottle of whiskey or vodka. That was when the rows would start—nasty, drunken arguments that usually culminated in Chris storming out and threatening to go off with someone younger, not some pervert who was only interested in young boys.

Is that what happened between the two of them? Maybe, maybe not, but at least I felt a sense that I was beginning to somehow know them a little more. Of course, while this kind of inquiry, this biographical empathy, was important, I had to be able to back up my insights with facts, with evidence. That was what I was short on.

I stood outside their house, number 7, and noted a description of it in my notebook. It was a two-story building with a front facade painted licorice gray and wisteria climbing to the right of the door. I stepped back a few paces to try and snatch a glimpse through the top window but couldn't see anything inside. With my camera I took a couple of images of the house; I had bought slide film because I wanted the photographs to be of good enough quality so I could use them in the book. Just as I pressed the shutter a second time and still as I was peering through the viewfinder of the camera, I saw the front door begin to open. I pushed the camera down out of sight, looked around me to see if I could run or hide, but instantly realized this would be not only foolish but impossible.

"Excuse me, young man. Can you tell me exactly what you are doing?"

The voice was female, fruity and theatrical, exactly like the woman now standing before me. She was in her late fifties or early sixties and had coated her moon-shape face in guano-white makeup and ringed her tired eyes in heavy circles of kohl. Brightly colored feathers—oranges and purples that winked in the autumn sunshine—stuck out of her excessively back-combed hair, giving her the look of a rather large, silly tropical bird.

"I say, come here, closer. Don't pretend—I saw you and your camera. What are you, one of these paparazzi?"

I walked toward her, more than a little afraid. I could see that the walls of her hallway and staircase were lined with black-and-white pictures of her in various poses and roles.

"Come on, show me."

I moved the camera from behind my back and gave her an apologetic look. I had to take a gamble, hoping that she did not know Crace. If word were to get back to him about my inquiries, my project—my future—was over.

"I'm just doing some research . . . about someone who used to live here," I said somewhat feebly.

"So you're not from one of the tabloids? What a terrible shame. I thought you might be on the point of reviving my fatally depressed, if not comatic—if that really is a word—career."

As I laughed, my mood lightened. I realized the sheer stupidity, the futility, of my earlier attempt at literary ventriloquism. I would really have to get a grip on myself. I knew I couldn't allow myself to get lost like that.

"So are you going to explain yourself or are you just going to stand there like a deaf mute?"

"Oh, sorry, of course," I said. "I'm doing some research on behalf on Gordon Crace, a man who used to live in this house. You probably don't know him, but—"

"That's where you are wrong, you see. You shouldn't presume to tell people—"

"Excuse me, did you say you knew him?" My voice sounded weak, cracked. "How?"

"Now I've got your interest, haven't I?" Her eyes glinted in a slightly deranged way. She clearly enjoyed the game, the tease, the pretense. "Don't look so worried, I don't know him personally, of course, if that's what you mean, but his name, you see. It was only a few months back I think that—"

"Yes?"

"That somebody else came knocking on my door. A lady biographer—"

The bitch. So she had started, had she?

"Lavinia Maddon? Was that her name?"

"Yes, now you say it, I think it was. But what's all the bother? What do you care? And more to the point, what are you going to do with those pictures?"

I lowered my voice to a conspirational whisper. I could tell she liked life elevated to the realms of the dramatic.

"You see, Mrs.—?"

"Miss—Miss Jennifer Johnson."

She looked at me hoping that I would recognize her name, her head turning and gesturing toward the portraits on the walls. I nodded and pretended to know who she was—or had been.

"You see, my employer, Mr. Crace, the writer, is extremely worried about people sniffing around about his past. He's against this biography and wants to go to any lengths to prevent it. So this lady, this Lavinia Maddon, is working on something totally against his will, and he wants to try and stop it. Muckraking, he calls it."

"Yes, I see. But why the photographs? Why the pictures?"

"Oh, that's purely sentimental. He has very fond memories of this house and just wanted me to take a few snaps for his own use. So you've no need to worry there. But can I ask, did this lady ask you any questions? What exactly did she want?"

She paused as she might once have done in some second-rate play or television series, her eyes focusing on some distant point on the horizon, a swollen finger rising to her fat red lips.

"I remember she asked if I knew Crace, knew what had happened back then. I didn't know what she was talking about, but she mentioned something about a suicide. I think she was trying to spare my feelings, but I eventually got it out of her. Doesn't bother me in the slightest if some silly queen topped himself in my kitchen. She asked if she could have a look around. She seemed well spoken and decent enough, had a good address if I seem to remember, so I thought why not? It was nice to have the company, in fact. You know, once I had friends clamoring around me. Now it's—"

"What else? I mean, did you give her anything? Did she find anything?"

"Oh no, nothing like that. She had a little notebook, a tiny little thing, and a darling sweet gold pencil, and she just wrote a few jottings down and then left. Haven't heard anything from her since. I hope I haven't gotten her into trouble; she was awfully nice to me. Bought me a bottle of gin. Such a sweet touch, I thought. You won't be angry with her, will you?"

"No, not at all. I just wanted to assess the situation, to see how far things had gone, that's all. I may have to see her though. Just to make things clear."

"But you won't mention my name, will you? Please tell me you won't."

"Of course not, Miss Johnson. But if I need to come back here, perhaps to have a look around, would that be all right?"

"I don't see why not. You could come in now, if you like. Have a little drink . . . "

I told her that I was in a rush and that I might return later. I took down her telephone number, and I left her standing there in front of all those photographs of her multiple, past, imagined roles, images that were possibly even more real than the woman herself.

⊹══⊹

Watching. Standing outside, watching. Always watching and waiting. The house was tall and grand with a stucco facade, one of those wedding-cake buildings with two fluted columns flanking either side of the entrance. On the first floor was a balcony on which one of the residents had placed two bay trees. In the middle of the square, to its western end, stood a tennis court surrounded by trees and shrubs, yet another symbol of the gilded life that had been denied me. Not for much longer, though. I was determined to shape my future for the better.

I took out my notebook and retrieved the letter from Lavinia Maddon to check her address: 47a Eaton Square. I just wanted to ask her a few questions, that's all. Nothing sinister. Perhaps just restate Crace's position in a polite but firm manner. I was in London to clear up a little business for Mr. Crace and thought that while I was passing through I would just drop in to see her. But wouldn't she think I was a little odd if I just called in like that? How did I know she would even let me in? After all, she might not be at home, might not even be in London. Perhaps I should phone her. Yes, that's what I would do. I took out the envelope again and dialed the number on the letterhead. Four rings and then the click of an answering machine. Her voice was deep and strong, oozing with privilege and confidence: did I want to leave a message for Lavinia Maddon, my name, number and time of call? I was about to speak when I saw a woman walking down the pavement. I cut the connection and watched her approach. I was sure it was her.

Tall, slender, a brunette; immaculate, glossy hair; well dressed, smart—she wore a charcoal gray tailored skirt and matching jacket, a crisp white blouse and a string of jet beads. As she walked closer, it appeared that she was deep in thought, her thin lips pursed together, her intelligent eyes focused, concentrated. In one hand she carried an expensive-looking soft black leather briefcase, in the other a book. I knew I had seen the cover before, a cubist portrait of three boys standing around a teacher, a brutal montage of red and black lines. I squinted, trying to get a better view of the title, half-knowing what it would be. The title of the book moved in and out of focus, the letters melting away as if they were mercury. She came to a halt outside the house and brought the briefcase up to her waist. As she fished inside it for her key, she lodged the book on top of the bag, where I had a better view. The title came into clear, crisp focus: *The Debating Society.*

I felt something like a sting inside me. I couldn't allow her to stand in my way. Not now, not after everything I had done, everything I had worked for. What option did I have? What was my future? If my Crace project fell through, I would have to return here to Britain, broke. A life at home with my parents. Rows with my father. Endless talk about what had happened. Desperate attempts to try and get a second-rate job. Thoughts of Eliza, unbearable memories of her.

I watched as she climbed the steps to the door, turned the key in the lock and walked inside the expensive house. I waited five or ten minutes before I rang her number again. She picked up the phone.

"Hello?"

"Can I speak to Lavinia Maddon, please?" I said, trying to enunciate the words as clearly and as precisely as possible.

"Speaking," she said.

"I'm ringing on behalf of Gordon Crace. My name is Adam Woods; I'm his assistant."

"Oh yes, thank you." Her tone changed. "Thank you so much for calling. I did receive your letter and, although I was disappointed, I had hoped that I would get a chance at least to speak to Gordon, to Gordon Crace, to try and persuade him that the book would be a very serious study."

"Yes, he's very well aware of your project," I said, pausing. I needed to find out exactly what she knew, how much research she had actually done. "Although Mr. Crace was doubtful about its validity—as you know he is an intensely private person—he now believes there is no point in trying to resist any further. I think he thinks that, as someone is bound to write a biography, it may as well be someone of your standing, of your caliber. So he is, in principle, interested."

"Really?" Delight infused her voice.

"Yes. I'm in London at the moment on business for Mr. Crace and wondered if perhaps we could meet."

"Of course. That would be wonderful. Whenever would be convenient."

I looked up at the top flat and saw her form walk toward the window, which overlooked the garden square. I stepped back out of view.

"I wondered if you had any time later. Sorry it's such short notice, but another meeting I had has just fallen through."

"That would be fine—absolutely perfect. Would you like to come over to my flat? It's in Eaton Square."

I told her that would suit me. She gave me directions, as if I needed them, and we arranged to meet at seven o'clock. I had an hour to kill.

I found a cafe where I recorded the recent events in my notebook, enjoyed a cappuccino and read through the cuttings once more. I had to assume that Lavinia Maddon had done all the necessary biographical groundwork—inquiries into Crace's background, parents, birth certificates, school records, university career—sweeping up anything that was in the public domain. If I went ahead with the plan, if I kept up the pretense that Crace was interested in her book, perhaps she would reveal to me exactly what she had discovered. If she found out about my book later, I would tell her that I was merely acting on Crace's orders to find out as much about her project as possible. I was simply doing my job. And Crace wanted an authorized account of his life, a biography done by a person whom he trusted, not some stranger like her.

Just before seven, I made my way back to her flat. The trees in the square cast long shadows across the tall white houses, like skeletal fingers caressing alabaster skin. I rang her bell and she buzzed me in.

"Fifth floor. Don't bother with the lift, it's easier to walk up," she said.

For a moment, as my hand trailed up the dark, polished banister, I felt gripped by a sense that I couldn't go through with this, whatever "this" was. I wasn't sure what I would do, and that scared me. I stopped on the stairway and turned to look at myself in a gilt-framed mirror. My skin looked even more ghostly white than usual, my blond hair adding to the bleached-out effect. I pinched my right cheek a couple of times, hoping to bleed some life into my face, but I still remained the color of a cadaver.

As I climbed the last couple of steps and turned the corner, I saw Lavinia waiting for me, her face beaming.

"Adam, hi. I'm Lavinia. So lovely to meet you. Please, come in."

She stretched out her hand and I felt the thin bones beneath her skin. Her handshake was just as weak as Crace's. As she smiled, a spiderweb of fine lines spread out under the surface of her lightly powdered face, rippling up from the corners of her mouth to her eyes and forehead. From a distance I would have thought her to be in her mid-forties, but she was at least a decade older.

She led me down a hallway into a large drawing room. Books lined every wall and spread across every available surface. The floor was carpeted in beige coir matting. A vase of white lilies spread their deathly aroma through the flat.

"Would you care for a drink? White wine?"

"That would be lovely."

"Please, sit down."

I lowered myself into a deep, wide gray sofa. A pile of bubble-wrapped books—a German translation of her Woolf biography—sat on the low coffee table in front of me. A *New Yorker* magazine, no doubt boasting one of her erudite, terribly well written, 10,000-word pieces, nestled next to the day's newspapers.

She came back and handed me a glass of cold white wine. She sat in the identical gray sofa opposite me.

"You can't imagine how pleased I was that you called."

I was sure that I could.

"From your last letter, I got the distinct impression that Mr. Crace would never agree to my book. I was in a quandary about what to do. Really quite at a loss."

"Had you done much work? I mean, background research and—"

"Oh yes, quite a substantial amount. I've already built up quite a file on him. I mean, of course, I didn't want to be presumptuous, just that if Mr. Crace did agree, I wanted him to realize I had done the initial research to indicate that I was serious, both in my intentions and as a biographer. But I wonder what it was that made him change his mind. He seemed so set against it."

I shifted in my seat and leaned forward.

"To be honest, it was because he had had an approach, another approach, from yet another writer."

She blinked, and for a moment her eyes flashed with fury.

"Of course, no one with the same literary credentials as you," I added. "Someone who proposed a book, well, nothing more than a sensational, vulgar book."

"Can I ask who it was?"

I did not say anything for a few seconds. A little punishment wasn't entirely out of the question, I thought.

"I'm sorry. I think it's best if I kept that quiet. I wouldn't want the name to get around."

"Of course. I understand," she said. She pretended not to care, but I watched as she bit the inside of her cheek. Her eyes darted back and forth. "So do you really think Mr. Crace would agree to see me?"

"I don't see why not. Obviously not at the moment, but certainly within the next few weeks or months. But before that, he would have to be sure of your intentions. I don't mean to be rude, Miss Maddon—"

"Lavinia. Please call me Lavinia."

"I don't mean to be rude, and I'm sure you only have the highest sort of book in mind, but I think what Mr. Crace would really like to see, what would put his mind at rest, is any kind of draft material you have on him."

"Well, that's really rather early in the day, I'm afraid. I haven't put pen to paper, yet, you see."

"Is there anything you could prepare for him then? Perhaps a synopsis, something you might have given your agent or publisher?"

"I do have something along those lines, but really I don't think it appropriate to show him."

She saw me look a little astonished. No doubt she was afraid that I would skew the deal, return to Crace and tell him to call the whole thing off.

"But having said that, I could easily rework it into a form that would suit Mr. Crace. Something more reader-friendly, without all that publishing jargon."

What she was really saying was that she would tone it down and fashion it into a more sanitized version.

"Yes, that sounds like something Mr. Crace would be interested in seeing. I know he is quite keen to get this sorted out in the next few days so—"

"Really as fast as that?"

"Yes. He's not one for letting things hang around. I'm going to fly back to Venice at some point next week, so perhaps if you could give it to me then . . . ?"

"Yes, that shouldn't be a problem."

I had well and truly hooked her. Could I go even further?

"You know, it's funny," I said, laughing, "you might even know more about Mr. Crace than the man himself. You see, soon after he moved to Venice, a great deal of his personal documentation was ruined during a particularly bad *acqua alta*."

"Really?"

"I'm sure he would be delighted if you could give him copies of anything you found—birth certificates, genealogical records, anything along those lines."

"Well—"

"I really do think it would make all the difference."

"Erm—"

"Make your case all the stronger."

"You think so?"

"Of course. Then he'd feel that he really could trust you. And it would only be to replace those documents he once had in his possession. But if you have a problem with that . . . "

"No, I'm sure that will be fine," she said, forcing a smile. "I'll give those to you next week as well so you can take them back to Mr. Crace."

"That's very kind. Mr. Crace will not be able to thank you enough."

For once the gratitude in my face was genuine. I think I really did feel something.

⊷⊶

By the time I arrived back at Jake's flat, I was exhausted. I threw myself onto the sofa, rubbed my hands over my tired eyes, and lay back on the cushions, feeling any remaining trace of energy drain away. Blackness enclosed me, and I must have fallen asleep as the next thing I heard was the ring of my mobile. I picked up it and saw my parents' number flashing on the screen. I rejected the call; I wasn't ready to speak to them.

I lay there in the dark, hardly moving, barely breathing, until Jake returned home. He walked in, switched on the light and found me sitting there, eyes open.

"For fuck's sake, man! What are you trying to do, give me a coronary?" he said, dropping his keys into the bowl on the sideboard.

I cleared my throat and laughed it off. "Sorry," I said.

"So how did you get on today? Find out anything interesting about your mystery man?"

I told him that the cuttings library had proved useful and thanked him again for his help. To prevent further questions, I asked him about his day. He'd been to a book launch that evening and sported red wine stains around his lips, like an extra mouth.

"I saw your favorite person there," said Jake.

"Who?"

"Can't you guess?"

I had a good idea who he meant, but I didn't want to think about him.

"Dr. Kirkby. God, you should have seen his face when he saw me. I think he thought you'd be around. But I was probably equally as astonished to see him. It was the launch of a biography of an obscure nineteenth-century female artist. Critics generally thought of her merely as a muse, but apparently she painted in secret. Quite a story, I suppose, and really—"

"Did you speak to him?"

"Only very briefly, just to be polite. His arm's better, out of its sling, anyhow."

We laughed.

"She wasn't with him, was she?"

Jake looked at me with concern, even anxiety.

"No, she wasn't there, mate," he said quietly. "You still think about her then?"

I nodded. I didn't really know what to say.

"You are better though, aren't you?"

"I think I am," I said. "It was one of those moment-of-madness things, I expect. Lost all sense. Like I was a different person."

"Yeah, right."

"But I've changed since then. I've got a real direction now." I couched the clichéd phrases with a certain amount of irony. "Know what I'm doing. Focused."

At that moment I remembered that last time with Eliza. I had just wanted to be with her, close to her.

"So what are your plans?"

"I'm off to Dorset tomorrow—more research for my writer. I'll probably come back to London again for a night or so—stay here if that's okay—and then back to Venice next week."

I'm sure anyone would have behaved just like I did in a similar situation. Provocation, that's what they call it. Parading her new man around like that. And so soon as well. He used to be her—our—lecturer. There was something so sordid about it all.

"How are you getting there? Dorset?"

"Train—two and a half hours, Waterloo to Dorchester."

I had waited outside the college building and followed him home. I made sure I kept out of sight on the Tube, moved to a different carriage and hid behind my newspaper. I trailed him from Finsbury Park, dropping behind him if he slowed down or if I thought he might turn his head.

"Where are you going to stay?"

"I'm not sure yet. Probably in a B & B somewhere or a pub perhaps."

Before he had turned the corner to his street, I had slipped on a balaclava. An overly theatrical touch, maybe, but at the time it seemed to make sense. That morning I had gone to a tacky clothing shop and bought a nasty nylon hooded top, a pair of jogging trousers and some trainers. I also wore a pair of black fake leather gloves.

"What are you going down there for?"

"Just a bit of research."

I had checked to see if there was anyone around. Good—no one.

"Which part of Dorset?"

"It's a village called Winterborne. It's about fifteen miles from Dorchester, toward—what is it?—Blandford Forum."

As he had turned the key in his lock, I ran up behind him and grabbed him around the neck. He tried to spin around and wrestle free, but I had him in a tight lock, his arms flaying around like an insect's. I decided it would be too risky to speak, but I gestured for him to give me his bag.

He dropped his briefcase and told me to take whatever I wanted. Just leave him alone. The pathetic fuck. His tawny beard quivered with fear, his slate-gray eyes rabbit-scared. How could Eliza choose someone so insipid, so cowardly, so pathetic?

I released the grip on his neck, causing him to fall forward like a rag doll. He greedily drank the air around him, a drowning man surfacing above water. I could have finished him off, I was sure. Perhaps I should have. Instead, I took hold of his right arm and twisted it behind his back, snapping it like a wishbone. The sound was really satisfying. I pushed him down to the ground, laughed at his whimpering, ransacked his bag, took a credit card, some cash, and then ran off. I heard him feebly call for help, but I disappeared down a side street. I took off the trainers, slipped off the joggers and hooded top, ripped away the balaclava and shoved the lot inside my rucksack. Underneath I was nice and respectable, a hardworking student— jeans, white shirt, black loafers, all of which I had carried with me. If I was stopped by the police, I could plead ignorance. Nobody would believe that I was the type of person who could do that kind of thing.

⊹⇒⇐⊹

In the end, I decided not to call my parents before leaving London. I didn't want to know about my finals. What difference would it make to my life now? Whatever class of degree I had been awarded, I knew it would never be good enough for my dad. There was no talking to him, he was just insane.

We had been sitting around the dining room table. Mum had tried to make the occasion a special one: pretty place settings, candles, bone-handled knives, crystal glasses. She had cooked Italian food in anticipation of my trip, and her lasagna wasn't at all bad. We had enjoyed a few glasses of Prosecco and then a nice bottle of red wine. Conversation was confined to a narrow, safe path— nothing that veered off into the danger zones of my past or my future—and it looked as though we were going to enjoy a perfectly civilized evening, culminating with kisses on both cheeks from my mum, a strong shake of the hand from Dad and a flurry of well-meaning parting words. All that changed in the space of a moment.

Mum brought in a dish of tiramisu, my father's favorite, and placed it in front of us on the table.

"Gosh, look at that. Doesn't that look splendid?" said my dad.

I probably should have said something then, or at least tried to have made some sort of inarticulate but appreciative sound. But I was thinking about Venice, my new job teaching English and the time I could spend on my novel. I was somewhere else.

I think he must have tried to pass me a slice, but I wasn't aware of this until I heard him slam the plate down.

"That's the problem with you, you think of no one else but yourself," my father said suddenly. "Your mother has gone to all this trouble for you and you can't even thank her."

"Oh, Peter, come on now, really—"

"I'm sorry, Sally, but this really has to be said. I'm not going to let him treat you—treat us—like this. He's got to learn a lesson."

"Sorry," I said. "Have I missed something here?"

"You know very well what's wrong. Why can't you just try, at least *try* to be normal?"

"Darling, now stop it. It's Adam's last night, and I wanted it to be really nice—for all of us."

My father's eyes blazed with anger. "There's no need for you to defend him. Remember, you were the one who was upset when you found out what he'd done."

"Peter, now is not the time—"

"No, Mum," I interrupted. "If Dad wants to say something, why not let him? He's obviously not happy, and I'd rather have him come straight out with it than let it fester."

I pronounced the last word with undisguised disgust, as if it encapsulated everything he stood for.

"Okay, okay," he said. "I'll tell you what bothers me. If you really want to know, I can't bear to even think about what you've done. When Eliza's father called me, I could not believe what he was saying. I was just so ashamed. Although that is disgusting enough in itself, what is even worse is that you don't seem to show any kind of remorse for your actions. Where's your conscience, Adam?"

"Peter, calm down. You know you don't mean it, really. Come on, say sorry now. Otherwise Adam's going to go off thinking—"

"For God's sake, Sally, don't you understand? We've been through all that with him before, but he just doesn't seem to take it in. I almost wish Eliza had called the police. Her father certainly wanted her to, and I can't understand why she talked him out of it. Maybe we should have turned him in."

"Don't be so ridiculous. You don't mean that," my mother said, tears filling her eyes.

"It might have done some good. At least it might have forced him, for once in his life, to stand up and take responsibility for his own actions."

No one said anything for a few seconds. My mother looked down at the table, desperately trying not to cry, and then she pushed her chair away, flinging her napkin into her seat.

"If it wasn't for you being so distant with him," she muttered under her breath as she walked into the kitchen, "none of this would have happened."

"So it's all my fault now, is it, that we've got a monster with no morals for a son?"

I couldn't stand any more. I got up from the table and, without saying anything, grabbed my coat and rucksack from the hallway. In the kitchen I kissed my mum good-bye as she scraped her plate of tiramisu into the rubbish bin. Of course, she half-heartedly tried to stop me from going but realized it was no use. On the way out, I caught my dad staring at me, his mouth open, docile and moronic. I looked at him with hatred. For once it felt good to be me.

"Don't fucking come anywhere near me or I'll kill you, you cunt," I said. I slammed the door behind me and left.

I hadn't spoken to him since. It was safer if we kept our distance.

I was back on Crace's trail. I felt as if over the past few days, apart from my encounter with Lavinia Maddon, I had let him slip away. The past had intruded too much, shadowing my thoughts and obscuring my real purpose.

On the train down to Dorset, I looked through all the material I had gathered on Crace. I flicked through my notebook, now full of my research, and examined the newspaper cuttings once again. If everything went to plan, by the end of my trip I would find out exactly what had taken place between Mr. Shaw's "stepson" and Crace, and I would be in possession of the diary. When I flew back to Venice next week, I would be armed with the basic biographical material provided by the very obliging Lavinia Maddon; hopefully the journal would describe the lead-up to Chris's death and tell me whether he had taken his own life or if he had been murdered. The word sounded so strange and unreal. I still couldn't believe that Crace was capable of killing.

The train, sheathed in a gray mist, pulled into Dorchester station. Outside, rain bulleted down onto the platform, sending people for cover, hunched and scuttling. I ran inside, past the ticket office and down a slope that led to the taxi rank where one car remained, its windows steamed up from the inside. As I ran my hands through my wet hair, I caught the attention of the driver, an overweight but youngish man with doughlike skin. I asked him if he knew the village, about fifteen miles from Dorchester, and we settled on a fee of £18.

As he drove through the streets, skirting around the edge of the town, the window wipers flicking backward and forward like the wings of a distressed mechanical bird, he attempted to strike up conversation.

"Down here for business?" he asked.

"Sort of," I replied.

"Been down this way before?"

"Not really," I said. "Nearest place would have been Bournemouth, I suppose, on holiday." That was true enough. And with that we fell silent, the roar of the dual carriageway and the wash of the water on the car the only noise.

We turned off the busy road, through a village, past fields and into an expanse of green. The trees were dripping with rain and the wind swept across the fields. The road was only one-car wide at times, the vehicle caressed by branches and twigs, a dark tunnel through an endless woodland. We descended a dip in the road and then up on an equally steep incline, around a sharp bend and into a clearing. On the left emerged the school where Crace used to teach, a perfectly symmetrical, neoclassical building set amidst acres of land. A few seconds later the abbey, standing slightly behind the school, came into view, a gothic monstrosity that looked out of place next to the Palladian-style building. The driver slowed down, jerked his head and stole a look.

"It's certainly some sight," he said, nodding as if to answer his own observation.

"It certainly is."

The car took us along the edge of a tree-covered hillside, over a verge and down again. The village lay before me, its church tower silhouetted against the sky. The driver dropped me off by the village pub, the Stag, which with its thatched roof and quaint lopsided doorway completed the pastoral scene. It was hard to imagine anything bad happening here.

I gave the driver a twenty-pound note and walked across the gravel pathway of the pub. I turned the handle and stepped inside to be faced by a wall of heat so strong it felt like I was being branded on both cheeks. Across the room, a log fire burned furiously, in front of which lay an old mongrel hound. The place was empty except for a member of staff, a red-faced middle-aged woman who stood behind the bar twisting a cloth, thrusting it deep inside a glass. I moved toward her, clearing my throat, but she didn't look up. It wasn't until I raised myself onto a stool and placed my bag on the wooden counter that she blinked and realized she had a customer.

"I just wondered if you had any rooms."

The deep furrows on her forehead rippled together, and she stared at me as if I had just spoken a sentence in a foreign language. Then she nodded, the loose skin around her neckline shaking, turkey-like.

"I'm afraid I'm not sure how long I might stay," I said.

She didn't seem to care. As long as she had her money up front—£35 a night—then it seemed I could do whatever I pleased.

The taciturn woman led me through a low-ceilinged snug room and up a back staircase. It looked as though there were three small rooms that ran along a central corridor. She showed me into the first one. It was a little tatty and not at all clean. A cluster of dead flies lay on the windowsill, which had dried in the autumn sunshine like sinister currants. I felt a cobweb brush against my hair. As I slung my bag onto an armchair in the corner of the room, a cloud of dust rose up from its cushion.

"You've most probably got everything you need," said my new landlady, gesturing around as if she had just accompanied me to a suite at the Savoy. In fact, apart from the bed, the dusty chair and the dead flies, there was nothing else in the room. "So I'll leave you to it."

She turned to go. "Oh, and there's a bathroom just down the corridor. Nothing special."

I didn't doubt her word for a second.

After tidying up the room and sweeping away the cobwebs and the flies, I unpacked my few belongings, stacking a spare pair of jeans and a couple of sweaters on the armchair. I took out my notebook and found Shaw's details. I checked my mobile. No reception. I grabbed a few coins from my wallet and went downstairs to the pub, where I had spotted a public phone. The dog still lay immobile in front of the fire; the landlady was back behind the bar, slowly and methodically drying glasses.

I dialed his number. After a few rings I heard a rasping noise that eventually formed itself into a "Hello?"

"Hello, Mr. Shaw. It's me, Adam Woods. You asked me to give you a call when I arrived. And, well, I'm here."

It took a few seconds before he caught his breath.

"Yes, so pleased to hear from you. Mightily pleased, indeed."

Obviously the lure of the money, the thought that within days he might be able to get his hands on £1,000, had raised his spirits.

"I just wondered when the best time was to come around. To see you . . . and to pick up the material you had mentioned."

"Ah, yes, the book, the book." He cleared his throat. "You could always come around later this afternoon if you like, if that is to your convenience."

I suddenly felt an overwhelming disgust for this nasty little man trying to make money out of his dead "stepson."

"That's fine, yes. I look forward to seeing you at . . . what . . . about five o'clock?"

"That suits me very well indeed, Mr. Woods."

After giving me directions to his cottage, he hesitated for a moment. "And y-you do have it with you, don't you? You know you won't be able to see anything unless I have the . . . the . . . due recompense first."

"You mean the money? Do I have the money?"

"Well—"

"Yes, Mr. Shaw, don't worry. I have that with me. You can count it in front of me if you like."

"No . . . I didn't mean . . . it was just—"

"That's fine. I understand."

I understood only too well what he was about, the scheming, grasping little blackmailer. As I put the phone down, I considered whether it was worth teaching him a lesson. An image of him flashed into my mind. I had no idea what he looked like, but I saw him as a wizened gray man, the color and consistency of ash. I was sure he would be as easy to crush as a piece of burnt paper.

As I walked back up to my room, I thought about the morality of giving money to a blackmailer. If I handed over the one thousand pounds, would that not make me just as much a sleazebag as him? The thought of dirtying my hands, soiling myself by associating with someone like him turned my stomach. Surely I was made of better stuff than that.

In my room I took out the original letter he had sent to Crace. What kind of game was he playing? Could I even trust him to give me the diary? Was it wise to pass over the cash without seeing some evidence? Suppose he didn't even have the diary. What if it didn't even exist? I felt a fluttering inside me; my throat tightened. A few beads of sweat boiled on my forehead. No, I would be letting Crace down if I didn't retrieve the journal. I had to safeguard his memory. I was the chosen one, after all. He relied on me; he trusted me.

I had to be prepared for every eventuality. I had to be strong. What happened later that afternoon could make the difference between ultimate success and abject failure. And I had failed too many times. I would not allow myself to shrink away from what had to be done—no matter what.

⊹——⊱⊰——⊹

I set off knowing that I would be early. Although the showers had stopped and the gray sky had begun to clear, the wind continued to blow rain from the trees. I ran my hands through my hair, slicking it back off my forehead. As I walked, I played with the bundle of cash in my pocket. Shaw would certainly see that I had the money; whether I would hand it over to him was another question. I hadn't quite decided yet.

His cottage was a small, run-down detached building that backed onto a field leading up to a wooded ridge. In front of the cottage ran a narrow track that eventually led down to the village church. At five, the church bell rang out, a pathetic attempt to symbolize order. All was not right with the world.

I stood outside the house, doll-like in its proportions. Honeysuckle tendrils snaked their way around the porch and up the primrose yellow wall. A wisp of smoke curled its way out of the chimney. I knocked on the door, which opened almost immediately. The man, small in form, wizened and gray, almost an exact match of the one I had pictured in my head, looked surprised to see me. His eyes twitched, his mouth fell open and he steadied himself on the door frame. Perhaps I had just roused him from an afternoon nap. But if that was the case, he would never have opened the door so quickly. Or maybe he was expecting someone older.

"Hello, Mr. Shaw? It's Adam Woods."

I stretched out my hand and after a slight hesitation he did the same. But as we greeted one another, I noticed that his palm was moist and sticky and that his fingers trembled.

"Please come in," he said, clearing his throat. "You'll have to excuse me if I appear a little out of sorts. It's just that I'm not used to this kind of thing—dealing in these matters. All a bit . . . above my head, if you know what I mean."

"There's nothing to worry about, Mr. Shaw. I'm sure we can come to some arrangement that suits us both. I mean, suits both you and Mr. Crace."

The door opened into a cluttered space that functioned as a sitting room at the front and kitchen at the back. Stale cooking smells—cabbage, liver and bacon—lingered in the air. A maroon V-neck jumper hanging over the back of a chair gave off steam as it dried in front of the wood-burning stove.

"Just got caught in that terrible downpour we had earlier," he said. "I hope you weren't . . . incapacitated."

His choice of words made me smile.

"No, I luckily avoided the worst of it," I said.

"Anyway, make yourself at home. Please take a seat, please do."

His hand, still shaking, gestured toward a two-seater sofa.

"Can I get you a cup of tea . . . or coffee? I've got coffee."

"Tea would be lovely," I said.

Shaw whistled to himself as he made the tea but made a point of looking over in my direction every couple of seconds.

"There you go," he said, presenting me with the mug. "Biscuit?"

"No, thanks," I said. "I'm fine. I was just wondering, did you know Mr. Crace at all . . . when he lived here?"

"No. Maureen did, of course. But I don't think I ever spoke to him."

"I see," I said.

He sat down in a chair opposite me, nearer to the door. I took a sip of the hot tea, put the mug down on the gray carpet and then fished out the money. I thought there was little to be gained from wasting time.

"I suppose you'll be interested in seeing this," I said, brandishing the cash in front of his face.

His eyes lit up.

"It is the least Mr. Crace can do for you . . . to cover your expenses for looking after the diary," I said.

He stretched out his right hand, eager to fondle the money.

"But I'm afraid I can't give it to you until you show me the journal," I said. "Mr. Crace is not a suspicious man. It's just that, quite naturally, he wants to know that he is putting his money to good use."

Shaw bit his bottom lip and his eyes darted nervously around the room. He lifted a finger up to his mouth and chewed on a piece of already red raw skin around the base of a stubby nail.

"I'm afraid we might have a little difficulty on that particular matter," he said.

"Excuse me? What do you mean exactly? You told me that you had the diary here, with you."

"I can get it—easily get it—"

I shoved the money back in my pocket and stood up. As I did so, my left foot brushed against the mug of tea, knocking it over. A dark brown stain spread out over the carpet like a fungal bloom. He pushed himself up from the chair. Panic paralyzed him, making him unable to decide whether to rush to the kitchen for a cloth or stay where he was so he could block my path to the door.

I walked toward him as if I had made up my mind to leave.

"Please don't go. Let me explain," he said between wheezes. "There's no need for you—"

I stopped in my tracks and stared at him, hard.

"I hope you haven't brought me all this way to mess me around. Mr. Crace would not like that at all, not one little bit. He would be extremely angry if he found out you were playing games with him. Do you understand, Mr. Shaw?"

His lips formed themselves into words he couldn't say. As I moved toward him, he flinched and steadied himself by taking hold of the armchair. I knew he was scared of me.

"Where is Chris's diary?" I raised my voice. "Where is it?"

"I can bring it here . . . I just need a little time, that's all."

"I'm afraid Mr. Crace has not got that luxury. Neither has he got much patience. I could call him right now and he could call off the whole deal."

"I doubt very much he would do that," he said.

Obviously he had just thought of something that invested him with a new sense of confidence, a horrible arrogance.

"Like I said, I'm sure he wouldn't want the police sniffing around . . . sniffing around his dirty linen, would he?" As he said this, he wrinkled his nose in exaggerated disgust. "The things he got up to, really quite unbelievable. I'm sure the authorities—and the press—would find them very interesting reading indeed. And it's all there, in black and white, so to speak."

Out of the corner of my eye I saw, next to the wood-burning stove, a basket containing a pile of logs. Behind this stood a pair of fire tongs and a sturdy looking poker. I could take hold of the poker and smash it into his skull, reduce his head to a bloody, pulpy mass. I turned, took a step in that direction and then stopped, pretending to warm my hands over the stove. I needed the journal. I couldn't do anything until I had laid my hands on it. After that, I didn't care what happened to him.

"Okay, let's calm down, shall we?" I said. "First of all, let me find a cloth. We don't want any stains. And then we can talk about this in a reasonable manner."

As I mopped up the tea, Shaw eyed me suspiciously, watching my every move. He was obviously on edge, nervous.

"Now, let's start again," I said, slowly. "You've got the diary."

He nodded.

"But it's not here. Is that right?"

"Indeed, that's right," he said.

"Are you in a position where you can get it and bring it back here?"

"Yes, that is possible."

"How long would it take for you to get it?"

Shaw hesitated, reluctant to reveal any more.

"Look, do you want the money or don't you?" I snapped.

"Very well, very well. I'll go and get it and you can wait here. But you promise to give it to me when I get back, when I give you the book?"

"I promise," I said.

"Help yourself to more tea. I'll only be ten minutes or so, perhaps a quarter of an hour."

Shaw slipped an oilskin jacket over his shoulders and disappeared out the front door, leaving me alone. As I heard his footsteps fade away down the lane, I looked around the room. On top of the small old-fashioned television set stood a few faded color photographs in cheap frames. There was Shaw in younger, happier times, with a woman, presumably Chris's mother, Maureen, a blond, apple-cheeked woman. Sun-kissed from a recent holiday, with arms around one another, they smiled into the camera. Similar pictures of the couple lined a shelf in a nearby alcove, but there was no sign of the boy.

I walked up the staircase that ran from the back of the kitchen to the first floor. I pushed open a wooden door and stepped into a darkened room, a bedroom. Cooking smells from below mingled with the stench of sweat and stale smoke. In the gloom of the curtained room, I could just make out that the linen on the bed was stained nicotine yellow and his pillowcase was circled with a halo of grease. By his bedside table there was a red plastic lighter, a glass ashtray overflowing with cigarette stubs and an asthma spray. I could just imagine him sucking in smoke with one breath and then puffing on his inhaler the next, a constant battle between the death instinct and his desire to carry on living. It was, most probably, one struggle he wouldn't have to worry about for much longer.

I left the bedroom and walked into the bathroom. The sight of

it—the basin ringed, the toilet smeared—turned my stomach. I
closed the door and walked into another room at the back of the
house that Shaw had filled with bags and boxes. I edged my way
around what little floor space there was, easing myself past a few
black bin liners. One of the bags had been slashed open, and
through its tear I could see a tangle of women's clothing: sleeves
of blouses, legs of trousers and feet of American tan tights, all
wrapped around one another like displaced body parts.

Squeezing past these, I pushed my way to the far side of the
room, where I had spotted an old filing cabinet. Rust peppered its
surface. I forced open the top drawer and, as it creaked and
whined, pulled it toward me. I ran my fingers over the green files
and selected one at random. Inside was a plastic folder containing
a stash of documents. I pulled out a cream-colored square of
paper emblazoned with red print, a birth certificate recording the
entry into the world of Maureen Frake on 8 August 1927, while
her wedding certificate told me that she had married John Davidson on 16 January 1946. I searched through the top drawer but
found no sign of her son's birth certificate, in fact, there was nothing to indicate that she had had a child at all.

I bent down to explore the lower drawers of the cabinet, but
as I stretched out my right leg to steady myself I felt something
sharp scratch against my calf. I twisted around to see a screwdriver poking through a piece of tarpaulin. I pulled back the thin
fabric of my trousers and rubbed the point of impact, straining
my head to see a red-rimmed puncture wound, a single red eye, in
the middle of my calf. I took hold of the screwdriver and examined it, running my fingers around its bloody tip, wondering what
kind of damage it could inflict. But then as I peeled back the covering over the packing case, I was faced with a range of possibili-
ties: a loop of a plastic washing line, a chisel, a mallet, a hammer

and a hacksaw. Just as I picked out the hammer, I heard footsteps outside. Shaw was back.

I concealed the hammer inside my jacket and traced my way out of the room. Knowing that Shaw would step into the house before I reached the kitchen or sitting room, I ran into the bathroom, averting my eyes from the dirt and the grime, and flushed the loo. Then I sauntered down the stairs, taking care to prolong the fastening of my fly button until the moment when I came face to face with Shaw. As he closed the door and stepped inside, the noise of the water tank continued to gurgle.

"Call of nature?" Shaw said.

In one hand, he carried a translucent supermarket bag. Through the thin sheen of the plastic, I could see the black spine of a notebook. I smiled as I walked toward him, feeling the sharp edge of the hammer underneath my jacket.

"So you have the diary?"

Shaw nodded as he took off his coat.

"Can I ask where you went to get it?"

"I'd rather not say, if you don't mind, Mr. Woods. Please, sit down."

He gestured for me to sit on the sofa, and as I did so, I maneuvered the hammer inside my jacket so that I could conceal its handle. Shaw sat beside me and placed the bag on his lap, slowly teasing away the sides of the plastic as if rolling down the edges of a delicate, protective sheathing.

As he revealed the contents of the bag, balancing the journal on his lap, he turned to me so I could see his unhealthy gray skin and his yellow teeth edged with black. I was also close enough to smell the stench on his breath. It didn't seem like he was long for this world.

"I've shown you mine; now you show me yours," he said, laughing.

A wave of nausea threatened to unsteady me. I felt the bitter taste of bile rise to my mouth, but I swallowed it down. I had to remain focused.

"Oh, yes, the money. Of course."

I concentrated hard as I visualized how best to manipulate the wad of cash out of my pocket without letting the hammer fall to my feet. Drawing the fingers of my left hand under me like an inverted claw, I moved my arm crablike so that it supported the hammer inside my jacket. Then with my right hand, I reached across myself into my left pocket and removed the money, dropping it into Shaw's lap.

"And now for the diary," I said.

"Here. Take it," he said, passing it over.

After flicking through the pages to make sure it was Chris's private journal and that it did indeed include details about Crace (I noticed the writer's name in several places picked at random), I stood up, intending to carry it over to a nearby table. After all, I didn't want the pages to get messy.

But as I tried to hold on to the hammer with one hand and the diary with another, it felt like the tool was about to slip away from my grasp and fall to the floor. I quickly shifted my position, attempting to steady myself. As I did so, I felt the journal slipping from my grasp. Either I let it fall or I would be forced to reveal the weapon I had disguised; I knew there was no choice.

The diary fell from my hands, hitting the tiled floor. Shaw looked up, concerned. He stood up from the sofa and shuffled toward me, bending down to retrieve the book. I stared at the back of his head, noticing a patch of dry skin at the base of his hairline. I manipulated the hammer so that I had it back in my control. Now was the time.

I took the hammer out of my jacket with my right hand. A

willing victim, the worthless man knelt before me. I raised the hammer up from my midriff to just above my shoulder so as to rain down as strong a blow as possible. I paused a moment and then, just as he was beginning to push himself upward, just as I was about to strike his skull and split his head open, I saw that he was holding something in his hands. It was a color photograph. I could hardly believe it possible.

I hid the hammer back under my jacket as I steadied myself on the nearby table.

"What's that? What's the photograph?" I asked.

Shaw supported his lower back with a hand, the pain of age creasing his face.

"Oh, it's a picture of Chris just a year or so before he died," he said, passing it over.

The photograph, bleached of most of its color, showed a young, handsome man with slicked-back blond hair. He was wearing an open-necked white shirt and a dark blue V-neck jumper and was standing by a group of newly budded trees. I could feel Shaw's eyes on me as I stared at the picture. I realized then why he had looked at me in that strange way when he had first opened the door, why he had taken one step backward. For him it must have been like Chris returning from the dead. For me, it was a vision of myself.

+≡⟞•⟝≡+

"Are you all right? Mr. Woods?"

I could hear Shaw wheezing behind me as I sank down onto the sofa. My body felt lifeless, deflated, and it took every bit of strength I had to keep hold of the hammer to prevent it from falling out of my jacket.

"There you go; get that down you," he said, pressing a glass full of brandy into my hands.

My hand shook as I brought the glass up to my lips. The brandy burned my mouth and throat, but I relished the sensation.

"The similarity struck me when I first saw you, couldn't quite take it in," said Shaw. "I must admit it gave me quite a shock when I opened the door and saw you standing there, the spitting image. Thought Chris had come back to haunt me. Punishment for what I'd done. Of course, it was silly of me to think like that, stupid really, but sometimes you can't help having those kind of thoughts, can you?"

As Shaw continued to talk, I gazed at the photograph, running my finger around its edges in an effort to persuade myself that it was real. I brought it up to my face for closer inspection and then held it out at arm's length, positioning it at every angle so as to try and spot even the slightest difference or inconsistency. But it was as if I was examining a photograph of myself that I could not remember ever being taken. I racked my brain to think whether I recognized the setting, but the spot with its cluster of lime trees could have been anywhere. I scanned the outer edge of the picture for clues.

"Do you know where the photograph was taken?" I asked, turning toward Shaw.

"Let me see again."

He held out his hand.

"Difficult to say, but it looks like somewhere around here. Oh yes, here we are, you see?"

He stubbed his forefinger on a point in the far left-hand side of the photograph.

"Look."

As he passed the picture back to me, he raised his finger up to reveal, in the background, a blurred segment that looked like terracing.

"What is it?" I asked.

"It's a couple of the grass steps that lead up to the old chapel, here"—he pointed to a spot an inch to the left of the frame—"on this hill, just out of the shot."

I had never really doubted the authenticity of the photograph, but the possibility of a picture being taken of me of which I had no recollection in a setting I didn't recognize was actually less bizarre than the one that I was now forced to face.

"Excuse me for a moment," I managed to utter, running upstairs.

In the bathroom I steadied myself by the basin. I splashed cold water over my face again and again, but it didn't do any good. My stomach felt like it was turning itself inside out.

I had to put the hammer back. In the storage room I skirted around the edge of the cluttered space until I found the toolbox. As quietly as I could, I slid it on top of the coiled washing line and covered the case with the tarpaulin. Then I went back into the bathroom and flushed the loo again.

Back downstairs, Shaw was boiling the kettle.

"Feeling better?" he said.

"Yes, much better, thank you."

"Fancy some more tea?"

"That would be lovely," I said. "Are there any more photographs in the journal?"

"To be honest, I didn't know that one was in there. Came as a surprise to me as well. Maureen was quite particular about her albums, you see. Liked to gather all the pictures together in one place. Drove her mad if one escaped or slipped out. She was a bugger for that, she was."

"So you still have the albums?"

"Oh, yes. They're upstairs."

As Shaw said this, passing me the cup of tea, I thought he looked at me knowingly, as if he was fully aware that I had sneaked around up there.

"But don't worry; you can tell Mr. Crace there aren't any of him. You see, Maureen burnt all those after . . . after it happened. So angry with him she was."

"I see."

"She was not happy with Chris and the situation, as you can imagine, but she just couldn't bear to destroy pictures of him. So there they sit, in album after album, just gathering dust."

"Would it be possible to see one or two of them?" I asked. "It's just that—"

"That you can't believe you look like brothers? I can well imagine. Must have given you quite a turn. Not surprising really that it knocked you for six. Odd though, isn't it?"

Shaw put his cup down and slowly made his way to the staircase.

"I'll see what I can find," he said.

While he was gone, I continued to stare at the photograph of Chris, standing before those trees like another me. A couple of minutes later, Shaw came back armed with a tower of photo albums. He placed them on the table and handed me one at random. As I flicked through image after image of Chris—walking along a coastal path, eating an ice-cream cone, standing proudly with arms crossed in front of the main entrance to Winterborne Abbey, gazing sleepily at the camera after being surprised in his bed—I felt like I was looking at an alternative life I could have led. The boy, the young man, in those pictures certainly resembled me, and in some shots he looked exactly like me, but the context, the surroundings, were totally unfamiliar and alien.

"So you say there are no images, no photographs of Mr. Crace?" I asked.

"None at all, I'm sure you'll be relieved to hear. You can tell Mr. Crace he can rest easy. The diary is the only . . . how shall we say . . . incriminating material."

"I see."

"But if you don't mind me saying, I'd watch my back if I were you."

"What do you mean?"

"It seems a little strange, don't you think?"

I gave him a quizzical look, pretending not to know what he was talking about.

"You know, you looking so like Chris. You're not telling me that's a coincidence, are you? I mean, what you two get up to in your private lives is up to you and—"

"Excuse me, Mr. Shaw, I don't know what idea you have in your head, but the relationship between Mr. Crace and me is purely a professional one."

"I didn't mean to imply—"

"Well, I hope not."

"It's just that . . . all I'm trying to say is that I'd be careful, that's all."

I cast my mind back to the time when I first delivered my letter to Crace's palazzo. The smooth feel of the marble as I pushed the letter through the dragon's mouth. The gentle eddy of the water all around me as I looked up at the candlelight flickering in the *piano nobile,* and the shadow melting in and out of the darkness. What had Crace seen when he had gazed down at me?

A young man who looked like the love of his life. The boy he had adored. The boy he had, perhaps, killed.

I said good-bye to Shaw and walked back through the village in a daze. The last few months appeared as insubstantial as a mirage. As I tried to compose a mental image of my time with Crace just to get a few things straight, the memories slipped and melted away, and I was left feeling unable to distinguish between the real and the imagined.

When I had arrived in Venice, I had seemed so certain of my future, so sure of my plans. Everything had been in place—a job, free accommodation, time to write. I had been presented with a new opportunity to start my life again, to forget about Eliza and the problems with my parents. I was ready to prove to everyone—and to myself—what I was capable of. I really had believed that I would write a novel, that I would find time to get myself back in shape and sort out all the weird stuff going on in my head.

It had not worked out like that. Since moving into Crace's palazzo, I had hardly had any time to write much of the novel apart from the occasional page or so. I had given up my time for Crace, sacrificed my independence and my life for him. And throughout those months, he had been playing some sick game.

Of course, now it all made sense, perfect fucking sense. Those sly, stolen glances he cast at me when he thought I wasn't looking. His lizard eyes darting around, snatching bits of me—a piece of forehead, a jut of cheekbone, a segment of fleshy upper lip. That strange expression that would descend upon him—a misty-eyed whimsy, part ecstatic reverie, part pain beyond measure—when he saw me first thing in the morning or when I handed him his early evening drink.

Back at the pub, I splashed my face with cold water. What

were the facts? Okay, Chris had died, but how did I know he had been killed by Crace? Why did I assume that Shaw was telling the truth? Couldn't Chris just have committed suicide like the inquest said? Surely if Crace had murdered Chris, then the police would have investigated the matter and there would have been a trial? It was time to examine Chris's account of what had happened.

I opened the diary, and as I flicked through it I noticed that certain pages had been torn from it. I turned to the front and immediately saw a four-line stanza centered in the very middle of the frontispiece.

> *If you turn these pages and look inside*
> *Read my words and attempt to read my mind*
> *Put thoughts of a happy future aside*
> *Always alone, always looking behind.*
> *C.D.*

The message sent a chill through me. I looked up from the pages. For a moment I thought about shutting the damned thing and delivering the diary back to Shaw. But, in truth, I knew I had no option. I turned the leaf-thin pages and started to read.

31 August 1959

I made my way through the boys to the schoolroom next to the library. Faces looked up at me as I entered the class. I looked around the room for a spare desk and found one right at the back. There was a boy with black hair and dark eyes next to me. I placed my satchel on the desk and sat down. I smiled and said hello, but he just stared back at me. I pretended to search for some-

thing in my bag, a pencil or a rubber, hoping that the fear would go away and that by the time I looked up again, everything would be all right. I counted out the seconds using my fingers, pressing my nails into my palm, but by the time the master arrived, I had lost count and my hands were all red.

The master said good morning. His name was Mr. Hamilton-Parker and he said he was going to be our form teacher for the year. He moved on to the register, calling the names. Adams? Yes, sir. Ammerson? Yes, sir. And so it went on until he came to me. Davidson? I couldn't speak. My throat felt all swollen. He looked up and called my name again. I tried to cough. Yes, sir, I whispered. The master didn't hear me, so I had to say it again. Someone at the back made a joke about my voice. The black-haired boy next to me, who I later learned was called Levenson, sniggered, and I saw other boys turn their heads to look at me. I felt my face redden. Mr. Hamilton-Parker told the boys to be quiet and got on with the register.

During assembly I kept trying to catch Dad's eye, but he didn't look in my direction, not even when he had finished playing. The headmaster, Dr. Hart, welcomed the new boys to the school and hoped that we would make him proud. He is sure that we have an exciting future ahead of us and that we will all be happy at Winterborne.

1 September 1959

Mum asked me how was it when I came through the door. I told her that it was fine, all right. What's wrong with your lip, she said. Nothing, I told her. Rugger, that was all. It must have been a rough game, she said. She told me to be more careful. Dad was at the sink, washing some vegetables he had just pulled from the garden. When I walked past him on the way to the stairs, he didn't look at me. In my room, I ripped the uniform off me.

I came downstairs and saw Mum's eager face. She told me to sit down and tell her about my day. She asked Dad whether he had seen me at school. Just at assembly, he said. Mum asked me whether I had made any nice friends. I nodded, but I didn't tell her the truth.

3 September 1959

In English Mr. Crace asked me to read a Shakespeare sonnet out loud. As I started to read I tried to imitate how the other boys spoke, but halfway through the sonnet I realized it was a stupid thing to do. I could hear Levenson and his friend Jameson sniggering at the back of the room, and by the time I finished the class-room erupted with laughter. The boys looked to Mr. Crace to join in on the joke, but he banged his fist on the desk and told the class to stop laughing. The room fell silent. I wanted to disappear.

The master turned to me and asked me to read the poem again, but in a more natural way, in my own voice. He turned to the boys and told them that Shakespeare would have spoken with a local accent. Making fun of dialect only showed one's ignorance, he said. I looked at him as if to say, please, no, but he nodded and looked at me with kind eyes. I stumbled over the first few words,

*feeling that my voice was coarse, ugly even, but when I
finished, Mr. Crace said it was beautifully done. He
then asked Levenson and Jameson to read out sonnet
18, taking one line each at a time. When the boys turned
to the sonnet in the book, the classroom echoed with
laughter once more. This time Levenson and Jameson
were the butt of the joke. Levenson went first, stumbling
over the words, "Shall I compare thee to a Summer's
Day?" and then it was Jameson's turn, "Thou art more
lovely and more temperate." By the time Jameson said
the last line, the two boys were blushing and squirming
in their seats. Even I found it funny. But when I looked
up, I saw Levenson staring at me with hatred.*

4 September 1959

*At the end of the afternoon, just as most of the other
boys were going off to their dorms or study rooms, I
walked down the long, dark corridor toward the front
entrance. As I stepped out, the sunlight blinded me. I
looked down at the gravel pathway, blinking. I turned
the corner and went behind the outbuildings, directly
into the path of the sun. My foot hit something and I
stumbled.*

*"Watch where you're going, Davidson," said a boy.
He had his foot outstretched. It was Levenson. "Not
only can he not speak properly, he can't even walk," said
Jameson. "What shall we do with him," asked the dark-
haired boy. They grinned at one another, and a moment
later I was being pushed behind one of the outbuildings,
out of sight. "Stop snaking around, blondie," Jameson
said to me, pushing me up against a brick wall. "Can't*

*your daddy afford to let you board with the rest of us?
Or are you too much of a mummy's boy? Was that it?"
The two of them laughed as they started to hit me,
lightly at first. I tried to fight back but they were too
strong for me. One of them smacked me across the face
and the other elbowed me in the stomach. As I bent over
double, I saw a drop of blood fall onto the ground. "Not
such a pretty boy now, are we?" one of them said. They
called me other names too.*

*I stood up and saw, in the distance, walking along the
path between the school and the music room, a man in a
tweed jacket. My eyes were smarting from the pain, but
I was sure he looked over in my direction. It was my
father. There was no need to shout over to him because
he had seen me. He would come over and stop it. He
would rescue me. But instead of running over to me, he
turned and carried on along the path until he disappeared. The boys punched me in the stomach and ran
off.*

23 September 1959

*I came downstairs after finishing my homework to see
Mum all red-faced. She told me that tea was nearly
ready. "Where's your dad?" she asked. "Not cleaning his
guns again, is he?" I told her I would go and check the
garden.*

*I went out the front door, across the narrow track and
through the blue gate that leads into the long garden.
"Dad?" I shouted. "Dad?" I walked down the lawn. In-
sects swarmed around the fruit bushes. I reached out to
touch a berry, but as my fingers began to form them-*

selves around the fruit, I felt a buzzing on my skin. It was a lazy bluebottle.

I caught a glimpse of Dad, his back to me, standing by the shed at the bottom of the garden. "Tea's ready, Dad," I said. He didn't appear to hear me, so I repeated the words. But as I walked toward him, he didn't turn to greet me. He just carried on looking at a patch of earth. I asked him whether he was all right and walked around the strip so that I could see his face. His eyes looked strange. His face was pale. Eventually he came to and told me he was just daydreaming.

19 October 1959

I didn't say a word at school today. I don't really mind. Not talking is easy once you get used to it. Anyway, I'd much rather write things down. Mr. Crace says the written word lasts forever.

20 October 1959

On the way to history, I saw Levenson and Jameson. I turned and started walking in the other direction. If I went out the main entrance, I could walk around the school to the back door. I thought I had given them the slip. But just as I was running up the side of the school, I saw Jameson in front of me. I turned to run, but Levenson was behind me. I thought about taking off across the fields, but if I did that I was certain to miss the lesson. I stood still, not knowing what to do. I heard their feet on the gravel as they came toward me. Jameson pushed me against the wall, and I saw Levenson's angry eyes. He raised his hand to hit me, but just as he was about to strike, an arm came to rest on his shoulder. It was Mr. Crace.

He asked them what was going on and the boys said nothing. Mr. Crace asked me whether that was true and I nodded. I could tell he did not believe us. We were just having a lively discussion, said Levenson. If that was the case, Mr. Crace said, then all of us would not mind coming along after school to take part in the debating society. Levenson and Jameson tried to protest, but he stopped them. The Pemberly brothers had both gone down with something, he said, and the society could do with a couple of extra loudmouths. He told them to go and then turned to me. He spoke softly, kindly. He told me not to worry. I did not need to join in with the debate if I did not want to. I could take the minutes.

20 October 1959

As soon as I heard the bell, I made my way to Mr. Crace's room. I knocked on the door. Mr. Crace told me to come in. I was the first to arrive. I opened the door to find him sitting at the desk, writing. He looked up, pleased to see me.

I heard a knock at the door and the boys started to file into the room. The last ones in were Levenson and Jameson, both scowling at me, as if it was my fault they were there. Mr. Crace told the group that today we were going to discuss democracy. He talked about it for a while and then split us into two groups—Levenson, Knowles, Miller and Wright in one group and Jameson, Dodd, Fletcher and Ward in another. He told me that I could be in charge of the reference books and help the boys find quotations and then take notes of what they say. The boys gathered round my desk, and Levenson and Jameson started to act as if they liked me. Levenson said he wished we had more interesting topics to discuss. Miller asked him what kind of things. "Girls," sniggered Wright. Levenson told him not to be so stupid. What he'd like to debate is whether the boys should be allowed to murder the headmaster.

I saw Mr. Crace look up from his desk. Levenson said in a funny voice, "Hereby this school passes the motion that its headmaster should be strung up and sacrificed." That would certainly get his vote, he said.

I caught Mr. Crace looking over and waited for him to tell Levenson off. But it did not happen. Instead, he opened his desk drawer, took out a notebook and scribbled something down.

21 October 1959

"Yesterday changed nothing," Levenson told me. Then he swiped me over the head and laughed. He called me a name and walked away.

2 November 1959

Today Mr. Cartwright, the music master, was ill, so my father took the class. The boys carried on talking as he walked into the room. He strolled over to the desk and tried to get their attention. They looked straight through him. He swallowed a couple of times. I wished he didn't have to teach. I knew he was only doing it for my sake.

"That's enough, boys," Dad said. The noise did not

die down. If anything, I think it got even louder. "Please, come on now," he said. His face looked tired. I sat there in silence while the boys teased and mocked him. Neither of us did anything about it.

When I got back home, Dad said nothing. I said nothing. But both of us understood. Dad looked old and very, very sad.

3 November 1959

I sat at the top of the stairs, listening. Darkness surrounded me. Mum and Dad were talking in the kitchen. They thought I was in my room, door closed, asleep. Their voices were low and murmuring, but I could just about make out what they said. Dad was upset and Mum tried to comfort him, but it was no use. The headmaster had made it clear that he would lose his job at the school if he could not discipline the boys better. And that meant that I would lose my place. Mum tried to calm him down and warned him about the risk of having another episode. He did not know what to do. There was silence. When I heard Dad start to cry, I crept back upstairs to bed.

4 November 1959

The boys are all excited because of the fire tomorrow night. They have spent the last few days collecting bits of wood from the forest and piling them high in one of the outbuildings behind the school. Some of the older boys have built little trolleys on which to carry the wood. They talked about how many firecrackers they have been given and how it was going to be the biggest bonfire ever. "It's going to light up the sky for miles around," they said. I'm looking forward to it too.

5 November 1959

After assembly I followed Dad outside into the music room. He looked worried. He told me he had lots to do and could not chat. He walked over to a music stool, opened it and took out a bundle of music scores. He said that he wanted to put them in order. He said he could arrange them according to composer or key. There was something odd about his manner. He quickly flicked through the scores and mumbled something under his breath.

I asked him whether he was all right. He has three classes—one at eleven, another at twelve and the last one at four. Mr. Cartwright was ill again, he said, and he had to stand in for him—again.

I ran through my own timetable in my head. I told him I would see him later. He did not say anything, and I left him arranging the music scores on top of the piano. The rest of the day passed slowly. I kept looking at my watch, waiting for the best time. At 4:15, in chemistry, I checked my pockets to make sure I had everything I needed. I raised my arm and asked if I could be excused to go to the lavatory. The usual taunts and teases echoed around me, but I did not care. Mr. Ormerod nodded his head, and I ran down the corridor and out to the music room. I crouched under the windows, gently easing myself up to peek inside. It was just as I had hoped. The boys were behaving badly. Some were throwing crumpled balls of paper at one another. Others were passing notes and sniggering. One boy had his feet up on the desk. At the front of the room, sitting at the desk with his head in his hands, was my father.

I dashed back to the school, quickly making sure nobody had spotted me. I ran into the loos, found a cubicle and locked the door. I slammed the lid of the toilet shut, sat on it and took out the piece of blank paper from my pocket, together with my pen and six-inch ruler. Using the ruler, I wrote out the letters in block form: TROUBLE IN MUSIC ROOM—NOW. I folded the paper in half, put it in my pocket just in case I was spotted, and then walked toward the headmaster's office. Luckily, the door was closed. I slipped the paper underneath the door and ran back to my classroom.

5 November 1959

Dad was not home, so Mum and me sat and ate our bangers and mash by ourselves. She put some of the food for Dad on a plate that he could heat up and have later. She was angry, but she tried not to let it show. At seven o'clock, with still no sign of him, she turned to me while doing the washing up and told me to get my coat and scarf on. We were going to the fire anyway. We were not going to wait around any longer for him, she said.

I stepped outside and breathed in the cold air. It smelt of smoke. As we walked from our house down the lane toward the school, I noticed that the sky looked orange. From a distance I could just make out the fire in the darkness. A crowd of boys and masters clustered around the bonfire. As we approached, Mum spotted one of her friends, Elaine Shaw, a neighbor's wife, and she stopped to chat.

I could feel the heat of the fire from where I was

standing, but I wanted to get closer. I walked nearer, conscious of the flames burning my face. Sparks spat and flew around me. Mum told me not to get so close to it, but I ignored her. I looked through the flames and saw Levenson. Next to him stood Jameson.

I told Mum that I had just spotted a couple of friends. She seemed pleased. It was probably the first time she had heard me use the word since I had started at the school. She told me to take my time and she turned back to talk to Mrs. Shaw, who has not been well.

I walked around the edge of the fire, as close to the flames as possible. If Levenson and Jameson did have a plan, I wanted it to be as far out of my mother's sight as possible. Behind me I heard a voice. "Watch it there." It was Dobbs, the caretaker. He put a hand on my shoulder. "Make way for the guy," he shouted. The crowd of boys parted to let him through.

Slung over Dobbs's shoulders was a horrid figure made from sacking and old pillowcases, stuffed with hay and sawdust, and wearing an old tweed jacket. The crowd began to cheer, and the flames of the fire seemed to leap higher into the sky. As Dobbs stretched out his arms, the guy's head flopped sideways, the glow of the fire lighting up its face. There was something strangely familiar about the way it looked. Dobbs flung it onto the top of the fire, the action greeted by cheers. Through the holes in the guy's skin, I could just make out that the figure had been stuffed with some kind of paper, what looked like dozens of screwed-up music scores. A moment later the whole thing burst into flames.

I had to get Mum away in case she saw. I told her I

was not feeling well. I wanted to go home. As we turned to go, some of the boys started to set off firecrackers. Then in the distance, I heard another, much louder noise. A gunshot. It came from the forest.

[Pages torn out here]

1 January 1960

Beginning of the new year. People say you are supposed to look forward to it. I'm not.

Mum is pleased because the school said she would not have to find the fees for my place. It's all been taken care of by Dr. Hart. Everyone is saying that it was a hunting accident, but I know the truth. I know what really happened.

I don't want to write any more.

I read through the diary quickly, almost eating the words as I went along, scanning the pages for any mention of Crace. As I did so, my heart raced, my breathing shortened, and I felt anger and panic begin to rise inside me.

Shaw had promised me an insight into why Chris had committed suicide, suggesting that Crace had had something to do with it. Apart from the entry about how Crace had come across the inspiration for *The Debating Society*, the diary gave me little extra information about the novelist. I threw down the diary, got up from my bed, opened the window and stared into the darkness outside. A murmur of voices came from below, locals enjoying a drink and warming themselves by the fire. Someone coughed, a loud rasping that reminded me of Shaw. I couldn't believe how stupid I had been to trust that weasel of a man. And I'd paid him a thousand pounds. At the sound of a woman's high-pitched laughter from the bar, I brought my fist down hard on the wooden windowsill. The pain, exploding from my hand and running up my arm, came as a relief.

I couldn't afford to abandon the project now. I had to make it work. I did not have a choice. In order to find out more about Crace, I knew I would have to gain access to the school. Yet I could hardly breeze in and start asking questions about Crace. Telling them about my proposed biography was completely out of the question, as there was a risk that word would leak out, either to Crace's publisher or even back to the writer himself. I thought about various options—presenting myself as a son of an old boy, pretending to be a tourist who wanted to look around—but realized that none of them would work.

What about the truth or something near to it? How would that work? What if I said I was an art history student who had taken an undergraduate course at London University—a fact that could be checked if necessary—and that I was embarking on an MA or PhD thesis exploring one particular art historical aspect of medieval churches? Crace had told me that Winterborne Abbey contained an interesting collection of relics, sculpture and statutory, objects that I was sure would have been documented in some way and the records held, I presumed, in the school archives. At least that would give me an excuse to get inside and hopefully strike up a conversation with the librarian. And if somebody checked with my old college and came up with the fact that I had not enrolled in an MA or PhD course, what would I say then? That I was doing this as research so as to strengthen my application for next year? It sounded just about plausible to me and certainly worth taking the risk.

At least this way I wouldn't have to dissemble that much. I needn't have to act. I could just be myself.

The next day, a Saturday, after an early breakfast, I decided to walk to the abbey to do a spot of research. Dark clouds cast shadows over the dense woods that enveloped the valley. As the wind roared through the trees, I stood outside and, in the back of my notebook, did a quick sketch of the building, which looked like an enormous Oxford chapel, complete with elaborate flying buttresses. What was unusual about it was the fact that the abbey did not have a nave, only a covered entrance where the central part of the church would have stood.

I turned the cold metal ring on the thick wooden door and pushed. Inside, the air was chilly and damp, as musty as the inside of a tomb. Weak sunlight filtered through the huge stained-glass windows, casting blood-colored shadows onto the tiled floor. I listened for the sound of other people, but I couldn't hear anything except for the wind high in the trees outside. Inside, the stillness was oppressive, unnerving.

To my right there was a table selling illustrated guides to the abbey for two pounds, above which a notice read, "This stall is run on a trust basis. Please place money in honesty wall box. Please do not abuse this trust." As far as I was concerned, my honesty was above question—in fact, I rather prided myself on my trustworthiness—and I promptly dropped two pound coins through the slot in the wall. As I did so, I remembered something I had read in Aretino's *Letters:* how the king of France had given the writer a heavy gold chain decorated with tongues enameled in vermilion on which was written the message LINGUA EIVS LOQUETUR MENDACIUM—his tongue speaketh a lie.

On the wall facing me, above which sat the huge organ, hung several old prints in ancient frames, one of which had an inscription describing the origins of the abbey. It was said that the church was built by King Athelstan in atonement for the death of his younger brother, for which he was responsible. Apparently Athelstan had accused him of a crime, falsely, it later turned out, and set him to sea in a boat with no sails or paddles and only one page for company. After his brother drowned and Athelstan learned the errors of his ways, he built the abbey, together with another monastery, and underwent seven years' penance in a bid to try and make his peace with God.

I noted all this down before walking underneath the curtained archway to the treasury that lay below the organ loft. According to my little guidebook, this is where I would find the relics of the church, all displayed beneath a glass panel. I switched on a timed light to illuminate the abbey's collection of precious objects, an ivory triptych of a nativity scene; cigar-shaped parts of a pectoral cross dating from the fifteenth century; a pewter chalice and paten from an abbot's grave; and on the very bottom shelf of the display, *Foxe's Book of Martyrs,* the only surviving book of John Tregonwell, who had left his library to the abbey. As I bent down to have a closer look at the book, its spine half-eaten away by age, the volume surrounded by clusters of silica crystals, I heard a footstep behind me.

"Not what you'd call a great collection, I'm afraid, but still quite fascinating, I think."

I turned around, startled, to see a woman in late middle-age wearing a tartan jacket, a gray skirt and black sensible shoes, carrying a pair of yellow rubber gloves and a large pair of scissors.

"Sorry if I made you jump," she said. "I was in the back of the vestry doing a spot of tidying."

She eyed me up and down and smiled.

"It's always pleasing to see young people show an interest in the past," she said, her gray-blue eyes twinkling behind her tortoiseshell-frame glasses. "I mean, so many of them haven't got a clue about what went on in their grandfather's day, never mind in the Middle Ages. Really quite a disgrace."

As she gestured around the abbey with the scissors, she looked down at the sharp point of the implement and laughed gently to herself.

"Sorry, so sorry, you must think me extremely odd, not to mention very rude," she said, stretching out her free hand. "I'm June Peters, the headmaster's wife. About to go into battle with the altar flowers over there."

"Hello," I said, shaking hands. "Yes, it is rather a fascinating group of objects. All extremely unique and actually quite moving."

"Do you think so?"

"Yes."

"Down on holiday? Beautiful countryside around here. Walking?"

"Well, sort of a working holiday," I said. "I'm an art history student, working on a thesis."

"Really? That's wonderful. How interesting. Some of these things go way back, as you most probably know. Anyway, I'll let you get on."

She waved her scissors in the air as a parting gesture and breezed down the aisle toward the altar. As I walked around the abbey, noting down its art and sculpture, including the rather fine reredos, an elaborate family tomb fashioned out of white marble and a wonderful nine-foot-tall oak hanging tabernacle, I came up with a plan to try and enlist the woman's help.

"Excuse me. So sorry to bother you," I said, walking up to her as she was beginning to trim the dead foliage away from a display overlooking the stone sedilia.

She looked up and smiled, only too pleased to help.

"I don't know whether you might know, but I'm trying to find out some more information about the collection here."

"Oh, yes?"

"I just wondered if you might know anything about any of the objects on display?"

"I'm not an expert, I'm afraid. You'll have to ask my husband about that. But there is a charming story about how the book came into the abbey's possession. Have you heard about that?"

"No, I haven't," I said.

"Oh, it's wonderful, quite amusing, really. When John Tregonwell, whose family lived in the house next door—are you sure you don't already know this? Did you not see the notice outside on the verge?"

"No," I said, smiling.

"Well, one day the little boy, John, who must have been no more than five at the time, was playing in here and climbed to the top of the tower. I suppose the wind must have been quite ferocious up there, or perhaps he got too close to the edge. Anyway, he fell sixty feet and was only saved by his nankeen shirts, which I suppose must have acted as a sort of parachute. As a gesture of thanks, he gave all his books to the abbey. And so it's thanks to his petticoats that we have this volume here."

"That's quite incredible," I said, doing a spot of quick thinking. "What a story. In fact, just the kind of thing I'm looking for."

"Really?"

"My thesis is going to concentrate on oral history," I said. "I want to ask local people what they think of art."

"I see," she said. "As I said, it's probably best if you talk to my husband. He's the real expert. He's at home this afternoon if you would like to see him."

"Would that be okay?"

"I don't see why not. In fact, I'm sure he would be delighted with the excuse to take a break from his work."

"Oh, I wouldn't want to disturb him."

"Now, don't be so silly. In fact, when I finish up here in a couple of minutes, I'll go over to the house and ask him."

"That's ever so kind. Thank you."

"That's no problem. Why don't you continue looking around while I go and check? I'm sure there's still a lot you would like to see. Oh, by the way, I forgot to ask your name."

"It's Adam," I said. "Adam Woods."

As she left the abbey, letting the thick wooden door bang behind her, I continued on my tour, past the altar and into the north aisle. I turned a corner and saw a tomb of a woman, her likeness carved in marble. In her left hand she held a book, presumably a missal, in her right, a skull missing its bottom jaw. The sight of the skull unsettled me, and I turned away from it without making any notes and walked down the aisle back toward the entrance. I stopped by another white marble tomb of a man gazing upon the supine form of a lady. The decorative flourishes—the brocading on the woman's dress, the twill cord around her waist, the tassels on the cushion supporting her—were all extremely fine, but at that moment I wasn't interested in aesthetics. It was the pose of the two of them there, the man gazing upon the lifeless body of his wife, that fixed me to the spot.

I used to wake up in the middle of the night and watch Eliza sleeping. I would rest my elbow on the pillow, my hand on my cheek, and gaze on her while she rested. At times her breathing was so inaudible that I thought she had slipped into unconsciousness and died. At that moment I loved her so much. But then her chest would rise and fall and she would begin to stir.

I heard the door bang shut and turned around to see the headmaster's wife staring at me.

"Good news," she said, walking toward me. "Just as I had said, my husband would be happy to see you later today. He suggests tea at four o'clock, if that suits you."

"That's wonderful."

She gave me directions to the house, which stood in the school grounds, before excusing herself.

"Sorry, I have to run, otherwise we could have had a chat. Even though I have to confess I'm quite at a loss to know exactly what it is you want to write about, I think it's just wonderful you are interested in art and in the past. Just wonderful. The way you were looking at that sculpture there almost brought tears to my eyes."

<hr />

"You must be Mr. Woods, the young man my wife was telling me about," said the headmaster, opening the door of his large Victorian house and stretching out his hand. "Hello. I'm Jeffrey Peters. Come in, come in."

The gray-haired, smartly dressed man led me through the entrance hall to a large sitting room where a fire cracked and spitted and cast a warm glow over the buttermilk-colored walls.

"Please sit down," he said, gesturing toward a bergère chair with olive-green cushions. "May I get you some tea?"

"That would be wonderful," I said, sitting down.

"I won't be long, but please make yourself comfortable," he said.

As he went off to make the tea, I stood up and took the opportunity to look around the tastefully decorated sitting room. On one wall stood an enormous bookcase, filled with books on church and cathedral architecture, spirituality and Christianity, while on the top of a highly polished mahogany chest of drawers stood a number of photographs of the headmaster and his wife and family. It was obvious that since the photographs had been taken, the headmaster, once quite a rotund figure, had lost a considerable amount of weight. In the corridor I heard the sound of the headmaster carrying the tea things, so I quickly resumed my seat.

"Here we are," he said, placing the tray on the low-lying table between our chairs. "Milk and sugar?"

"Just milk," I said.

"And cake? June does rather pride herself on her fruitcake."

"What a good idea," I said. "Thank you."

"June told me a little about your proposed thesis," he said, passing me a plate, "which does sound rather intriguing, but I wondered if you could outline it in a little more detail."

"Yes, of course," I said, trying not to think too much about the library of specialist books on the shelves above me. "I'm not an expert in church or cathedral architecture—I've only just finished an art history degree—but I wanted to research the way objects in places like Winterborne Abbey are displayed and experienced."

The headmaster reached out to take his teacup, but his intelligent eyes registered a keen interest in the subject.

"For instance, when you go to a museum, a world-class museum like the Tate or the V & A or the National Gallery, you see objects of great genius and beauty and intelligence, but often I believe you don't feel a personal connection with the art. Whereas if you live or study or work in close proximity to a place, such as the abbey, that can trace the provenance of the objects in its collection way back in history, I think a viewer has a very different experience of the things on display."

"Yes, I see what you mean," said the headmaster. "It's an interesting idea."

"Your wife told me that fascinating story about the little boy who fell off the tower."

"Oh, yes, terribly charming," he said, laughing. "The famous nankeen petticoat."

"And how he went on to leave his library to the school. I would be really interested to research the history of the book on display, of course, together with the ivory triptych, the chalice, cross, and other objects. And also some of the sculptures in the abbey as well, some of which are very fine indeed."

"Yes, we would have had a great deal more, I should think, if the Norman church that stood on the site had not been struck by lightning and consumed by fire in the early fourteenth century."

"Really?"

"Yes, I'm afraid so. A case of *totalier inflammavit, columnis decrustatis.*"

"I see."

He took another sip of tea and fixed me with his eyes.

"Of course I will help in any way I can, but I really can't see what I can do."

"I wondered whether the school keeps records of the objects, whether there is an archive of any sort."

"Yes, there is something in the library I seem to remember, a ledger of some kind, I think. You're welcome to have access to that if it helps."

"Thank you, that's extremely kind of you. And also, as I'm interested in the way people perceive these objects, I wondered whether it would be possible for you to put me in touch with any former staff members, for instance, or old boys of the school. I think it would be good to hear from as wide a range of people as possible, those from older and younger generations."

"What kind of questions will you ask them?"

A currant from the fruitcake lodged itself in my throat.

"Sorry, excuse me," I said, coughing. "It would be things like, what was your reaction when you first saw the particular object? Did you consider it to be an historical exhibit or a work of art or both? And how would you say it differed from the objects on display in a conventional museum?" I thought about the religious books on the shelves. "And did the relics or the objects have any kind of religious significance for you? Were they invested with a sort of spirituality?"

The headmaster looked down at the floor as he thought this over. As I waited for his decision, my heart began to race. I forced myself to keep my composure. Finally he raised his head, looked at me and smiled.

"I can see that could be very interesting indeed," he said. "And I presume you will study other places as well."

"Yes," I said. "I'm not sure which ones yet, but basically it will be anywhere that has a collection of art objects on display that have been there for years and that have a local, quite specific connection. So it may be things in a church, a local museum, a school or wherever. Of course, I am going to have to limit myself to the number of places I study, but if you have any suggestions, I'd be very happy to hear them."

By the time I had finished, I had almost convinced myself that it was a worthwhile, and even quite interesting, subject for research.

"I think it's a splendid idea, but I just have one question," he said, staring intently at me. "Why on earth did you choose Winterborne Abbey? After all, we are hardly, as they say, in the center of things, and the collection here, although we have a number of very fine pieces, is extremely modest."

It was one question I had not prepared myself for. I pretended to clear my throat once more to give myself a few extra seconds to think.

"Sorry about this," I said, as I coughed. "Oh, rather a silly reason, I'm afraid. When I was a teenager, I read *The Debating Society,* which I think was written by a former teacher here, Gordon Crace."

On the mention of the name, the headmaster's eyes narrowed. The atmosphere in the room changed in an instant, but I had no choice but to continue.

"The book made a great impression on me at the time," I said, "especially the descriptions of the abbey, the school and the landscape. A few years later, my family came down to the Isle of Purbeck for a summer holiday, and I pleaded with my parents to make the drive over to Winterborne Abbey to see it. I was astonished by its beauty and I suppose I never forgot it."

I laughed at myself for being so foolish, but the headmaster's stern expression did not soften.

"I had rather hoped the world had forgotten about that silly book," he said, sighing. "In fact, I think the less said about it the better."

The headmaster rose to his feet.

"But come to my office in the school on Monday morning, and we'll see what we can do," he said. "Mrs. Fowles, the librarian, is bound to be of some help."

As he led the way out of the room and to the front door, I got the impression that he couldn't wait to get rid of me, as if the mere mention of Crace's name had polluted the air.

⊹⊱━━⊰⊹

"I think that is the last of them," said, the librarian, a sad-eyed, gray-haired woman, as she placed three slim, green, leather-bound books on the table. "If you want anything else, just let me know and I'll be glad to bring the volumes over. I'll be in the library if you need me. You do know where that is, don't you?"

"Yes," I said. "Mr. Peters pointed it out to me. Thank you."

Earlier that morning the headmaster had offered me the use of the records held at the school and had informed the librarian of my project, suggesting that it might be best if she brought the material to the anteroom outside his office so that I would not be disturbed. The headmaster had also promised to give me contact details of former members of staff or old boys, but, of course, I couldn't ask for these straightaway. So for the next few hours, I looked through the books, noting down details about the provenance of the various relics, sculptures, statues and paintings displayed in the abbey. I knew I might need this kind of information if questioned about my project.

Through the door that separated the anteroom from the study, I could hear the occasional ringing of the telephone, followed by the headmaster's low voice. Sometimes I heard him open the door to staff members or pupils, but I could not make out their muffled conversations.

I closed the last of the ledgers, picked up my notebook, and walked out of the headmaster's anteroom and back to the library. The corridor had filled with boys—some fresh-faced, others who had greasy skin, spots and lank hair—who eyed me with a mixture of shyness and curiosity. I knocked on the door of the library and stepped into a grand and spacious room that had an elaborate fretwork ceiling and an imposing marble fireplace. Through an open door I saw a smaller room where Mrs. Fowles was sitting at a desk, reading. She looked up as I entered.

"Can I help you, Mr. Woods?"

"Yes, I wondered if you might. I've finished with the ledgers now—they were extremely helpful, so thank you."

"I'm pleased they could be of some use. Is there anything else you'd like to look at?"

"I wondered whether it might be possible to see anything that might help me track down some former staff members or old boys."

"As Mr. Peters probably explained, we would need a list of names from you first. Then we could check the records to see if we have any details for the boys in question."

"Yes, Mr. Peters did mention that, which is why I thought it might be a good idea to start with, I don't know, school magazines or a list of the boys in each particular house."

"There are a number of magazines, the production of which was overseen, I think, by the English department, but I must warn you that we don't have them for every year. It disappears completely for a couple of years here and there. But we do have a list of the boys in each house dating back, I think, to when we first became a school in the early fifties. And there's also a few scrapbooks, odds and ends really, photographs, reports of certain achievements and the like."

"That sounds perfect," I said, smiling.

"I'm sorry I won't be able to help you straightaway as I'm expecting a class of thirteen-year-olds at any moment," she said, looking at her watch and pausing for a second. "But if you can do without my help, you're very welcome to start browsing through the books in the back room, if you like. The actual school records aren't kept there, of course, just an assortment of books relating to the school. The boys are only allowed in the back room if they have permission, so you'd be quite private, and there's a little table and chair you could use if you like."

Mrs. Fowles looked down at the desk and started to play with the corner of a blue-colored folder, as though she were slightly

embarrassed by her act of kindness and half-expecting her suggestion to be met with an outright rejection.

"That is extremely kind of you," I said, really meaning it.
"Thank you so much."

She looked up. The noise of boys walking down the corridor
moved closer toward us.

"Gosh, they're almost upon me," she said, moving toward the
door that led into the back of the library.

I followed her into the narrow, cramped room, and as we maneuvered our way through the tightly packed shelves, she began
to blush.

"I think it's all quite self-explanatory. Books about the school
are mainly on this shelf here," she said, gesturing toward a tall
wooden bookcase. I heard the door to the library open and the
boys walk into the room. "The school magazines are in the box
files on this shelf there and the scrapbooks begin," she said, pointing to the bottom of the shelf, "yes, around here."

"Thank you again," I said.

"I'll be with you in an hour," she said.

As she turned to leave, she smiled and her eyes, so sad earlier
that morning, lit up with something approaching delight. It was
obvious that not many people appreciated her. It felt good to
bring a little bit of joy into another person's life.

I scanned the shelf of books in front of me, running my fingers
over the surfaces of the spines as I read the titles: *History of Winterborne Abbey; Winterborne Abbey, the School and Abbey; Capability Brown and the Eighteenth-Century Landscape; The
Architecture of Dorset Churches and Abbeys;* and Pevsner's *The
Buildings of England.* After my morning studying the ledgers, I
had had enough of dusty archives detailing the abbey's architecture and its collection of art. I wanted to get on with my real job,

the unearthing of material that would give me a clue into Crace's
time at the school or anything about Chris that would offer an insight into his state of mind prior to his suicide. I wasn't sure what
I would find, or even whether I would discover anything at all.

I bent down to study the untitled, oversized volumes bound in
pale blue leather on the bottom shelf of the bookcase. I pulled out
one by random. On the front of the cover were the words "Winterborne Abbey School in photographs, 1957" embossed in gold letters. As I opened the book, a couple of black-and-white prints fell
out, a photograph of a group of what looked like sixth formers
standing in front of the school entrance and another of a curly-
haired boy smiling widely as he clasped a trophy to his chest. I
placed the two pictures on the floor beside me, intending to put
them back when I found where they had come from, and began
looking through the album. Under each of the photographs, someone had written, in neat handwriting and in black ink, a small
caption explaining the subject above. There were details of the
appointment of the head boy, the scores of each of the houses,
photographs of sporting, musical, and dramatic triumphs, and at
the very back a reduced-size print of the staff and pupils gathered
on the lawn, with the house serving as a backdrop.

I scanned the photograph, searching the dozens of faces staring out at me, running my finger slowly over the matte surface of
the photograph. There, at the very end of the first row, sandwiched between a thin elderly man in wire-rimmed spectacles and
a portly woman in tweed, was Crace. It was hard to reconcile the
fine features of the man in the photograph, with his full head of
hair, handsome face, youthful skin and playful smile, with the
man I knew in Venice, but there was no question it was him.

After easing the album back into position, I pulled out the
volume next to it, for the year 1958, and found a similar selection

of photographs: rugger wins, cricket victories, musical recitals and dramatic performances, including *A Midsummer Night's Dream* and *Journey's End*. There was a typed cast list for Sherriff's play that showed that it had been directed by Crace, yet the only image I found of him was the one in the group photograph, again stuck onto the last page of the book, looking more or less the same as he did the previous year.

I turned to the back of the 1959–1960 scrapbook and scanned the faces looking for Chris, my other self. There was Crace, again, staring out with an amused expression, but there was no sign of Chris, nor was there any sign of his father. I looked at the date of the photograph—6 June 1960. John Davidson would have been dead for seven months.

I turned the pages of the album and, a couple of pages into the book, I saw a photograph of a man standing on a stage. Dressed in a badly fitting, cheap-looking tweed jacket, he looked embarrassed, astonished that anyone, let alone someone with a camera, would show the slightest interest in him. Underneath the picture was the caption: John Davidson, organist and music teacher at Winterborne Abbey, after his performance of Bach's Preludes in October 1959. It was hard to see any similarity between Chris and his father. Whereas the photographs of Chris I had seen at Shaw's showed him to be quite a handsome boy with a square jaw, blond hair and intelligent-looking eyes, this man looked as if the life had been sucked out of him. Dark circles shadowed his eyes, and his skin looked sallow and unhealthy.

Just as I was about to close the volume and swap it for the next one, I flicked past a notice that caught my eye. I turned the pages back to where I had spotted the words "the debating society." There was no photograph, but a page had been glued into the scrapbook detailing the victory of the Winterborne Abbey debating society over nearby Pemberton College, together with a list of names, some of the boys Chris had mentioned in his journal—Matthew Knowles, Timothy Fletcher, Adrian Levenson and David Ward. The motion, proposed by Winterborne Abbey, was "this house believes that manners maketh the man." At the bottom of the page were the words "Mr. Gordon Crace also extends a very warm thank you to Christopher Davidson, who acted as the team's valued amanuensis."

I copied the details into my notebook and turned to the scrapbook for the following year. There, at the back, was what I had been searching for: a photograph showing both Crace and Chris, taken after another of the debating society's wins. Master and pupil stood facing the camera, a few lines apart, Crace looking enigmatic, teasing almost and Chris with a more pained and uncertain expression on his face, as if he were biting the inside of his cheek. The date underneath read 7 March 1961, two years after Chris's father's death and six years before his own.

From the library I heard the sound of boys' voices. I stood up and peered around the shelves to check whether Mrs. Fowles was on her way to see me. There was no sign of her. I took hold of the scrapbook containing the picture of Crace and Chris and eased my right index finger underneath the tabs of glue at each of the four corners of the photograph. Applying a little pressure under each edge I prized the photograph away from the page, leaving behind the trace of four white paper marks. I slipped the picture into my bag, taking care to make sure it was well hidden between the pages of my notebook and an old newspaper. I felt a little ashamed of myself, especially since Mrs. Fowles had been so kind to me, but as I understood it I was just doing my job, gathering evidence in any way I could. It would all count, I was sure of it, every little scrap.

I turned around to the shelf that Mrs. Fowles had said held the school magazines. I took down a box file, opened its cardboard cover, and eased forward the spring mechanism that kept the mass of documents in place. The first few pages were nothing more than loose papers from an old annual report, columns of figures detailing the spending on building work. Beneath this was a buff-colored folder, inside of which was a slim publication dated autumn 1960 and emblazoned with the school's crest. Somebody, one of the boys, I presumed, had quite cleverly designed the cover arranging the title, "The Blast," around the crest so it looked as though it was exploding from the coat of arms. I flicked through the pages quickly, past passages of purple prose, including one boy's sub-Wordsworthian description of wandering through the sublime landscape and another's poem about loss and death, a sonnet that revealed in its last line that the object over which he was grieving was his dog. There was, however, no trace of Chris, and the only sign of Crace was a two-sentence acknowledgment on the inside cover that thanked him for his help in overseeing production.

I ploughed my way through the magazines, combing them for clues, but came up with little of interest. It was dreary, boring work, almost mechanical in its drudgery. I stifled a yawn as I closed the first box file and sat back down at the table. I suppose at least I had some full names now, ones that could be checked against the official school records. Of course, I would pretend that I had just chosen them at random from the scrapbooks and the like, hoping that no one would see the hidden connection—that the boys had all belonged to Crace's debating society.

Then I remembered something: the date of Crace's novel. I checked in my notebook. *The Debating Society* was published on 4 March 1962. I took down the next box file along the shelf, prized open the spring and, instead of carefully and painstakingly going through the magazines page by page, turned out the contents on the table and scanned the magazines for the one with the corresponding date. Everything in the box was from 1961. I tipped the lot back into the file, with a promise to myself I would tidy it up later, flipped down the spring, set it to one side and took down another. As I opened it and saw the year 1962, I felt a thrill pass through my body. But then I remembered Mrs. Fowles's words about the irregularity of publication. Would Crace have bothered to oversee the production of a school magazine just before the release of his own novel? Even if he had, would it have survived?

I turned the pages greedily, quickly finding the magazines published in winter and autumn. There was nothing that bore a spring date, but at the back of the file, its cover creased and torn at the top right-hand corner, was the summer issue. In addition to the explosive graphics emanating from the crest, a boy had fashioned the coat of arms into a sun motif, and below the title someone had drawn the words "Have a blast for summer."

I opened it at the page that featured a question-and-answer interview with Crace. I couldn't believe my luck. At the top of the piece was a byline: Interview by Christopher Davidson. Chris started the feature by outlining, in one paragraph, the reason why he was interviewing his English master.

Mr. Crace, for all his merits, which there are many, would normally not be featured in the interview slot in The Blast. *But on this occasion, we are making an exception. What has drawn our interest is not his fine ability to teach us how to take apart a poem or analyze a dramatic scene, but the fact that he has written a re-*

cently published novel called The Debating Society. *After its initial publication in March—and I hope Mr. Crace wouldn't mind me pointing this out—sales were extremely modest, but recently, thanks to a review in the* Times *and many other notices, it has won a place on the bestseller list. As we go to press, the book stands in the number-three slot, and there is even talk of it being made into a feature film. Mr. Crace very kindly agreed to take time out from his busy schedule to grant* The Blast *a short interview.*

Q: *The news that you had written a novel came as something of a surprise to many of the staff and pupils at the school. How long had you been writing it?*

A: *I started it in the first few months of 1960, and after I had done the initial plotting, it seemed to write itself. I didn't mean to keep it a secret at all. I was writing very much for my own entertainment, well, certainly to begin with, and I never dreamed that it would be published. And I have to say it very nearly did not see the light of day. You see, after I had finished it, I sent the manuscript off to several different London publishers, all of whom rejected it. But finally a small house bought it for a very small sum of money. Of course, the amount I was paid didn't bother me in the slightest as I was just delighted someone had accepted it. It astonishes me that the publisher took it on and, quite frankly, amazes me that anyone wants to read it.*

Q: *What's your reaction to it being a bestseller?*

A: *I am shocked. Really, quite honestly shocked. That's*

the only way I can describe it. But, of course, I'm de-lighted that people seem to enjoy it. I think it's sold in the region of 60,000 copies, and the publishers seem to have high hopes for it when it comes out in paper-back next year. They are also in the process of selling it around the world, including America.

Q: How has the book changed your life?

A: Well, not really at all. I know people may not believe me when I say that, but it's true. I mean, I still teach here, and contrary to some of the rumors, I'm staying on at the school next year. Of course, I will try to write another novel, but I haven't started on anything yet.

Q: What kind of reaction have you had to the book?

A: Well . . . [he laughs] I think some of the staff members here weren't that keen on it when they realized that its subject matter was—how shall I say?—a little dark. They thought it might bring the school into dis-repute and all that. Of course, I understood their con-cerns, but after all, it is a work of imaginative fiction, nothing more. While Winterborne Abbey is, quite clearly, a model, architecturally speaking, for the school, it's obvious that the classics master could not possibly be done away with by one of the boys. Apart from anything else, I don't think Mr. Gibson would stand for it. [He laughs.]

Q: What was your inspiration for the book?

A: [A long pause] Inspiration is so difficult to talk about, isn't it? [Another pause] I suppose the inspiration for the book must have grown out of my time as a teacher here, but as for specifics—the basis of the plot, the

line of the story and so on—I have to take sole re-
sponsibility for those. Probably grown out of the murk
of my imagination. Far from a pretty sight, I'm
afraid.

As I finished reading the interview I heard footsteps coming toward me. It was Mrs. Fowles.

"How are we getting on?" she asked.

"Oh, very well indeed," I said. "It's a mine of information. And so well kept."

Her creamy cheeks began to turn a shade of strawberry pink.

"No, you've done a remarkable job," I said. "First-rate, it really is."

"You really think so? I've only tried to do my best, keep things in order, in their proper place, nothing more than that."

"It's been a great help to me. I can't thank you enough."

Mrs. Fowles looked down and started to play with the seam on her flowery blouse.

"If there's anything else you need . . . "

"I wondered if you could take me around to see the school secretary? As I've got a few names now, I thought she might be able to give me some contacts and addresses. Then I thought I could write to them with a few questions."

"Yes, of course. I've got another lesson in"—she looked at the clock on the wall—"about a quarter of an hour, but I would be happy to introduce you. Did you see her—Mrs. Barwick—this morning?"

"The headmaster's secretary? Oh yes, I did see her, briefly, but we weren't introduced."

I followed Mrs. Fowles down the corridor to the headmaster's office. She knocked on the door of the headmaster's secretary and held the door open for me. Sitting at a neat and tidy desk was an attractive, blond fiftysomething woman.

"Katherine, this is Adam Woods. I think the headmaster may have mentioned him to you," said Mrs. Fowles. "He's the young man who is doing his thesis on the relics and art of the abbey."

"Oh, of course," she said, standing up to shake my hand. "How do you do? Yes, the headmaster did tell me you might be dropping by."

Her blue eyes sparkled as she spoke and she seemed to be constantly smiling.

"I'll leave you two to it," said Mrs. Fowles. "Thank you, Katherine. And, Mr. Woods, if you need anything else, you know where to find me."

"Yes. Thank you again for all your help," I said.

Her cheeks colored slightly as she edged back toward the door.

"Good-bye," she said, closing the door behind her.

"Thank you, Jeanette," said the secretary, taking up a notepad and pen from her desk. She turned back toward me. "Now, what can I help you with?"

I cleared my throat.

"As you know, I'm working on an art history project, a thesis, on the objects on display in places like the abbey here."

She nodded, keen to hear more.

"I think the success of the thesis depends on my ability to talk to people who came in close contact with the art, these relics and statuary. This morning Mrs. Fowles very kindly gave me access to the school's scrapbooks and magazines so I could pick, at random, a few names."

"Yes, I see," she said, combing her right hand through her hair.

"I wondered whether, if I gave you a list of names, you could find contact details for them so I could write to them and ask them a few questions."

"And Mr. Peters knows all about your request?"

"Yes, he does."

"I'd better just check with him first, if you don't mind. I won't be a moment."

She knocked on the headmaster's door and walked in, leaving me in the office, alone. Her desk was bare, except for a computer and a large diary. Today's date had various appointments scheduled for the headmaster, written in exquisite, tiny handwriting. At eleven o'clock he had had a meeting with a local planning officer, regarding the building of a new science block. At four in the afternoon he had a staff meeting. And there at the bottom of the page, in the space that served as a sort of horizontal margin, the secretary had written my name, followed by a question mark.

As I looked at the computer's screen saver, a picture of a greyhound, which I presumed to be the secretary's dog, I thought about the possibility of trying to log in so I could retrieve some of the records before Mrs. Barwick came back. My hand hovered over the mouse. The idea was absurd. I couldn't risk her walking in to find me messing about with her computer.

I moved my hand away from the computer, but it lingered over the diary once more. Out of curiosity I turned the page. I glanced at the door. There was no sign of her yet. I looked down at the headmaster's agenda. There was an appointment with a Mr. Perth-Lewis at 9 AM about his son, Neil. The secretary had arranged a telephone call with the parent of a prospective pupil at 10:30. And there, scheduled for a meeting with him at noon, was Lavinia Maddon. Next to her name the secretary had written, "Biography of Gordon Crace." I remembered the way the headmaster had reacted when I had mentioned Crace's name during our meeting. I had assumed it was because of something I had said. Now I knew differently. He was obviously dreading the appearance of Lavinia and the prospect of dredging up an old scandal, one he thought had been long buried.

I heard the door open and quickly turned around.

"Mr. Woods? I've just had a word with the headmaster and it's as I'd thought."

I tried to gather my thoughts. My mouth had dried up. My heart was racing. My blood felt like acid running through my veins.

"Yes?" I said, desperately trying to control my anger.

"He's happy for you to contact whomsoever you please, but he would like me to write or telephone them first just to make sure they are happy with that. I'm sure that's okay with you."

She looked at me with her bright, twinkling, happy eyes. I felt like poking them out.

"Yes, yes, of course," I said, hating her for what she had just told me and what I had seen written in her hand.

"If you give me a list of the names you want me to look up, I can start straightaway, if you like."

"Yes, that would be very kind. Thank you," I said.

I looked in my bag and took out my notebook.

"Excuse me. Sorry, but do you have a sheet of paper?"

"Of course, yes. Here you are," she said, opening a drawer in her desk and taking out a sheet from a neatly stacked pile of paper.

Everything was so ordered, so regimented. Did nothing go wrong in this woman's life?

I wrote out the names on the paper, making sure that those from the debating society (Matthew Knowles, Timothy Fletcher,

Adrian Levenson and David Ward) were mixed up with ones I had picked out at random from the scrapbooks. At the bottom I added one extra name, that of Ruth Chaning, the young art teacher Crace had known while at the school. I passed the list, on which I had written twelve names, over to the secretary.

"I think, unless I'm very much mistaken, I can give you the details of one of these already," she said, smiling to herself.

"What do you mean?"

She walked over to her computer and tapped in a name.

"Do you know which year Adrian Levenson left the school?" she asked.

"I suppose it must have been at some point in the mid-sixties."

"Yes, thought so," she said, looking at something on her screen. "Here we are. It is the same one."

"What do you mean?"

"Unlike most of us newcomers, Mr. Levenson has been here since the early days. In fact, I suppose you could say he has never really left the school. He's the games master. Would you like to speak to him?"

"Oh, yes," I said, trying to disguise my surprise.

The secretary used the phone on her desk to call Levenson, but as there was no answer, she left a message briefly explaining my project and asking him to call the office. Then she said she would go straight down to the basement to search for the records.

"If you don't mind waiting for a few minutes, it may take me a while," she said, gesturing toward a chair.

As I waited, I felt panic rising inside as I thought about Lavinia Maddon and her imminent arrival. I couldn't quite believe she would be here the next day, stalking these grounds and looking for clues about Crace. How much did she know? Most probably much more than she was letting on to me. It was obvious she was trying to get to the bottom of the mystery of Chris's death and Crace's part in it. It was too late to stop her now. What would she think if she saw me here? She, for one, wouldn't be taken in by my story about my thesis and the relics in the abbey. In fact, she had the power to blow my cover. All she needed to do was causally mention to the headmaster that I was the personal assistant to Gordon Crace and the foundations of all my hard work would be swept away.

There was only one thing for it: Lavinia would have to be stopped.

An image of her, pale, lifeless, her face masklike, came into my head. I saw her lying in the undergrowth of the forest, her smart, gray skirt soiled with mud, her white blouse sprouting a bloom of blood, the contents of her handbag spilled out over the loamy ground. Her mouth dropped open in an horrific grimace and her lips were beginning to turn blue. Her hair, once so perfectly coiffured, now lay in a tangled mess, and there was a thick red-black liquid oozing from her head. Most of her long, manicured nails had broken or splintered, and her hands were dirty and covered in scratches. A sloe worm slithered over her ankle; a black beetle scuttled into her ear; a slug left a silver trail over her left shoulder as it edged its way closer and closer toward her mouth.

It was impossible. I would have to think of some other way.

Then it came to me. Just as I had told the staff of Winterborne Abbey more or less the truth, I would also tell Lavinia exactly what I was doing here. Pre-empting her was the only way forward. It was the best solution to the problem. I would call her, tell her that I was down here, express my astonishment that she was due to arrive the next day, and suggest we meet up. Then she would be the one doing the squirming. She would be the one who felt guilty, not me. I left the secretary's office and walked outside. I took out my mobile, relieved that I had a signal. I found her London number in my notebook and dialed. Four rings. No answer. Click. The answering machine. I didn't leave a message but tried her on her mobile. As she picked up the phone, the line crackled and hissed.

"Hello?" I said, shouting into the phone.

"Sorry, I'm driving. Can you just wait for a moment?"

I heard the noise of traffic zooming past her and the loud, screeching brakes of a lorry. She was obviously on her way down here. I wondered how far away she was.

"Sorry about that. I just had to pull over."

"Hello, it's Adam Woods here."

"Oh, hello, Adam. Look, it's a terrible line. Can I call you back?"

"Yes, of course."

"I'll call you back on this number."

A minute or so later, my phone rang. I checked to see that no one could hear me before answering. The line was much clearer.

"Adam?"

"Yes, hello, Lavinia. How are you?"

"I'm fine actually. Just taking my life into my hands by driving on the M3. How are you?"

"Very well, thanks. I'm down in Dorset at the moment, just doing some work for Mr. Crace, getting some details for him about his old school, Winterborne Abbey."

I could hear the shock in her voice.

"How extraordinary," she said.

Obviously she didn't know what to say.

"Sorry?"

"J-just that I can't quite believe it. That's exactly where I'm

driving to. I have an appointment with the headmaster tomorrow."

She had opted to play the honesty card as well.

"How incredible," I said, pretending to sound surprised.
"What are you coming down for?"

There was a slight pause on the other end of the line.

"W-well, I thought it would be helpful for everyone to get as
much information about Mr. Crace's life as possible. Just to speed
up the process a little."

"I see," I said.

"Obviously it was information I was going to pass on to you so
you could it take back to Mr. Crace."

"That's just wonderful," I said. "Since we're both down here,
we should meet up at some point."

"Yes, I would like that very much. But what are you doing in
Dorset?"

"Just a spot of research for Mr. Crace," I said. "As you know,
Mr. Crace is a terribly secretive man, and he gave me express instructions not to reveal my true intentions. He told me to come
down here and try to find out details about his school without
anyone knowing the real reason. He told me he didn't even want
them to know he was alive. So I've had to go to the slightly ridiculous lengths of pretending I'm an art history student doing research on the abbey so as to gain access to some of the records."

"Really?" She sounded intrigued, but was there a note of suspicion in her voice?

"Yes. I know it sounds a little far-fetched, but Mr. Crace insisted. He came up with the plan himself: how old boys and staff
members view the objects displayed in the abbey, their personal
connections to the relics and the statuary. I've had a hard time
pulling it off, I can tell you."

"I don't doubt it," she said.

"Look, I'd love to carry on talking, but I've got another appointment in a couple of minutes. Where are you staying?"

"At the Hazelbury Manor Hotel. Do you have the number there?"

"No, but I can easily get it."

"Why don't you call me there tomorrow after breakfast?"

"That sounds fine. I'll do that."

I made my way back to the secretary's office, but Mrs. Barwick was not there. It was obviously taking her longer than she had thought to locate the old records. As I waited, I looked around the room. The office was the very picture of efficiency, with everything neatly filed away in clearly labeled cabinets. There was a shelf of books, including a dictionary, the Bible, a thesaurus, a set of encyclopedias, and a well-thumbed *Who's Who*. The walls were lined with faded photographs of the school, etchings of the abbey and a few framed typed letters from well-known old boys. Although I spotted an actor, a television presenter and quite a few famous sportsmen, there was no sign of Crace's name.

I heard the door open and turned to see Mrs. Barwick there.

"You've had your fair share of celebrities," I said, smiling, "all with good things to say about the school."

She did not reply. Her eyes, so bright and sparkling a few moments ago, looked stern and serious. She looked older, sadder. In her hand she clutched a piece of paper.

"I've got the names you wanted," she said, finally.

"Oh, good."

"Well, I'm afraid it's not all good news."

"What do you mean?"

She sat down at her desk and placed the piece of paper before her.

"I'll show you," she said, gesturing me over.

I looked over her shoulder at the paper on which I had written the list of names that I had requested. By each of the names, Mrs. Barwick had scribbled little notes in pencil, but her handwriting was so small that I could not read her annotations.

"Look," she said, running her finger down the paper. "I've got the addresses for these old boys. Greason, Downing, Simmons, Cooper-Lewis, Alderman, Jones, and Booth-Clibborn."

They were the names I had picked out at random.

"Levenson you already know about, so that's good. But Miss Chaning, I'm afraid, has left no forwarding address, so we've no contact for her. And as for the rest, I'm sorry to tell you—I really don't know how best to say this—well, it's just that Matthew Knowles, Timothy Fletcher, and David Ward are . . . well, they all passed away some time ago."

"Are you certain?"

"Yes, it's all there in their records."

"When did they die?"

"All at different ages." She looked closely at her pencil notes on the paper. The three names had little crosses next to them. "Mr. Knowles in 1970, Mr. Fletcher in 1982 and Mr. Ward in 1973."

"All of them so young," I said. "Did the records tell you how they died?"

"No, I'm afraid not."

"Yes, it is bad news." I started to think out loud. "I wonder what happened to them."

"God only knows," said Mrs. Barwick. "But whatever happened, it doesn't much help your research, does it?"

As I turned to go, the secretary said she would just check the answering machine in case Levenson had called. He had, obviously during the few moments while I had been speaking to Lavinia. Although he said he probably would not have much to contribute, he suggested meeting outside the abbey in twenty minutes.

✛⟩══⟨✛

Adrian Levenson was a physically commanding man even though he was in his mid- to late fifties. Tall, at least six feet two, with broad shoulders, he looked exactly like what he was: a former rugby player turned games master. He was still strikingly handsome, with a rugged, lined face, a squat nose that looked like it had been broken several times, unreadable dark eyes, and a full head of silver-gray hair. As we greeted one another, I noticed that his hands were almost twice the size of mine; his grip left my fingers aching and weak.

"How do you do, Mr. . . . ?"

"Woods. Adam Woods."

"That's right. Good to meet you. I'm Adrian."

He was superficially extremely friendly, but I'm sure the bully that Chris had described in his diary was not far from the surface. I would have to be careful.

"As you can see," he said, gesturing at his blue jogging pants smeared with mud, "I'm very much an outdoors man. Always have been. Never really interested in indoor pursuits. Spent as little time in there as possible."

"It will be interesting to hear your perspective. I'm trying to gather together as many different opinions as possible."

"And what did you say it was for?"

"It's for a thesis I'm writing for my art history course. About objects on display—"

"Probably all above my head, I'm afraid," he said, wiping his dripping nose with the back of his hand. "Give me the thrill of a game any day. Doesn't matter what it is—football, rugger, cricket, even rounders with the younger boys. Enjoy them all. Do you play?"

When I told him I did not, he looked slightly disappointed in me, as if I had let him down.

"Never mind. Anyway, what do you want me to do?"

"I thought we could just start with a walk around the inside of the abbey. I know you told me you never really paid much attention, but seeing a few of the things may help jog your memory or whatever."

"Very well," he said, wiping his mud-encrusted running shoes on the coir mat. "But I warn you, I don't think I'll be of much help."

We stepped inside the cold, damp building, silent except for the sound of our breathing. The weak, gray light cast the abbey in an eerie gloom.

"To be honest, I only come in here when there's a three-line whip that comes from the headmaster's office," said Levenson. "Never liked it, even as a boy. It gives me the creeps."

I took out my notepad and started to scribble down snatches of our conversation. I had to make it appear as though I was interested in his thoughts on the building and its collection. We walked through the archway, beneath the organ loft, and stopped by the treasury. I pressed the light to illuminate the glass panel.

"Do you remember any of these relics having any particular impact on you when you were a pupil here?"

Levenson looked down at the collection, the ivory triptych, the disintegrated cross, the pewter chalice, the ancient book, as if he'd never seen the objects before.

"As I said, not much of an impact, I'm afraid. I was—still am, most probably—a terrible ignoramus when it comes to things like this. Sorry."

"Don't worry, it's no problem."

When the timer turned the light off, I didn't bother to press it again. Instead, we carried on walking down toward the altar into the north aisle. As we turned to face the statue of the woman holding half a skull, Levenson appeared to shiver.

"That's the only thing that really made an impression," he said, pointing at the sculpture. "That woman and that godforsaken skull. When I first arrived, some of the older boys used to talk about the curse of the screaming skull, how it was the skull of her lover, a man who had been murdered by her husband. All a complete fabrication, of course, but when you're twelve and away from your parents, you believe any nonsense like that. Don't get me wrong, I thought I was pretty tough, but that's one thing that used to give me nightmares. Not much use to you, though, eh?"

"No, no," I said, busy scribbling away, "it's fascinating. Exactly the kind of thing that I can use."

"Really?"

"Yes," I said. "Good personal detail. Do you know if it affected any of your school friends in the same sort of way?"

"Oh, it must have. It was one of those stories boys would start to tell after lights-out."

"And are you in touch with many of the boys you met then?" I said, turning to a page in my notebook where I had listed the names of the boys in the debating society.

"No, not that many. A shame, really."

"What about . . . let's see . . . Timothy Fletcher? David Ward?"

"No," he said, blinking.

"Matthew Knowles?"

He shook his head.

"Jameson?"

"No," he said, trying to keep his voice under control.

I took a deep breath, still pretending to read the names from my book, as though I had selected them completely at random.

"Christopher Davidson?"

His dark eyes seemed a shade darker. His fleshy lower lip twitched like a fat worm exposed to air.

"And what about Gordon . . . Gordon Cra—?"

As his hand whipped up onto my throat, I dropped my notebook onto the cold, hard floor. He pushed me against the statue with such force that my head hit the marble with an audible crack. His black eyes burned into mine with a fierce violence.

"I don't know what kind of game—"

"You may have bullied those boys in the past," I blurted out, suddenly amazed by my own forthrightness, "but you're not going to bully me."

His grip tightened around my neck.

"I know what you did to Christopher Davidson."

He seemed to freeze.

"Drove him to his death."

His mouth gaped open.

"And his father before him."

"What are you talking about?" he said, quietly, his grip on me relaxing slightly.

"Chris's diary. I've read it all. It's all there. All about what you did."

"I don't know what you are talking about," he said, but it was obvious my words had resonated within him.

As he let go of me, this great hulk of a man looked as if he were shrinking before my eyes. His shoulders began to droop down, his chest collapsed in on itself, and his legs appeared like they were about to give way. I had knocked the fight out of him, just with a series of little words, a couple of sentences about something that had happened years ago.

"Look, you've got it all wrong."

"Not according to the evidence Chris left behind. And God knows what you must have done to those other boys."

"No," he shouted, but then started to speak quietly. "No, really, it's not how you think—at all."

At that moment we heard the door to the abbey bang shut and footsteps whisper across the floor.

"We can't talk here," he said, looking around. "I haven't been up to the tower in ages, but I think I have a key. It will be quiet up there, private. We won't be disturbed."

From the pocket of his sweatpants he took out a large bunch of keys and sorted through them until he had found a small key, similar to the one Crace had used to open his letter box.

"Yes, here it is," he said. "Follow me."

I picked up my notebook and walked behind him to the organ loft. By the treasury he pulled back an old black velvet curtain to reveal a narrow stone staircase, which was covered by a latticework wooden door secured by a padlock. Using the key, Levenson unlocked the flimsy door, no more than a delicate crisscross of wooden slats, and started to climb the stairs that led to the tower.

Hesitantly, I started to follow him up the staircase, my fingers brushing against the rough stone and centuries' worth of accumulated dirt. A few twists of the stairway and the light from below faded away; a few more and it was almost pitch black.

"Don't worry, just follow me," said Levenson.

I guided myself up using my hands, occasionally grazing my knuckles against the hard stone. I heard something creak and the sound of Levenson breathing heavily as he tried to push himself through a trap door. From the top of the staircase I saw a slash of weak, gray light and felt the chill of a cold wind.

"This way," he said. "Here, let me help."

He stretched out his enormous, callus-hardened hand and pulled me upward, through the trap door and out onto the roof. He slumped back, breathing heavily. I stood up and walked along the roof, taking smaller and smaller steps as I neared the edge. The ground down below jumped up to meet me, and I stood back quickly, feeling dizzy. In the distance, I saw the tree-covered hills colored by the weak sheen of the last rays of the sun; the path from the school to the village clearly etched into the landscape; and, nearer to me, a few groups of boys slowly moving on the grass like black worms spilling their way across a stretch of lawn.

"Before we start, I think you owe me an explanation," said Levenson. "Do you want to tell me what you're really up to?"

"What do you mean?"

"It's obvious you're not really interested in all that shit about art."

I didn't say anything for a couple of moments. Then I decided to take a gamble and tell him the truth.

"Very well," I said. "I'm writing a book about Crace, a kind of biography."

"I see," said Levenson. "I'd be extremely careful if I were you."

"Why?"

"Haven't you looked in a mirror?"

I didn't respond.

"Isn't it obvious? I mean, you and Davidson could be brothers."

"What of it? Probably just a coincidence."

"I don't think so, somehow. I'd just watch your back if I were you. Seems odd to me."

"I'll bear that in mind, Mr. Levenson. But I don't think you need worry yourself."

He took a deep breath. "Crace . . . you think he merits a book then, do you?"

"By all accounts it seems he led what could be described as quite a colorful life."

"Indeed he has," he said, snorting with derision.

"But I'd appreciate it if you kept the fact that I'm writing a book to yourself. It's not something I would like to get around, just as I'm sure you wouldn't like the headmaster and parents to know about your past."

"I had nothing to do with those boys' deaths," he said, his anger rising again. "Absolutely nothing. All right, I did bully Davidson, the stupid sissy that he was, and his pathetic father. But how did I know he suffered from depression? To me—and to the rest of the boys—he was just another inadequate, bumbling teacher who couldn't control a classroom. I wasn't the only one."

"So you are admitting to bullying."

"Well, yes, but only when I was a boy. It was stupid, and silly, and immature, and yes, of course I regret it now. You can't imagine what it was like when I heard that he, Mr. Davidson, had killed himself. The headmaster told everyone it was a shooting accident gone wrong, but of course, Jameson and I knew the truth. Despite what you may think of me—despite what Davidson might have written in his diary—I'm not a complete monster. I went to pieces afterward. Yes, I tried to cover it up, probably played the tough man even more, but inside I was falling apart, especially when I . . . I . . . "

Levenson coughed to clear his throat.

"Yes?"

"When I remembered that he'd seen us, Jameson and I, carrying that effigy, that Guy Fawkes, to the caretaker's office. He came out of the music room and saw . . . saw it dressed in his jacket. We'd taken it from the back of his chair when he wasn't looking. We thought he was going to go mad, start shouting, but he just went quietly back inside and closed the door. We thought that was hilarious and couldn't stop laughing, congratulated ourselves on getting away with a fine prank, until, of course, we learned what had happened later."

He fell silent and looked down, ashamed of himself.

"I see," I said.

"And after that I really did make an effort to be nice to Davidson. Well, not exactly nice, but at least not like I was before. I mean, although I wasn't keen to begin with, we worked together on the debating society—"

"Exactly. Now, that's what I'd like to ask you about."

"Okay."

"You did know that Crace got the idea, the idea for his novel, from you?"

"What do you mean?"

"The fact that, as far as Chris describes it in his diary, you were in the classroom talking about, I think it was democracy, wasn't it?" My words flooded out, almost too quickly to enunciate properly. "It must have been your first time there, after Crace had spotted you trying to bully Chris in the corridor, and you said you had an idea for a good debate, that you should put forward the motion that you should kill the headmaster. And Crace heard you and wrote it down in his notebook, and that idea formed the basis of his book."

He looked astonished, taken aback.

"I can't really remember one way or the other; it was so long ago. But if that was the case, good luck to him. At least he used me for that and not for anything else."

"Sorry?"

I knew what he was going to say.

"The reason why those boys killed themselves, the reason why Davidson killed himself—it was all the same thing. I'm telling you this for your information. What you do with it is up to you. You can put it in your book or whatever, I don't care. Just as long as you don't attach my name to it. Okay?"

I nodded.

"Right, then," he said, taking a deep breath. "He was messing about with them. You know, abuse or whatever you want to call it. He chose his boys carefully. Always a particular type, sensitive, I suppose you'd say. Obviously knew better than to try it on with me, though."

Everything was beginning to make sense—awful, horrible sense.

"And you knew this at the time?"

"Oh, God no," he said. "Of course not. None of us did. Only later, much later."

"How did you find out?"

"It was Knowles. He told me about what had been going on, just before . . . before he died. We had kept in touch after leaving school. He'd gone off to university, and I was trying to make it as a rugby player. Too many injuries, not enough breaks, whatever the reason, I never made it, which is why I ended up back here. Anyway, we met up at a pub in London, he got terribly drunk, both of us did, and it all spilled out. I thought he was joking at first, but he was in a flood of tears, like he was having some kind of breakdown. It was terrible to see him like that. He said he had tried to forget about it, and seemed to have done so for a few years, but he'd just started going out with a girl at college and, well, the memories of it all came flooding back. I tried to help as best I could, but soon after that, that's when I heard that he'd . . . he'd killed himself."

"How awful," I said.

"Yes, it was. And all because of that bastard Crace."

He spat out the name as if it were poison.

"After Knowles's death, I didn't think anything more about it until I heard that Ward had killed himself and then Fletcher nearly ten years after that," he said. "It was too much of a coincidence. All the boys were in Crace's fucking debating society. I can't believe none of us knew. Going on under our fucking noses, and none of us knew."

"How did it start? With Knowles, I mean."

"He told me that Crace had treated him as though he was his favorite pupil, encouraging him in his studies, giving him extra tutorials, promising him great things, that he would go to Oxford, how one day he might grow up to be a famous writer—all that crap! But Crace's real intentions, they were different.

"After Davidson died, Knowles said he had become increasingly depressed. The two, Chris and Matthew, had become close friends in the debating society, but Knowles had had no idea that anything was going on between Davidson and Crace. That night, when he was drunk and he told me all of this, he had said the worst thing was the fact he no longer felt special. Knowles hated Crace for what he had done to him, but he told me that he loathed him even more for betraying him. Fucking sick, isn't it?"

"Did he tell you anything about Chris? About how he had died?"

"No, not really, except for the fact that after the funeral, Knowles went to see Davidson's mother. During the course of the conversation, he asked her whether she had any idea why her son might have wanted to kill himself. She was obviously distressed—

God only knows, the poor woman—and didn't want to talk about it. But she kept repeating one phrase: 'His life wasn't his own anymore.' The fucking pervert! I mean, I know I always thought Davidson was a bit wet, but to do that to him . . . "

He walked over to the parapet, crouched down, and, as if to cleanse his mouth, spat into the darkness.

"I think I've said enough." He heaved himself up and turned to go. "And remember what I said—watch yourself."

***

I felt the pain the moment the back of my head came in contact with the water. I ignored the throbbing and the stinging, and eased myself down into the bath. The noise of the pub downstairs, the tinkling of the glasses and the occasional boisterous cry of one of the customers, disappeared as I slipped underwater. I closed my eyes and heard my heart beating inside me, a fast, irregular rhythm.

I had started off if not exactly liking Crace, then at least feeling able to be amused by him. I respected his accomplishments, admired him for the purity of his vision, and looked up to him for his abilities to forge a strong, definite identity for himself, even if it was one that was slightly peculiar. But now—what did I think of him now? The revelation that he had taken me in because I had reminded him of Chris was one thing; finding out that he had been a serial abuser of boys something quite different. The thought that I had lived with him over the summer turned my stomach. The idea of him looking at me, his lazy, reptilian eyes preying on me, was disgusting. The way he touched me, his bony, etiolated fingers running up and down my neck, caressing my shoulder. Levenson was right. Crace was a fucking pervert.

An image of Crace and a young blond boy flashed into my mind. Crace had a grip on the boy's shoulder and was forcing him to spread his legs wide. The boy attempted to scream, but Crace clasped his hand over his mouth. I looked into the boy's face. He looked like me.

I pushed myself up and out of the water, gasping for air. It had been a daydream, nothing more than that, but it had seemed so real. I quickly soaped and rinsed myself, and then washed my hair. As I patted myself dry, using one of the damp towels the landlady had given me, I noticed there was a sheen of gray gossamer-like hairs covering my skin. The towel was completely covered in dog hair. The comic surreality of it all lightened my mood for a few moments until I remembered that I had, in fact, little to laugh about. I was writing a biography of someone who did not know what I was up to, someone who could cause a lot of trouble for me if he ever found out. My subject was not only mentally unhinged but a criminal, responsible for the abuse and subsequent deaths of a number of his former pupils. And the most daunting prospect of all? I was due back at his palazzo in a matter of days.

I sat down on the edge of the bath, feeling weak and anxious once more. What would happen if I gave it all up? After all, so far my research had given me nothing but trouble. I had found myself in a number of situations that had necessitated a great deal of quick thinking on my part so as to prevent exposure. I thought about the little episode with Shaw and remembered what I had so nearly done. I knew my history, my own potential, and realized that I had to avoid any form of stress. And yet what was I doing?

If I jacked it all in, I would be free of Crace and his dirty, sick little mind forever. I wouldn't have to worry about worming out more connections between his life and work. I could forget about Lavinia Maddon and her powerful publishing connections. I needn't concern myself about waiting for Crace to die before I could publish my book—because there would be no book.

No book? I just couldn't imagine it. I was a writer, after all. That's what I had always wanted to be ever since I was a child. It's what I felt inside. It was what I *was*. If I stopped, it would be like I had never existed. I had to carry on. I had a duty to tell the truth about what Crace had done to those boys. And I had a responsibility to myself.

⊹⊱══⊰⊹

I called Lavinia after breakfast and arranged to meet her after her appointment with the headmaster. I could tell she was keen to get off the phone, but I liked the idea of stringing out the conversation a little longer.

"I still can't get over it—you being down here at the same time as me," I said. "I mean, it's such an unbelievable coincidence, don't you think?"

"Yes, it is rather—" she said.

"Fascinating, yes. I wonder what your interview with the headmaster will throw up."

"Yes, I'll tell you all about it when I see you later. I'd better—"

"I'm sure Mr. Crace will be impressed by your diligence."

"What do you mean?"

"When I tell him that you've been doing all this background research just so you could help me. I mean, it's rather like you've been doing my job for me."

"I did want to try to be as helpful as possible."

"Very helpful indeed. Mr. Crace will be delighted. And so kind of you to volunteer all that material for Mr. Crace as well, all those documents you've unearthed. When I go back, I guarantee he'll think he's made the right choice in you, the perfect biographer."

"Yes, thank you, I—"

"Do you happen to have them with you?"

"Have what with me?"

"The material relating to Mr. Crace that we spoke about."

"I do have some of the documents, a few notes. I was looking at them this morning, here in my hotel room."

"Wonderful. Actually—just a thought—wouldn't it be better if I met you at the hotel after your meeting with the headmaster?"

"Well, I—"

"It's just that I thought it would be easier for you show me what you've got. Save you from lugging everything over to the school."

"Oh, I see—"

I enjoyed listening to her squirm. If only I could have seen her face as she wrestled with the situation.

"I mean, if you'd rather not . . . if you've changed your mind, I can easily tell—"

"No, no. That's fine. It's just you caught me off guard. I didn't realize you wanted them quite so soon. I haven't copied any of them yet, you see."

"Never mind. I could have a quick look at them and take some of them away for copying. There's no reason why you should have to bear the expense. Mr. Crace would be happy to pay for it. After all, you are doing him a great favor."

There was a pause at the end of the line.

"Yes, very well," she said, sounding flustered. "Sorry, I really do have to go."

"So I'll see you at Hazelbury Manor, then, at one thirty. Perhaps we could have lunch? Mr. Crace's treat."

"Yes, yes. See you then. Good-bye."

I spent the morning writing in my notebook and making myself presentable for lunch with Lavinia. I managed to persuade the landlady to lend me an iron and ironing board so that I could press my linen jacket. I polished my shoes using some paper towels I had found in the bathroom, put on a clean white shirt and ran some grease through my hair. The area at the back of my head was still tender and a scab had started to form over the cut, but in the mirror I looked presentable and respectable, the very picture of a young, up-and-coming writer.

The landlady told me it usually took half an hour for taxis to arrive, so at half past twelve I ordered one to take me to Hazelbury Manor. I stepped out of the pub into bright sunlight; it was one of those gloriously bright, crisp autumn days. Even though everything was dying back and the leaves were rotting on the ground, it seemed as though there was a prospect of a new beginning. I had a sense that I could do anything I wanted and that nothing could stand in my way. Despite all my doubts, fears and anxieties, I was certain I was doing the right thing.

The taxi took me past the school and across a stretch of open countryside that had views down into a vale. Through the enormous rhododendron bushes that lined the meandering drive, I could glimpse a white building in the distance. The taxi turned a corner onto a more direct approach, and the house—a splendid classical villa with a later, probably Victorian, addition at the back—came into view. As the car drew nearer to the hotel, I saw, through the tall front windows, a number of well-heeled guests drinking coffee in the morning room. The car park was full of BMWs, Mercedes, Saabs and Audis; I even spotted a bottle-green Bentley. It was certainly rather different from my establishment with its low ceilings, clusters of dead flies, cobwebs and dog-haired towels. I had to give her credit. Lavinia certainly knew how to live in style.

How had she made all her money, I wondered. Not just from writing, surely. Was she married? Perhaps she had a rich lover? A wealthy investment banker or the head of a national museum? Had she any children? Fiercely intelligent young men and women, my age, I suppose, who after Oxbridge had easily established themselves in good jobs, or perhaps more bohemian types who had shunned material gains to develop their talents as musicians, painters, and photographers. Of course, with Lavinia's help, they could afford to do whatever they pleased.

I realized how little I actually knew about her. That would have to change.

I paid the taxi driver and walked up the gravel path to the front door, on either side of which, in pots, stood two immaculately manicured bay trees. I opened the door into the hallway, which was paneled in wood, and walked across to the reception desk, where a pretty, fresh-faced blond girl sat reading a magazine.

"Hello, sir. Good morning," she said, looking up. "Can I help you?"

"Yes, I'm here to meet one of your guests, but I think"—I said, looking at my watch—"I'm a little early."

"What's the name, please?"

"Maddon. Lavinia Maddon."

She smiled and said she would ring the room. There was no answer. Lavinia would still be with the headmaster or perhaps driving back from the school. I wondered what Mr. Peters had said to her. Would he have mentioned me at all? Or would she? As long as Levenson kept his mouth shut and didn't say anything to either of them, I would be safe. And it didn't appear that he wanted to say anything more on the subject.

"I'm afraid she's not in her room, sir. Can I leave a message for her?"

"I'd hoped we could have lunch here."

"Yes, of course. I'll ring through to the restaurant and book a table. For two?"

"Yes, please, for two."

She told me I could wait in the bar. She would tell Ms. Maddon where to find me as soon as she arrived back at the hotel.

At the bar, which was quite busy with what looked like a group of sales or advertising reps, I ordered a glass of Sancerre from the barman and took a seat by the window. I was confident about my meeting with Lavinia, but a little extra help wouldn't hurt. I took a sip of the dry, chalky tasting wine and then another before gulping down the whole glass. I asked the barman for another. I was halfway through that glass when Lavinia walked in.

"Lavinia, hello, so good to see you again," I said, standing up and stretching out my hand.

"Yes, you too," she said.

"Let me get you a drink. What would you like?"

"Well, it is a little early for—"

"We are here to celebrate, though, aren't we?"

"What do you mean?"

"I'll get you a drink and then I'll tell you."

She looked a little nervous, smiled weakly and finally relented.

"I'll have a glass of white wine as well, please."

At the bar I ordered a bottle of Sancerre. On the way back from the bar, I stopped and looked at Lavinia. Everything about her was so perfect. Her dark hair was shiny and neat, her gray woolen skirt and jacket obviously well cut and expensive. As I came up behind her, I saw her writing in a small, black leather notebook with a tiny gold pencil, the same notebook she had used when she had spoken to Jennifer Johnson at Crace's old house in Bloomsbury. I squinted to see if I could make out anything, but her handwriting was so small that it was impossible.

"Drinks are on the way," I said, sitting down and smiling. "Did you have a profitable meeting with Mr. Peters?"

"Oh yes, quite interesting," she said, putting her notebook away in her black leather handbag. "Of course, he didn't know Mr. Crace personally, but he gave me some good information on what the school was like back then and pointed me in the direction of some people I could talk to, people who might have known Mr. Crace."

"Really?" I had to hide my astonishment. "Such as?"

"Former teachers, old boys and the like. But I'm sure you know just as much as I do."

What did she mean? Had she found me out?

"Funnily enough, Mr. Crace has kept me rather in the dark. He is quite a mystery, even to me."

"I can't quite believe that," she said, laughing. "You have lived with him, after all."

"I know, but—"

Just at that moment, the waiter came over with the wine and two fresh glasses. He uncorked it and asked if I would like to taste it.

"Please, Lavinia, will you?"

The waiter handed her a glass with a little of the wine. She swirled the glass in her hand and then placed it beneath her nose, her nostrils flaring and constricting a couple of times.

"Yes, very nice, thank you," she said, placing the glass back down on the table. "You said there was something to celebrate?"

"Of course, yes, there is," I said. "I spoke to Gordon . . . to Mr. Crace this morning and filled him in on you a little more. And he's definitely come to a decision. You've got the job."

Her frostiness melted away instantly.

"Really?" she said, smiling. "Well, that *is* something to celebrate."

I held out my glass.

"So here—cheers. This is to you and your book. I'm sure it will be fascinating. Cheers."

"Cheers. And thank you for all your help. I really couldn't have done it without your help. You've been absolutely invaluable."

"No, I'm only pleased that Mr. Crace has found the right person for the job."

Lavinia was in high spirits as we walked into lunch, telling me how relieved she was that a decision had been finally made and relating to me just how stressful the last few months had been. When she had received my initial letter, she had seriously considered giving up the book. But now her publishers would be pleased, she said. She couldn't wait to tell them.

"I think it's best that if you do say anything, please ask them to keep the project confidential for the time being," I said, as we took our places in the restaurant. "As you know, Mr. Crace is not the kind of man who would like this to be greeted with a fanfare and trumpets. In fact, he could do a sudden *voltafaccia* if it got out or if he thought it was being talked about in the press."

"Yes, I understand," said Lavinia, placing the starched napkin over her lap.

The waiter refilled our glasses, another good opportunity, I thought, for another toast.

"To your secret project," I said.

She laughed girlishly, the fine lines around her eyes crinkling like crepe paper.

"To *our* secret project," she said, correcting me. "And thank you once more."

"Have you thought of a title yet?"

"It's in the early days yet, but I have toyed with a few."

"Oh, really? Such as?"

She paused, hesitant.

"One I do rather like is *The Silent Man,* after Jonson's *Epicene,* because, as you know, I am keen on exploring the idea of literary and commercial success and then subsequent silence. And also, of course, it's a reference to Malcolm's book on—"

"That's wonderful," I said. "I'm sure Mr. Crace would like that too."

"But please don't tell him. I wouldn't want him to think I was running before I could walk, if you see what I mean."

"No, of course not. I promise to keep it just between us."

The waiter came over to take our order. Lavinia decided to have the smoked trout and horseradish sauce and then the sea bass, and I went for the wood pigeon with beetroot followed by the lamb shank with beans. We ordered another bottle of wine.

"How long have you been a writer?" I asked.

"Oh, gosh, over thirty years now, it must be. What a thought."

"How did you start? I mean, how did you get into it?"

"After university I took a job on the literary pages of a Sunday newspaper. While I was there I wrote my first book, a biography of Constance Fenimore Woolson, which did very well and won a couple of prizes. Anyway, that enabled me to leave and write full-time."

"That was very fortunate."

"Yes, it was, rather. I always say it's the only thing I'm fit for."

"I noticed on the way back from the bar that you keep a notebook."

"Yes, I do."

"Is that a diary or—"

"It's not really what you'd call a diary, nor is it a proper writer's notebook. More just a reminder of whom I've met and occasionally what they've said. First impressions, feelings, physical descriptions, those kinds of things. Aspects of a person you cannot capture on an audiotape."

"Yes, I see. What a good idea. Do you carry it with you everywhere?"

"Yes, I suppose I do. It's become second-nature now. Scribbling things down here and there."

I took another couple of gulps of wine and leaned forward toward her.

"So you'd write about meeting me, would you?"

She smiled, her gray eyes sparkling.

"I might, if I felt so inspired."

"I see," I said. "And what might you say?"

"I'm afraid, Mr. Woods," she said in a mock-pompous tone, "that would be between my notebook and me. Strictly for my eyes only."

"You mean you don't even show your husband?"

She laughed.

"Especially not my husband!" she said as the waiter placed a plate in front of her. "The truth of the matter is that Ian and I have not really spoken since our divorce seven years ago. Silly really, after bringing up two children together, all those years, but—"

"I see. And is there anyone else? Anyone you—"

"If you're trying to find out whether I'm single, well, the answer is yes. And resolutely, determinedly so. And happy with it. And what about you?"

"Me?"

"Yes."

"I did have a girlfriend—Eliza—at college, but that ended on a bit of a sour note."

"I'm sorry."

"No, I'm over her now, as they say. Got her out of my system."

"Good. Good for you."

Lavinia started to laugh again, forcing her to bring her napkin to her mouth.

"I'm sorry, sorry, excuse me," she managed to say, waving her hand in the air in a gesture of apology.

"What is it?"

"No, I couldn't, really. Just me being ridiculous."

"No, what?"

"Oh, very well. But you promise you won't hold it against me?"

"Yes."

"Promise?"

"Yes."

"Just that I thought—I don't know why—that you were, you know, you and Mr. Crace were—"

"What?"

"That you were . . . together."

"What?"

"It was just a stupid thought, a whimsy, nothing more."

"What on earth made you think that?"

"I don't know. My impression is that you seem to be so close to him, that you hold him very dear. And little things, like when you talk about him, your eyes light up. I haven't offended you, have I?"

"No, of course not. Don't be so silly."

"Really? You would tell me if I had, wouldn't you?"

"Yes, I would. But after what you've just said, I could do with another drink."

I smiled, but I was seething inside. What had made her say that? Why did everyone seem to think that?

"If you don't mind me asking, how did you become friendly with Gordon Crace?"

"I rather fell into the job by accident," I said, cutting into the wood pigeon. "My original job—teaching English to the teenage son of an Italian family—fell through after he got himself in a little hot water. I wanted to stay on in Venice, because I had this mad idea of wanting to write a novel partly set there. And so when the job with Mr. Crace came up, I took it. It seemed to suit my needs at the time."

"I see. I didn't realize you wrote."

"Well, the book is not going quite as planned."

⊢══•══⊣

After lunch, which I insisted on paying for, we took our coffee in the elegant morning room at the front of the house. Sunlight streamed through the grand windows, casting everything in a pale, golden glow. As I ran my fingers through my hair, I caught Lavinia gazing at me with a puzzled expression, her eyes almost squinting, her brows so knotted that a very definite line seemed to split her forehead in two. Then a moment later, her eyes widened ever so slightly and her mouth dropped open.

"I don't believe it," she whispered.

"Sorry?"

"No, it's just too ridiculous," she said as she continued to stare at me in bewilderment. "It can't be."

"I'm afraid you've lost me, rather."

I knew what she had seen.

"Why didn't I ever see it before?" she said.

"What?"

"Have you ever come across the name Christopher Davidson?"

"No," I said. "Should I have?"

"And you've never seen a photograph of him?"

"Not that I know of."

"Come with me," she said, placing her cup down on the table and standing up.

"Sorry?"

"Upstairs. I want to show you something."

She almost ran out of the room and up the wide, wooden staircase.

"Are you going to tell me what you're talking about?"

We walked down a corridor lined with prints of the house and Dorset landscapes.

"In a minute. I just want to show you something."

At the end of the corridor, she fumbled in her bag for her key.

"Come in," she said.

She threw her bag onto the large bed and walked across the room to the triple-mirrored dressing table. As I shut the door and followed her, joining her by the mirrors, our reflections looked back at us, a strange triptych. She started to search through a pile of papers, some of which were in plastic wallet files. So it was true—she had built up quite a substantial amount of material on Crace, documents that might prove very useful indeed.

"I know it's in here somewhere," she said, her brows furrowing once more.

"What are you looking for?"

"Here, I've got it," she said, holding up a copy of a black-and-white photograph. "Have you seen this before? Seen a picture of him before?"

"No. Why?"

"Can't you see?"

"See what?"

"You and him—that you could be twins."

I took the photograph from her hand and pretended to study it.

"I suppose there is some kind of superficial resemblance," I said.

"No, it's more than that. In a certain light, you look exactly the same. And when you ran your hand through your hair—"

"So what? Who is this?"

"It's Christopher Davidson. Gordon Crace's lover."

I did the best I could to look shocked.

"Oh my God," I said. "Yes, I see what you mean. But—"

"Exactly. Why did Gordon Crace choose you?"

"What happened to him, to this Christopher Davidson?"

"He died—committed suicide in 1967."

I didn't say anything, just continued to stare at the photograph.

"Do you think you're going to confront him with this?" she asked.

"I don't know," I said. "It does seem odd, unsettling."

"Yes, I can imagine," she said, biting the corner of her lip. "Do you feel he's been totally honest with you?"

"Come to think of it, no, I don't—especially after seeing this," I said, gesturing toward the photograph. "I can't quite get my head around it."

"I suggest you think it over," she said. "Give it some time."

I took a deep breath. I wanted to give her the impression I was thinking aloud.

"Even though it is very strange, I'm sure there has to be some logical explanation for this. There must be. And to be honest, I do have to go back to Venice anyway. I need to get on with my novel."

"Oh, really? So what will you do?"

"So, I'm going to return to Mr. Crace and, for the time being, not say anything at all."

"Are you really sure? I wouldn't want you to do it just for my sake."

"No, no, I'm totally confident that's the right thing to do. And I can't afford not to go back."

"And what will you say about Christopher Davidson?"

"Nothing. I'll keep it to myself. After all, Mr. Crace's private life is hardly my business, is it?"

Lavinia sat on the bed and ran her fingers through her hair.

"It does seem rather noble of you. I mean, if I were you, I'm not certain how I would have reacted."

"Best not to think about it, that's always been my philosophy," I said, looking around the room. "But as I am going to go back, I may as well as take those documents you were talking about."

"Oh yes, of course."

She stood up and went over to the dressing table once more, where she began rifling through her files.

"Which ones did you say would be helpful?"

"I think Mr. Crace said he was missing things like his birth certificate, genealogical records, material that he said would help fix his place in the world."

"You should be able to find a few things in here."

She passed me a plastic file bulging with pieces of paper.

Inside was a copy of his birth certificate, a large folded A3-size piece of paper on which someone had traced a spider's trail of a family tree and some typed notes about Crace's early life growing up in Edinburgh and the school where his father had once taught science.

"Thank you," I said. "Mr. Crace will find this very helpful indeed. And. . ."

"Yes?"

"Did you manage to lay your hands on the synopsis we talked about as well?"

"Oh, surely now Mr. Crace had made his decision, he won't be needing to see that any longer."

"I do think he would feel more comfortable if he did see a copy of it."

"I'm afraid I can't give it to you just at this moment."

"Never mind," I said. "I'll get this copied, and perhaps when I give the papers back to you, you could have it ready then. I'm conscious about not leaving Mr. Crace for too long."

"Very well," she said as she walked me to the door. "Thank you again for lunch, Adam. It's really very kind of you."

"No, it was my pleasure."

As I opened the door and turned to say good-bye, Lavinia stepped forward and kissed me, lightly, on the cheek. She smelt of honeysuckle, the same sickly sweet fragrance that Signora Gondolini had been wearing the first time I heard Crace's name.

"Thank you," she said. "For everything."

She thought she was so clever. She thought she had me wrapped around her little finger. I imagined her in her hotel room, sitting quietly and smiling to herself, enjoying the twinned sensations of anticipation and achievement. Not only did she believe that she was going to write Crace's biography, that she had been given approval by the reclusive author himself, but she had spotted the physical similarity between Christopher Davidson and myself and, as such, had started to understand that she had a much stranger—and even more salable—subject on her hands than she had previously thought.

All that rot about her not wanting to put me under any pressure—I wonder what she would have said if I'd completely freaked out and had refused to go back to Venice. It almost made me wish that I could play the scene again just so I could see her reaction.

The truth of the matter was that I had her exactly where I wanted her. She had given me everything I needed—dates, places, context, genealogical documents, all the basic research on Crace's early life that I could ever possibly want. Combined with my first-hand research, my day-to-day experience of living with Crace and Levenson's evidence, the book was beginning to take shape.

+≍≍+

Back at the pub, I cradled the clutch of pound coins in my sweaty palm, took a deep breath and dialed my old mobile number, making sure to prefix the call with 141 so he wouldn't know where I was calling from. I knew it might take a while for Crace to ease himself out of his chair, place his book or glass of wine down, find the mobile, pick it up and work out which button he had to press, so I let it ring. Finally there was click on the line, and I started to feed the phone with money.

"Buon giorno?"

"Hello, Gordon. It's me, Adam."

"Adam? My dear, dear boy, I'm afraid you'll have to speak up."

"How are you?" I shouted.

"Much better now that I've heard from you. I thought you had run off and deserted me."

"I'm sorry I haven't been in touch, just with everything to do with the funeral, you know. And my mother has been in a real state—tears, constantly questioning why, reliving memories from her childhood."

"I'm sorry to hear that. But yes, the death of a parent is an intimation of mortality."

I told him the details I had prepared earlier so as to give the invented experience a gloss of authenticity.

"Anyway, it's all over now," I added. "And I should be able to get the return flight I booked."

"Oh, thank God. It's been a nightmare without you."

"But you are all right, aren't you?"

"I have been feeling a little weak. Nothing major, so don't worry. Just off-color, that's all."

"But has the girl from the shop—what was her name . . . Lucia—has she been coming in to check on you like I'd arranged?"

"Oh yes, she's all right, nothing more than a little slip of a thing. Drops off the food and then goes. Actually, I'm pleased she doesn't want to hang around."

I was down to my last pound coin.

"Listen, Gordon, I'm going to have to go now, my money is running out."

"Oh, really?"

"I'm afraid so. But listen, I'll be back soon and we can catch up then."

"Well, I'm pleased everything has gone to order over there."

"Thank you."

"I know death hath ten thousand several doors for men to take their exits."

"What was that?"

The phone started to pip.

"Death—"

And we were cut off. I looked in my wallet for more change but had none. I could have gone to the bar to get some from the landlady, but I decided against it. As I went upstairs to my room and looked out of the window over the dark, brooding landscape, I thought of what Crace had just said to me. Death hath ten thousand several doors for men to take their exits. I wrote the sentence in my notebook, wondering where it was from. And then just the one word—death—over and over again.

⊹≒≒⊹

The next day was glorious, crisp and bright, and I spent the afternoon walking, turning the various options over and over in my head. On my return, as I made my way back to the village in the fading light, I passed a pretty, dark-haired girl walking a border collie. There was something about her that reminded me of Eliza. I smiled as she walked by, but she seemed nervous and on edge. The collie caught a whiff of something, the trace of a rabbit or the scent of another dog, and bounded over to a nearby tree. The girl called for the dog, but it ignored her. She tried shouting its name, Robbie, once more, but her voice cracked, betraying an undertone of fear. I looked around us; we were alone. Our eyes met and I knew, in that instant, that she was afraid of me. She turned her head and started to walk away. I felt like running up to her, putting my hands on her dark red velvet jacket, telling her that she had completely the wrong idea about me. I could almost feel her soft skin on the tips of my fingers, almost smell her sweet aroma.

"Sorry, I—" I said to myself as she walked away, her dog now running after her.

I watched as she moved into the distance, disappearing through the trees and into the forest beyond. If only I'd had a chance to stop and talk to her, who knows what might have happened?

I continued to walk into the village, thinking about Eliza. As I approached a couple of farm outbuildings, I saw a figure walking in the woods ahead of me. I spotted a flash of red among the glow of the autumnal russets. Was it the girl I had just seen? I caught another glimpse of the color and then it disappeared. I carried on through the trees, following the sound of someone ahead, and watched until the figure came into view. It was a man wearing a maroon V-neck sweater, holding the branch of a tree with his right hand as he tried to catch his breath. His face was obscured as he bent forward, his left hand resting on his knee, and he was wheezing. It was Shaw.

I was about to call out to him when he eased himself upward, took out his asthma spray, inhaled quickly, coughed a little and then started to move forward. He was walking in the wrong direction for his cottage. What was he up to? I kept well back, making sure I was hidden by the trees, and started to follow him.

A few minutes farther down the track that skirted along the edge of the wood and from where you could see the village, Shaw emerged at the corner of a recently ploughed field. I watched as he walked down the dirt path, near the fence, and over the stile at the end. Waiting until he had gone out of view, I ran across the field, making sure to hide myself as I approached its bottom. I crouched down by a hedgerow but peeked over it and saw him disappearing into what looked like the shell of a derelict house. I checked to see if anyone was looking and then walked down a track toward him. On one side was an old wooden gate with traces of blue paint visible underneath a mass of ivy that led down an overgrown garden; on the other, a small, two-story house that looked like it hadn't been lived in for years. There was no front door to speak of, merely a dirty wooden panel covered in traces of graffiti. Shaw disappeared inside. I waited, listening for Shaw's wheezing, but heard nothing, so after a couple of minutes, I put my head through the opening. There was nothing but darkness.

After a while my eyes became accustomed to the gloom. I thought I could make out the outlines of a table and some chairs; the floor was covered in newspaper and old beer cans, and the walls were marked with rings of damp and yet more graffiti.

I edged my way in, careful not to upset anything on the cluttered, rubbish-strewn floor. I heard something creak upstairs and then the sound of footsteps. I moved over to the far corner of the dark room, using my fingers to feel the way, until I came to the bottom of the stairs. I pressed my foot down lightly and slowly crept up, but as I stood on the second from the last step, the old wood emitted a painful groan, as deep and haunting as the last breaths of a dying man. My body froze, my breathing stopped. It was only a matter of seconds before Shaw came out from one of the rooms and found me on the stairs. I waited and waited, but nothing happened. I looked behind me and thought about how I should leave before he discovered me, but then, at more or less the same moment, it came to me: I realized exactly where I was. I was standing at the top of the stairs in Chris's old house, outside one of the rooms where he most probably wrote his diary. There was no way I was going to turn back now.

I moved slowly onto the top step and felt my way around the landing, guiding myself forward by the groove of an old picture rail. I felt the rail join the frame of a door and listened. Nothing. I moved on down the small corridor, around the corner, and stopped outside another door. In the space between the bottom of the door and the floorboards, I saw a dim glow, a light that seemed to be moving around the room. Shaw had a torch.

I heard the sound of something being moved, a piece of furniture perhaps, and then the creaking of some wood. Then nothing but Shaw's interminable wheezing, followed by a few snorts and coughs and footsteps. The light from his torch was getting brighter. He was walking toward me.

I stepped back into the darkness. As he opened the door, I knocked the torch from his hand. It fell onto the floorboards, casting shards of light up and around the dusty space and onto Shaw's frightened face before I grabbed it and shone it right into his eyes. The light bleached out any remaining life from his already ghastly face.

"What—" he said, gasping for breath.

"Do you want to tell me what you've been looking at in there? Or do you want me to beat it out of you?"

Shaw was so scared he couldn't say anything.

"Let's go and have a look, shall we?" I said, grabbing his puny hand and pulling him back into the room.

"There's n-nothing here," he said finally.

"I'm afraid I don't quite believe you," I said, shining the torch over the room.

An old dressing table, complete with a cracked, dirty mirror, was swathed in cobwebs; a small frame hung on the wall, its canvas so blackened it was impossible to make out the details of the image; and the walls, once covered in rose-print wallpaper, were streaked with what looked like burn marks.

"It's just my little retreat, somewhere where I like to get away from it all," said Shaw.

"If you're not careful, you'll end up here on a permanent vacation—under the fucking floorboards."

His eyes twitched. I looked over toward the dressing table, shining the torch in that direction.

"There's nothing under the floorboards. Nothing, I tell you."

"Well, Mr. Shaw, why don't you show me?"

I pushed him toward the other side of the room.

"This isn't the place you were telling me about, by any chance?" I said. "Or should I say, the one you didn't want to tell me about—where you kept Chris's diary."

"No, no," he shook his head. "I don't know you what you mean."

"Don't you think one thousand pounds is an awful lot of money, Mr. Shaw?"

"Pardon?"

"I said, don't you think one thousand pounds is an awful lot of money?"

"I suppose so."

"That's something we agree on."

"It's not that I'm not grateful, Mr. Woods, for the money. I am, I really am."

"I'm glad to hear it. But for one thousand pounds, I expect the truth. You wouldn't want to keep anything back from me, would you?"

"No, no, of course not."

"Good. So now show me."

The sound of his wheezing seemed to fill the dusty room.

"It's not good for me health."

"No, it's probably not. So the sooner you show me, the sooner both of us can get out of here."

"I was going to show you, honest I was."

"So you are telling me there's something else. Something you neglected to show me."

"Yes, but—"

"Good. Let's see it then."

"I was going to contact you tonight."

"Oh, really?"

"Only that as it is something very special I thought Mr. . . . Mr. Crace might want to place a . . . a separate price on it."

I laughed in his face.

"I don't think you're in much of a position to bargain, do you?"

He hesitated, unsure about what to do, his eyes darting back and forth between the dressing table and the floor.

"Very well."

He shuffled over to the dressing table, placed a hand on the darkened mirror to steady himself, and slowly lowered himself onto his knees. From his pocket he took out a screwdriver and with its edge prized up the side of one of the floorboards near the far skirting board. He pushed his hands into the space between the joists, moved whatever he was looking for closer to him, took up a neighboring floorboard, and brought out a shallow, rectangular biscuit tin with a faded image of the Queen on its top. He eased open its rusty lid, took out a couple of sheets of paper covered with writing, and then gestured for me to shine the torch onto the letter that lay in his hand.

"It's Chris's suicide note—to his mother," he said. "He wrote it the night before he died."

"Is there anything else in there? Let me see."

"No, nothing," he said. "That's it."

I shone the torch inside the box. He was telling the truth.

"Here you are," he said, passing it over to me. "At least Chris can rest in peace now."

He hadn't given a thought to Chris. All he was interested in was money, the dirty blackmailer. I took a deep breath as I remembered what had very nearly happened on my last visit. What a fool I had been. After all, if I'd gone through with it, I would never have found out about Chris's letter.

"Thank you," I said.

"At least Mr. Crace will keep everything—the diary, the note—in a safe place—out of prying eyes, so to speak."

"That's right," I said. I couldn't be bothered to tell him my plans. He'd learn about them soon enough.

"Maureen never forgave him for what he did, though."

"Yes, that was unforgivable. I may work for him, but I can't excuse him for that."

"Stealing his life like that."

"Yes, just awful. But best if we keep it to ourselves, don't you think? I'm sure Maureen wouldn't have wanted a scandal. Causing all that upset, the name of her son being dragged through the mud. And then there are the other families, as well, to consider."

Shaw wheezed, a puzzled expression creasing his white face.

"Other families?" he asked.

"Yes, the others."

"What do you mean?"

"Chris wasn't the only boy. He wasn't the only one . . . to be . . . to be abused by Crace. There were others as well."

"But Chris wasn't abused."

"What?"

"I'm not sure when they first, you know, got together, but Maureen told me that it was hard for her at the beginning, really hard. But she saw how happy it made Chris, how happy they were. She didn't like it, but she came to realize that if she wanted to keep Chris as her son, that's how it would have to be. But abused? No."

"So, you're saying that—"

"That's not why he did it."

"But why then?"

He passed the letter over.

"It's yours now," he said. "Read it."

Dear Mum,

I don't know how to say this. It's about Dad. Do you remember that Guy Fawkes night all those years ago? Stupid question, of course you do. It's probably branded into your memory just as much as it is into mine. It was all my fault.

Earlier that day I watched from outside his classroom as he failed to control his pupils. I seized my opportunity and ran to the loos, where I wrote a note and slipped it under the headmaster's door. I know it was an awful thing to do, but at the time I thought it would be for the best. Dad might lose his job, but he'd get another one, and I'd move schools, to a place where I wouldn't be afraid to open my mouth.

I couldn't go without telling you that. Sorry. But that's not why I'm doing this.

I'm not sure when it started to go wrong—probably soon after I dropped out of university. I know you were set against me leaving the course, but Gordon really did think that I had a future as a writer. He looked at my work—a few short stories and character sketches—and proclaimed it good, fine writing, almost ready for publication. But what I needed to do, he said, was channel my energies into a novel. Most first novels, he said, were really nothing more than thinly disguised autobiogra-

phies, but there was nothing wrong with that, and so we decided that the best thing to do was to start off with something close to my heart, something I felt was true. So I started to look through my old diary. That was the hardest thing, I can tell you, reading things I had written years back.

Gordon suggested trying to relive some of my memories, ones perhaps I'd recorded already in my journal, and write down what I felt. He said I could take one incident—for instance, my first day at Winterborne—and then try and write about it over and over again, each time from a different perspective or using different vocabulary. It was incredibly stimulating and it really seemed to work. Some days, if I got really stuck, which was quite often, he told me just to talk. According to him, speaking about an experience was sometimes enough to kick-start the unconscious into processing it into a form ready for expression on the page. Occasionally, Gordon would take notes. "Why are you bothering to write all this down?" I'd say. "Just for the record, that's all. You never know when you might need it," he'd reply.

Gordon, of course, did not actually need to write another book after the success of The Debating Society, *yet every morning he went into his study and emerged at 12:30, confident that he had written his allotted words for that day. He was so self-assured. My production was far from steady, however. Most days, I have to confess, my "writing" consisted of nothing more than looking through my diary and writing out, over and over again, scenes I'd already recorded in my journal. When-*

ever I tried to tell Gordon about my worries, he insisted that I was doing splendidly. Just as long as I was working every day, that was the most important thing. I was instilling a sense of creative discipline, which was essential in any writer. He told me not to worry too much about narrative or plot, as that would come with the development of character; rather, I should try and capture the experience of living—consciousness, he called it.

I'm not sure how best to tell you what happened next. But I don't want you to do anything to hurt or damage Gordon above and beyond what I ask of you. The last thing I want, believe me, is you being dragged into all of this. I couldn't bear it if I knew that was going to happen.

It started with little things, a sense that Gordon was preoccupied, anxious. He had a faraway look in his eyes that worried me. Whenever I tried to ask him whether he was all right or tell him how I thought he seemed a little distant, he said it was nothing more than problems with his book. But then Gordon started to disappear in the afternoons. He said he was going for a stroll, to get some fresh air. The first time he did this, I went to get my coat, and he told me he needed time alone, to think. Writer's block, he said. I helped myself to a large whiskey and soda that afternoon. I'd already had a couple that morning—Gordon said the drink might help me relax, might encourage me to write—and soon it became a regular fixture, as normal as a cup of coffee first thing or a bite to eat at lunchtime. It wasn't a problem. Both of us could carry it. In fact, I'm having a drink while I write this and I can hardly feel its effects.

Anyway, Gordon's strolls shifted from afternoons to late at night, walks that seemed to last a few hours. And then there were the mysterious telephone calls, callers who would hang up whenever I picked up the receiver. I didn't tell you any of this before because I didn't want to worry you. And I thought it would all blow over. Writers are supposed to be temperamental souls, after all, aren't they? As you know, I've always respected Gordon's privacy. He was always a little funny about his so-called sacred spaces. We used to laugh about it. But I prided myself on the fact that he could trust me. I wish now he hadn't. I wish he had regarded me as no better than a common snoop. Perhaps things would have been different.

It's hard for me to admit this to you, but you have probably guessed by now that I suspected him of seeing someone else. I'd heard a few things said about him, but I'd never believed them. Nothing more than bitchy comments by jealous types. Gordon wouldn't stoop to such a level. But then why did he keep spending so much time away from me? He stopped talking to me, but whenever I tried to question him, he told me to stop being so pathetic and hysterical. I tried to leave him once, I really did. I was going to come home to you. But he told me that he needed me, that he loved me, that he'd never be able to write without me. He started to cry like a little boy. I found that I couldn't do it.

I did not want to give in to the temptation to search his things. It just wouldn't be right. But last night was different. That's when it all changed. I hate him now for making me do that. But I hate myself more.

At about ten o'clock Gordon came into the sitting room from his study and announced that he was going out. I asked him where, but he responded, as usual, with the words, "For a walk." He said it in such a way as if it was perfectly normal, as if I was the odd one for questioning him. I probably made a bit of a scene, I'll admit that much, but what else was I to do? He stormed out, and that's when I told myself I was going to find out about his little walks. I went into the bedroom and started to look through his things in the wardrobe, tossing jackets and ties and trousers all over the place. I found a couple of tickets to an exhibition, some matches from a restaurant—places I was sure I'd never been to— and a handkerchief stinking of cheap aftershave, but nothing that gave me a clue to his strange behavior. What if the rumors had been right? No, I refused to believe it.

I'd never been inside his study—it was, he had said many, many times, completely out of bounds—but as I stood outside the door, I felt that if I just had a quick look inside, I would discover, once and for all, the reason why he was behaving so oddly. I almost convinced myself that I was going to do something that was, in a way, quite noble. After all, if I discovered nothing amiss, then Gordon had been telling me the truth all along, that he loved me and no one else.

I pushed open the door, tentatively, almost afraid that I would see him there sitting in his chair by his desk. But, of course, there was no one there. I quickly set to work, searching through the pockets of his corduroy jacket that hung over the back of the chair and then his desk. I suddenly felt shoddy, dirty, and very, very stupid, and I was about to give the whole thing up and pour myself another large drink when I opened the bottom drawer. Underneath a pile of old newspapers and magazines there were two boxes of typing paper. I don't know what made me think of opening them; perhaps it was the way they were covered by all that newsprint, as if they were being deliberately hidden away. I put the newspapers to one side and lifted the first box. It was quite heavy. I eased open the top of the box and inside was a manuscript.

On the front page, in bold capital letters, were the words THE MUSIC TEACHER, *followed by Gordon's name. I can't tell you the feeling of dread that came over me. I wanted to die there and then. The second box contained a carbon copy. As I flicked through the manuscript, familiar phrases jumped out at me; there were sentences I could complete without even having to read to the end. It was all about a boy—me—and his relationship with his father, a music teacher and organist at a minor public school who suffers from depression. Of course, I didn't need to read its final pages to know what happened, but there it all was—a climax in which the man blows his brains out on Bonfire Night.*

As I looked at these final pages, I heard the front door click. I didn't bother to move. I didn't care what happened to me anymore. Gordon came in, found me in his study and started screaming and shouting, but I remained deathly calm as I showed him what I had found in his bottom drawer. He couldn't deny it, of course. But when I asked him what he was playing at, using my story in this way, he turned on me. He told me that I would have to face up to facts, that I would never be a writer, that I just didn't have it in me. Someone may as well use the material, he said, as I was plainly not going to do anything with it. I tried to tell him that this was my experience, that these were my words, but he wouldn't let me speak. He was just drawing on the life around him, he said. He was a writer, a published writer, and writers take other people's lives. I was nothing more than an amateur.

I told him I couldn't go on. That I didn't care anymore, I wanted to end it all. Then, stupidly, I told him I still loved him. He brushed me off and stormed out of the room. He came back with a couple of packets of sleeping pills. He'd had enough of me, he said. Just do the decent thing, he said. Try not to leave a mess. Then I heard the slamming of the door. I haven't seen him since.

I don't want to write any more. Like I said, I can't. I haven't much time left. With this letter you should find the carbon copy of Gordon's book, which should, I hope, now never see the light of day. It will be dead, like me.

I'm leaving Gordon a note telling him what I have done, as well as one that should satisfy the police. If Gordon ever does try to take his book further, all you need do is show him or his publishers this letter, together with my diary, which I'm sending you as well and which will tell you in more detail what happened on that Bonfire Night. I hope you will be able to forgive me. If Gordon agrees not to publish his novel, please don't say anything. I don't want any fuss.

Your loving son,
Chris

"You seem preoccupied," said Lavinia. "Are you all right?"

"Sorry?"

"There—I think I've proved my point," she said, laughing.

After leaving Shaw, I had returned to the hotel and met Lavinia in the bar. She had insisted on buying me drinks to thank me for acting as a go-between. She was in a celebratory mood and had already knocked back nearly a bottle of wine. Her self-satisfaction blinded her to the truth. But how was she to know what my real intentions were? I had given back her documents, which I had copied, and she had passed over her synopsis, which, although most probably heavily censored by her, nevertheless gave me an insight into her methods. I wasn't so stupid as to try and copy from it, but at least it would provide me with an arc to the story, a structure from which I could work. As I poured her another glass of red wine, I tried to tell myself that I was the one who should be celebrating.

"Oh, I'm sorry, Lavinia," I said. "I can't stop thinking about my resemblance to that boy in the photograph. What was his name?"

"Christopher. Christopher Davidson."

"That's it. I know I said I'd try to put it out of my mind, that it didn't mean anything, but the more I think about it, the odder it seems. Sorry. I suppose I'm not making much sense."

"No, don't be silly. Of course it must be extremely odd. I can't quite work it out myself."

"You asked me why Mr. Crace had hired me. At the time I had been naive to assume it was because he liked me, or at the very least thought me capable of doing the job. But now—"

"What?"

"I just wonder what he's really getting out of it."

"I see what you mean," she said, gulping back her red wine.

"So if I seem a little out of sorts tonight, that's why. Sorry."

"But you are going to go back?"

There was slight note of panic in her voice. She obviously thought that she had won me over with her charms and that, most probably, I would do anything for her. I hesitated longer than I needed to so I could watch the terror of uncertainty creep into her face. Without me near Crace, she would lose one of her closest allies.

"Yes, I am," I said, rather wearily. "In fact, I'm catching a train to London tomorrow and then flying back to Mr. Crace. But only because I can't afford not to. I've got to get on with my book."

"Oh, yes, I meant to ask you about that," she said. "So it's set in Venice?"

"Yes, part of it is set in Venice and part in England."

"How intriguing. In the present day?"

"Mostly," I said, "except for a small segment in the past."

"So you've started writing—"

I hesitated, not knowing what to say.

"Sorry. You probably don't want to talk about it," she said.

"No, it's not that, it's that . . . that photograph . . . I don't know—"

"I understand completely," she said, placing a hand gently on my knee. "What you need is a breath of fresh air." There was a note of flirtatiousness in her voice. "Do you fancy a stroll?"

"What? Now?"

"Yes. It might help get things in perspective."

"Okay."

"I'll just go and get my coat," she said, smiling. As she tried to stand up, she had to steady herself by her chair. "Oh, gosh. That wine has gone to my head." She ran her hand through her hair and laughed nervously, girlishly. "Wait for me down here. I won't be a minute."

During those five or so minutes alone, I realized that I had been presented with the perfect opportunity. It had to be now. She had served her purpose.

"Are you ready?" she said, slightly slurring her words. In her room she had applied a sheen of plum-colored lipstick and an extra covering of powder to try and make herself appear more presentable, but it was obvious she was a little drunk.

"Yes," I said. "But I've just thought of something."

"What?"

"I don't know how it could have slipped my mind."

"Yes?"

"And to think that I was about to leave without showing you."

"Oh, for God's sake, Adam. What is it?"

"Mr. Crace's favorite place when he worked at the school, the spot where he said he had the idea for *The Debating Society.*"

"What?"

"The chapel up on the hill. Have you come across it?"

"No, I've never heard of it."

"Mr. Crace just mentioned it in passing to me one day. There was something about its atmosphere, he said, that was conducive to creation. But . . . it's out of the question."

"What is?"

"Walking up there. It's too far from here. But I suppose you can always go and explore it by yourself tomorrow."

I could tell I had caught her interest.

"What a shame," she said, maneuvering the strap of her handbag over her shoulder. "It sounds fascinating." Her eyes, which until a few moments ago drooped with drink-induced contentedness, now burned with a new intensity. "No, we're going."

"How?"

"I'll drive. It's not far. There won't be any police out here, will there?"

"Even so," I said, "I really don't think you are in any condition to drive. I haven't had as much as you, so if you don't mind being chauffeured—"

"Are you sure?"

"Yes, of course."

"That's super," she said, smiling.

As she took the keys out of her bag, I slipped a pair of gloves on, remarking how I had heard one of the guests telling the receptionist that the temperature outside had dropped by a few degrees.

"I must admit, I feel I have had one celebratory drink too many," she said as she handed the keys to me.

We walked to the front door and out into the cold night, the purple-black sky full of stars, an expanse of crushed diamonds. Lavinia took a deep breath and exhaled.

"You know, seeing the place that inspired Mr. Crace might help us both," she said. "Before a book, I always feel the same way—half nervous, half excited. Each time I feel I'm going to be incapable of capturing the essence of another person, getting them *right*. No matter how much I tell myself I've done it before and I'll most probably do it again, it's always the same. Ridiculous, isn't it? But I suppose it must be the same with you, I mean, now that you are trying your hand at fiction."

As we walked toward her silver-gray Audi, I pressed the key and the doors unlocked.

"Sorry, I know writing fiction is very different from biography," she said as we climbed into the car. "Novelists often don't want to discuss their work, especially if it's in progress. Forgive me."

I felt her fingers brush against my hand as I reached for the gear stick and started the engine.

"No, don't worry. It's just that I'm a little uncertain about it, that's all."

"I understand. I have to say I do admire you, though. It's certainly a brave move."

I guided the car slowly down the winding drive, past the tall rhododendron bushes and out onto the country lane. I tried to speak, but my words disappeared in my throat. I had to pretend that everything was normal.

"H-have you tried?" I said, coughing. "Writing novels, I mean?"

"Oh, gosh no. I'm much too admiring of my subjects' work to even try and imitate them. But that's not to say I don't get a thrill out of writing. To be honest, though, the research is my favorite part. Digging around in someone's past, trying to unearth secrets, sorting through archives in the hope of finding a piece of paper that might shed light on a particular person. I mean, I can't tell you what pleasure it brings me to know that in a few minutes I'll see the place that inspired Gordon Crace."

"Yes, I'm pleased I remembered to tell you about the chapel," I said, turning the car into the lane that led up to the church. "You never know—it might help."

The road narrowed, and I stopped the car in a passing place off the lane. By the driver's seat there was an empty plastic bag that I slipped into my pocket. As we got out, I realized that the canopy of trees leading up to the chapel would shield us from the moonlight. I smiled to myself.

"I'm sure I've got one in here," said Lavinia, pushing forward her seat and fumbling in the back of the car. "Yes, here it is."

A beam of light temporarily blinded me. I shielded my eyes with my hand. She was holding a torch.

"Great," I said, my mouth forming itself into a fixed smile.

"It's not far, just at the top of this track, but it's a bit unsteady un-
derfoot."

She took a couple of steps, but I could tell she was having
problems negotiating the rough terrain.

"Do you want me to help?"

"Yes, that's kind, thank you," she said, taking my arm and
passing the torch to me.

We walked slowly up the track, the light cutting through the
darkness. Occasionally I let the torch drop down to the pathway,
where my eyes searched the ground. In the distance I heard the
cry of an owl.

"What did Mr. Crace actually tell you about this place?"

"Oh, just that he would often come up here when the teaching
was getting on top of him. He'd walk up here from the school and
sit on the bench and think, sometimes write in his notebook. It
also gave him quite a good view of the abbey and the school down
in the valley."

"Oh, really?" she said, her body now pressing closer to me.

"Apparently it's Norman and built of flint. I think Mr. Crace
said that there was an inscription inside that granted a 120-day
indulgence to passing pilgrims."

"Do you think that applies to us?" she said, laughing.

"I don't see why not."

At that moment, just as the dark outline of the chapel came
into view, I switched off the torch, pretending to drop it on the
ground.

"Sorry," I said. "It slipped out of my hands."

"Don't worry," she said. "Can you see it?"

"Yes." I said.

I bent down to the earth where I had already spotted a rock,
a large piece of flint. I clasped it in my hand, feeling its sharp

edges bite into my skin. I quickly stood up and raised my arm above me.

"What—" she said. But she didn't have a chance to finish her sentence.

I brought the heavy rock down hard on Lavinia's head, immediately stunning her. There was a crack and a faint cry, and I followed through with two more blows. She tried to stretch her arm out into the dark night, swayed from side to side for a moment and then slumped to the ground. The stone in my hand felt wet and sticky as I continued to pummel her skull.

Finally, I switched on the torch and shone it into her eyes. There was no reaction. If she wasn't dead already, she would be in a matter of minutes. Blood poured down her face from several deep wounds. I pulled out the plastic supermarket bag from my pocket and placed it over her head. I didn't want her blood staining my clothes. I crouched down and lifted Lavinia into my arms and carried her down the track, checking that there was no one around. I left her body slumped against a tree, out of sight of the road, and opened the car door. I got into the driver's seat, made sure I had secured my seat belt, and started the engine. I took a deep breath and put the car into first gear. Although I had planned what I was going to do, I still couldn't quite believe it. Hesitation was not an option. I slammed my foot on the accelerator and the car lurched forward. I quickly moved up a couple of gears until I was going about forty miles an hour. Then I deliberately steered the car off the road, down a track, and in the direction of a clump of trees. All my instincts told me to slam on the brakes, but I knew that I would have to resist until the very last moment. Just as a tree loomed into view, I braked, pressing down as hard as possible on the floor pedal. Two conflicting forces fought for control of the vehicle as the car crashed through the undergrowth, sounding as if it were splitting into two. I jolted forward, the shattering windscreen coming perilously close to my eyes. As my forehead slammed down hard on the steering wheel, I heard myself cry out, but the seat belt pulled me backward, tightening against my chest.

Shocked by the sudden stillness of the moment, I sat and watched the steam from the engine spiral up into the cold night air. I felt a painful throbbing all across my forehead and soreness across my right shoulder, but apart from that I was unhurt. I undid the seat belt and tried to force open the door. It didn't move. I tried again, but it was stuck. Something was blocking it, a branch perhaps. I eased myself over to the passenger seat. That door opened easily. The front of the car looked like it had collapsed into itself, a mass of twisted metal.

I ran down to the spot where I had left Lavinia's body. Making sure there were no other vehicles coming toward me, I took hold of her slight frame and carried her up to the car. She did not weigh much, but even so I had to stop a couple of times to catch my breath. As I supported her by the car, I checked the pulse on her neck. I could not feel anything. I pulled the bag from her head, lifted her into the passenger seat, and gently moved her over to the driver's seat. Then I grabbed hold of her hair and slammed her face hard into the windscreen. Shards of glass embedded themselves in her fine skin, now black with blood.

All that was left for me to do was rearrange her limbs in a grotesque tableau so that it appeared she had suffered a car accident. When the police tested her blood, they would find that she was over the limit, while the staff at the hotel restaurant would testify that she had indeed enjoyed a copious amount of alcohol. By the time the police got around to questioning the young man she had dined with, he would have fled the country. If they did ever catch up with me, I would tell them that, despite my protestations that she had had too much to drink, Lavinia had insisted on driving me to the pub. Obviously she had lost control of the vehicle as she traveled back to her hotel. The fact that she had not worn a seat belt had reduced her chances of surviving the crash. Checking that I hadn't left anything in the vehicle, I slammed the door and said a silent good-bye.

The plane lurched to the left, tipping through the sky as we made our descent into Venice. I looked out of the window, but all I could see was an expanse of cloud. I remembered the first time I had made this journey, running onto the plane bound for Venice in a bid to escape my past. I had thought that by starting afresh, in another country, I would be able to forget about everything that had happened to me. I would lose myself in writing and escape into a magical, imaginary world. Little did I realize then that the book I would ultimately write would be rather different from the one I had intended. But don't they say that all the best writers always create something that, despite their careful planning and preparation, ultimately develops a life of its own?

I was ready to present Crace with the truth. I would lay out all the evidence in front of him. I couldn't see how he could possibly argue with me. I would tell him everything I knew about his past, all the details about his inspiration for *The Debating Society,* how he had abused those boys at Winterborne Abbey and how he had taken Chris's life—both literally and figuratively. I would present the facts clinically, objectively, without passing judgment, but make him realize that things could not carry on as they were. Obviously I knew he wouldn't want me to go to the police, but I was sure there was an arrangement we could come to that would be mutually beneficial.

I would tell him that I was going to write his biography, authorized by him, and in return for his cooperation I might consider erasing certain "facts" from his history, elements of his story that, if made public, would no doubt ruin him, if not land him in jail. Exactly which parts of his biography I glossed over and which ones I concentrated on was open to discussion. If he refused to cooperate, I was armed with enough material to write an unauthorized account of his life, over which he would have no control whatsoever. Of course, after his death all such verbal agreements would be null and void and I would be free to tell the story. I wondered what had happened to the manuscript copies of *The Music Teacher* that Chris said he had seen; perhaps Crace still had the novel in his possession.

I stepped out of the airport, feeling a light dust of fine drizzle on my face. As I waited by the *motoscafi* stop for the boat into Venice, together with a group of businessmen, a young couple and a smartly dressed elderly Venetian man, I had a sense that I was moving toward a future that had already been prescribed for me. I remembered that as a child I always had a sense that I was different, special somehow. I knew that one day I would make my mark. I suppose it was only a matter of time now before I would attract the kind of attention I always thought I had deserved but that had so far eluded me.

Fog had settled over the lagoon, and as we traveled through the water, it was hard to make out anything beyond the mist. But, like Crace, I had a mental image of Venice that had become a substitute for the real thing; I no longer needed to see the actual squares, bridges and canals. And as Crace said, it was best to leave the reality of the city to the unfortunates who could only see with their eyes and not their imagination.

In the middle of the lagoon, I took from my rucksack the plastic bag I had placed over Lavinia's head. Inside was the rock I had used to kill her. I tied the ends of the bag into a secure knot and, making sure nobody was watching me, surreptitiously dropped it over the edge of the boat. As it sank, I felt a reassuring sense of satisfaction, of completeness. Lavinia was out of the way now and I would never have to think of her again.

As the launch approached the Arsenale, the fog was so thick that it was difficult to distinguish between the land and the water. I was the only person to disembark, as all the other passengers had opted for the San Marco stop. I stood on the Riva and listened as the engines of the boat faded away into the mist, the sound of bells tolling somewhere in the distance. I turned up the collar of my jacket and started to walk along the promenade, which seemed deserted, empty except for the occasional stray pigeon from St. Mark's, until the fog finally released a couple of other figures from its grip. I considered getting my guidebook out of my bag to study the map, but I couldn't bear to see the form of that question mark staring back at me again, so I continued in the direction of St. Mark's. I knew, obviously, that at some point I would have to take a right turn down one of the alleys that led toward Castello. I picked one at random and followed its trail, through a campo and over a bridge by a side canal. The water seemed to be whispering to me, imparting some coded message that I failed to understand. At points I could only see three or four feet in front of me and, as the fog seemed to suffocate any sound surrounding it, I was surprised when I saw someone emerge out of the dense, opaque cloud. It was as if residents and visitors alike had been reduced to ghosts, destined to walk around the watery city for an eternity.

I crossed another smaller bridge and took a street that I was convinced would lead me to the back of San Zaccaria, from where

I was confident I could find my way to Crace's palazzo with ease. As I neared the end of the narrow alley, I began to feel the hairs on the back of my neck prick with fear. I heard the noise of a fluttering pigeon hovering above me but could not see it. I reached out into the mist but felt nothing but the damp air. I thought I heard breathing behind me, but when I turned around, no one was there. Finally, as I neared the end of the alley, I saw that there was nothing ahead of me but a brick wall, its surface mottled with moss. I had walked down a dead end. I traced my steps back up to the little bridge and down another street that did eventually bring me to the back of San Zaccaria. By the time I approached Santa Maria Formosa, the mist had started to clear a little.

Outside the palazzo, I took the key from my pocket and walked over the bridge that separated the house from the rest of the city. The dragon carved into the marble gate looked at me as if passing judgment. I turned the key in the lock and pushed open the heavy door. Wisps of fog snaked their way around the courtyard, eel-like in their movements. I called out Crace's name, but there was no answer. I walked up the staircase, the latticework of the metal banister cold to the touch, and unlocked the door that led into the portego. I shouted for Crace again; again there was no response, and I assumed he was sleeping. It was dark inside the palazzo, so I turned on some of the lights in the grand hall.

As soon as I saw one of the frames lying face down on the floor, surrounded by splinters of glass, I knew there was something wrong. I ran to the side of the hall, feeling the glass crunch under my feet, and bent down to examine what had happened. I picked up a couple of shards, and turned over the frame to see the image from the *Triomphi di Carlo* by Francesco de' Lodovici. I placed the woodcut and glass to one side and ran down the portego to the corridor that led to Crace's bedroom.

"Gordon? Gordon? Are you all right?"

I didn't bother to knock on his door, pushing my way in instead. He was lying fully clothed on top of the bed with his back to me, not moving.

"Gordon?"

I walked over to him and hesitated before touching him lightly on the shoulder.

"What the—?" said Gordon, turning over, his eyes opening.

For a moment, as he flapped and wrestled with an invisible enemy there on his bed, halfway between waking and dreaming, he reminded me of a trapped bird, its wings bound with wire, desperate to free itself.

"For fuck's sake, Adam," he said. "Thank God it's you."

"What's happened? Are you all right?"

"I thought he'd come back—it was awful," he said, easing himself up into a sitting position. He hadn't shaved for days, and yellow-gray stubble covered his face like a rash of iron filings.

"Who? What?"

"Him. The boy who was here before you."

"What—you mean someone you employed?"

"Yes, the one before you," said Crace, his words spilling out. "He had had a copy of his key cut. Thought he'd been dismissed unfairly, without due reason. Reckoned he deserved something for all his trouble, so he stole in here last night. Thank God I couldn't sleep. I was tossing and turning in my bed and on the way to the bathroom to get a sleeping pill when—"

"Gordon, slow down, slow down."

He took a deep breath. "—When I heard a noise in the portego. I don't mind telling you that I was scared out of my wits. I tried to tell myself it was a cat that had somehow climbed in through one of the windows, but when I heard the noise of one of the etchings being removed from the wall, I couldn't stand there any longer. I went into my study, got the gun out of the urn and walked out into the portego, where I saw him . . . him . . . taking down the Francesco de' Lodovici."

"And what happened then?"

"I told him in no uncertain terms to put it back where it belonged. I pointed the gun at him, told him that I would use it, but, of course, I couldn't. I was shaking all over. He knocked it out of my hand, and then the little thing got all nasty, started spouting all sorts of horrible language and filthy accusations. Oh, Adam, it was just awful."

"What did he want?"

"It was quite clear I wasn't going to get rid of him. I didn't want him to take one of my favorite works—you can understand that, can't you?—so I offered to give him some money."

"Why didn't you call the *carabinieri*?"

"No, I didn't want them involved. No, that was impossible."

"You didn't give him any money, did you?"

"It was that or the Francesco de' Lodovici. So I offered him five hundred euros to go away and never come back."

"But did that satisfy him?" I thought of the woodcut on the floor in the portego.

"Yes, it did seem to. I got the money, gave it to him and felt relieved it was all over. But then as he was on his way out, he suddenly got all violent again and grabbed hold of my jacket. He pushed me against the wall, and I felt myself crash into the glass of the etching. He told me not to go around brandishing guns, that someone could get killed like that. And with that he pushed me down, dashing the etching off the wall as he did so. He threw the key at me and then he left."

Crace ended his story and started to sob quietly. As he raised his thin, bony hands to his face to cover his eyes, I noticed that his skin was covered in cuts and his cream jacket had a cluster of small dark stains around the lapel.

"I'm sorry. Look at me, making a fool of myself," said Crace, sniffing.

"Don't be silly, Gordon. I just feel so awful for not being here."

"Yes, that couldn't be helped. But thank God you're back. It made me realize just how much I've come to depend on you. Please promise you won't leave me again, Adam. Promise?"

I nodded.

"I promise."

"But what's wrong with your forehead?" he said, noticing the bruise. "What happened?"

"Oh, nothing. Just a silly accident, that's all."

+≡≡+

When I walked around the palazzo that day, it looked as though every room in the building had been ransacked by the intruder. Trousers, shirts and vests lay strewn around Crace's bedroom. The drawing room floor was full of books, their spines sticking out at odd angles, and the kitchen was littered with used food packets, empty tins and half-eaten meals. The only damage Crace's former employee seemed to have caused was breaking the glass of the etching that hung in the portego; everything else was a manifestation of Gordon's self-neglect. Crace had told me that Lucia, the girl who had come in to bring him food, often just left without saying a word and, as he didn't take to her, he didn't want to encourage her to stay around. No doubt she felt the same.

It was astonishing to see how far Crace had let himself go in the week that I had been away. Not only had he not shaved, but he had not washed or changed his clothes either. When I asked him why, he told me he thought there was little point in making an effort since he had nobody to make himself decent for. Each morning, he said, he had gone through his clothes, picking out various items he thought he might wear that day, but felt so apathetic and without purpose that he dropped them on the floor, where they had remained. It was as though, in my absence, he had simply lost the will to live. What would have happened, I wondered, if I had stayed away longer. I imagined him lying in bed, the heavy tapestry covers pressing down over his skeletal frame, his body slowly withering away, turning to dust.

"But why didn't you tell me how you were feeling on the phone?" I asked, picking up the clothes in the bedroom.

"I knew you had enough on your mind without worrying about me. I didn't want to upset you any more than you were already. How was it, by the way?"

"Sorry?"

"The funeral."

"Oh, it was very sad, of course. But everyone decided to try and think of it more as a celebration of her life."

"Very wise," said Crace, looking at the scratches on the back of his hands.

"Do you want a plaster for that?"

"No, my skin is not what it was, but I'm sure it will heal in good time. But my back—" he said, grimacing as he stood up from the bed. "Gosh, that's another story. Would you mind awfully running a bath for me? I think a good, hot soak is what I need."

"Good idea," I said.

In the bathroom, I quickly cleaned the sink and the loo while the bath was running. Steam filled the space with a thick mist, frosting over the mirror, and when Crace stepped into the room a few minutes later, he reminded me of one of the ghostly figures I had seen earlier emerging from the fog.

"I'm such a pathetic creature," he said. "Look—my fingers are shaking so much I can't even take my own clothes off. I hate to ask you, Adam, but would you mind."

His fingers danced up and down his shirt, ineffectually pulling at the buttons, but it seemed he couldn't get his hands to stay still long enough.

"Of course. Here, let me," I said.

Starting at his collar, I slowly undid each of the buttons, unfastening the shirt down to his waist. As I did so, Crace lowered his eyes as if he was enduring a necessary humiliation. Using me to balance against, Crace unzipped his trousers and I guided him toward the loo. I flipped down the seat, eased him down to a sitting position and gently removed his trousers. I felt for him, sitting there in his pants, vest and socks looking like the sad, tired, elderly man he was. Although I knew he had, no doubt, done some awful things in the past, it was clear now that he was incapable of doing anything more than simply existing, biding his time until the moment his life was snuffed out.

I picked up his clothes and set them to one side to be cleaned. Considering that he had not washed for some days, he did not smell that bad; the aroma that emanated from him was not so much body odor as that of musty books. He smelt like an old, airless library.

"Thank you, Adam. It's so very kind of you," he said, still looking down. "I don't know what I'd do without you."

Stretching out his thin arm, now without any muscle definition whatsoever, he held on to the sink and tried to lift himself upward, but he winced in pain as he moved.

"Here, let me help," I said, cupping my hands underneath his armpits.

"It's so humiliating. I don't know what's wrong with me."

"You'll regain your strength in a few days. You've had a terrible shock and just need a bit of looking after, that's all."

"You are kind, Adam. So kind."

Making sure I had him fully supported, I used my weight to lift his light body toward me. As I did so, I felt his cold hands slide around the back of my neck, his fingers caressing the base of my hairline. I winced as I felt our skin touching, and as I brought him nearer, I tasted his metallic breath.

"Thank you, thank you," he whispered as I steadied him against me.

"There you are . . . good," I said, making sure that he found his footing before gently unclasping his arms from behind my neck. "That's right. Now, do you think you'll be okay if I leave you? Can you manage in the bath by yourself?"

"You know I wouldn't normally ask you, Adam, but would you mind terribly if you helped me in? I realize I do sound rather pathetic, but my back feels like it's gone into some kind of spasm."

As he tried to reach around to feel his spine, his face creased with pain.

"I don't know what that boy did to me, but it bloody well hurts."

"Come on then; let's get you into that bath."

I bent down to check the temperature—it was as hot as it could be without being scalding—and added some citrus-smelling salts, mixing the crystals in by swirling the water with my hands. I dried my fingers and then, trying not to think about what I was about to do, I took hold of the bottom of Crace's vest and gradually eased it upward, past his concave chest and sharp shoulder bones and over his head. Then I helped him sit on the rim of the bath and knelt down to remove his socks. His gnarled, crooked toes looked like the knotted roots of an old tree. I stood him up again and, from behind, gently pulled down his white cotton underpants, supporting him as he stepped out of them. His buttocks were hollow, and as he turned around I caught a glimpse of his long, thin penis surrounded by a patch of gray pubic hair. After helping him into the bath, I held him as he lowered himself down.

"Gosh, that's hot," he said, sucking in air through his teeth as he came in contact with the water.

"It should help, though," I said, taking hold of his shoulders and easing them backward.

"Yes, it is feeling a little better already," he said.

"Why don't you have a soak," I said, drying my hands, "and then give me a shout when you're ready to be washed?"

"I know I'm being a terrible bore, but would you just mind sitting with me for a while? I'm still not feeling quite myself."

"Of course. No problem," I said.

I watched as Crace's body began to relax. He eased himself down a little deeper in the bath so that his head nearly disappeared underwater. As he closed his eyes, he crossed his arms across his chest and exhaled.

"How are you getting on with your story?" he said, still with his eyes closed.

"I'm sorry?"

"Your novel. I just wondered how it was going."

"I haven't made much progress on it recently, what with the funeral and everything."

"Yes, I can quite imagine," he said, opening his eyes and sitting up in the bath. "But before you went away, you did promise me you'd read me something from it."

"I'm afraid it's still in rather a rough form. I'm not sure whether it's suitable for public consumption."

"That is a shame," he said. "I was looking forward to it, I must say. I would have thought your notebook must be quite full of scribbles by now. Could you pass me the soap?"

I reached over to the tray at the bottom end of bath and handed him the bar of olive oil soap, his fingers lingering a little too long on mine.

"But it's only me, Adam. You wouldn't be reading in front of an audience."

"Well—"

"Please. And it would help take my mind off all this awful business."

I had not much to show him apart from a few scenes, but nevertheless I agreed.

"But I warn you, don't have high expectations."

"Don't worry," he said, smiling. "I won't."

━━◆━━

After bathing, drying and dressing Crace, I finally managed to find the time to unpack. My room was the same as I had left it— sparse, bare and functional. I noticed, as I stepped into it, that it was devoid of any of those little touches—pictures on the wall, mementos on shelves, books, cards—*things* that make a room personal. Perhaps I had always known that I wouldn't stay long in the palazzo, that I would move on. Or was I afraid of giving Crace any insights into my character?

Out of my rucksack I took my wash bag, placing it on the floor near the door as a reminder to take it into the bathroom later, and some clothes that needed cleaning. I'd tackle the rest of the jobs that needed to be done—the washing of clothes, the tidying of the kitchen, the restoration of order—the next day. I felt exhausted, not only by my early start and my flight, but also, I think, by the stress of arriving back at the palazzo to find Crace in such a state. I tried not to think of the proximity of his reptilian body next to mine in the bathroom, the feel of his skin, the sight of his nakedness.

The incident with his former employee, who did seem like a thoroughly unpleasant character, had unsettled him. I was sure that his injuries were not serious; the cuts on his hands would heal in a few days and his back strain would ease off too.

In the bath I had asked him again if he was certain about his decision not to involve the police, but he repeated that he wanted no further action taken. In fact, he was so insistent that I began to suspect whether Crace was telling me the whole truth. Why had the boy before me left so suddenly? What had Crace done to him? Now that I knew about his past, it was highly likely that he had tried to seduce him, the boy had taken umbrage, a dispute had arisen, and the employee had obviously felt he had no choice but to leave. It was no wonder the boy, feeling angry and hurt, had come back seeking some kind of revenge.

I took out my notebook from my rucksack, sat down at the desk under the window and flicked through it, a feeling of pride surging within me as I looked at all the evidence I had amassed on Crace. Although certain aspects of Crace's life were still opaque and, so far at least, unknowable, I almost had enough information to start sketching out a rough draft of a biography. On a page at the back of my book, I started to make a list of possible titles, but none of them seemed as apposite as Lavinia's *The Silent Man*, which I toyed with taking as my own.

Turning around to make sure the door was closed and that Crace wasn't about to walk into the room, I thought about the best place to hide the journal. Before going away I had kept it at the bottom of my luggage, under an old T-shirt, but now, as the material it contained was so much more detailed, I knew I would have to find a better location if I wanted to keep its contents secret. I walked over to the windows and pulled back the shutters. It was dark outside now, but from the dim lights of a balcony opposite, I could see that the canal below was still sheathed in fog. Occasionally a gondola would emerge from the mist, remaining visible only for a matter of seconds before it disappeared once again. In the distance I heard a woman singing, practicing her scales in series of minor keys, and the barking of a dog.

Outside my window was a narrow ledge that contained an empty planting box, under which I thought it might be possible to hide the notebook, obviously wrapped inside a number of plastic bags. I surmised that it would be feasible to attach the notebook to the window box by using string or a plastic band, but I couldn't risk placing the package in such a vulnerable location, as a rainstorm could easily sweep it off the sill and wash it down into the waters below. Also, if Crace happened to stand by the window in the kitchen next door and look toward my bedroom, he would be able to see it nestling by the planting box.

The shelves of the built-in wardrobe were another possibility, but far too obvious, as was placing it under the mattress of the bed. Also, now that Lavinia had given me all her research notes, the amount of material I had to hide was quite considerable and, as a result, the space would have to be big enough to store it all comfortably. For a moment I considered exploring the empty floor above me, a whole level that remained unknown to me, but as Crace had told me not to bother going up there, he would soon get suspicious if he heard my footsteps through the ceiling. Then the image of Shaw taking out Chris's diary from underneath the floorboards came into my mind. I remembered the hollow sound of the floor in my room. Of course; it was the perfect idea. All I needed to do was lift up a piece of the wooden paneling and I would have the ideal hiding place, a dark, secret space that I was sure Crace would never dream of. But in order to lift one of the sections, I would need some kind of tool. I recalled the chisel I had used to remove the moss from the Corinthian column in the courtyard. I bent down and crawled underneath the desk, searching for the loose piece of wood I had often felt with my feet as I worked there. If I could just ease it up a little, I could spread all my material into the void, out of sight and away from prying eyes.

I stood up and walked to the door. Outside in the corridor, I listened for signs of Crace. The palazzo was silent, except for the soporific sound of the water outside. Crace was probably still in his bedroom, putting the finishing touches to his outfit. In the bath he had declared that tonight we were going to have a celebration to mark my return, a special evening to show his appreciation of everything I had done, all my little kindnesses. He had a bottle of Château-Margaux 1967 that he had set aside, which he wanted to open and share with me. It was the least he could do, he said, for helping him. He had apologized that there wasn't much food in the kitchen; he'd eaten everything the girl had left for him except for some overripe tomatoes and a piece of hard Parmigiano, so we had settled on a simple supper of spaghetti with a tomato sauce made with a generous amount of butter and sweetened with sugar, which I said I would make for him later. He was looking forward to listening to me read from my novel after supper.

In the kitchen I washed and dried a heavy pan and placed it on the stove. I opened a tin of tomatoes, emptied the contents into the pan, together with the chopped ripe tomatoes, added the butter and sugar, and gave the mixture a good stir. Then I bent down under the sink and, from among the bottles of bleach, detergent and cleaning fluid, took out the chisel. I gave the sauce another quick stir, turned down the heat and then walked back to my room, closing the door behind me.

I knelt down by my desk, found the piece of wood that I had selected earlier, tried to loosen it a little and eased the chisel into the cavity. The floor creaked as I pushed the chisel down. Slowly, I raised the panel and peered down into the dark space beneath, a mass of cobwebs, old traces of sawdust and dirt. A damp, deathly smell rose up from beneath. I didn't like the idea of confining my nice, clean notebook in this rank, filthy space, but knew it had to be done. I stood up, wrapped all my material in two plastic bags and pushed them deep into the cavity. I hurried back into the kitchen, where I continued to stir the sauce.

"You seem much better," I said, twisting the last of the spaghetti onto my fork.

"Oh, yes, I am. A great deal better. My back is not so painful now, and that bath did me the world of good. Your return has really lifted my spirits."

"Good. I'm pleased to hear it. I still can't believe that that boy came back and behaved like that. He must be a truly awful person. I'll bet you are pleased you fired him when you did."

"Indeed," said Crace, using his napkin to wipe a smudge of tomato sauce from the corner of his mouth. "He was insufferable.

And anyway, if I'd stuck with him, I would never have found you."

He gave me that look again, the one that turned my stomach. I smiled, pretending that I was pleased by the compliment. It was only a matter of time, I kept telling myself, before we would have to have our little talk, when he would have to face facts. I doubt he would be smiling after that.

"That was delicious, Adam. Really lovely. You caught the sauce just in time."

"And thank you for this," I said, taking another sip of the Margaux. "It's wonderful."

He held out his glass.

"Cheers," he said. "Here's to you—for everything."

"Cheers," I said, looking down. "Right, let me clear away these plates."

"Oh yes, you'll be keen to get on with your reading."

I cleared my throat.

"Gordon, about the reading—"

"Yes?"

"I just wondered if you could give me an hour or so. I just want to look over the piece, rewrite a couple of sentences here and there."

He looked disappointed.

"It's just that I want to make it as good as possible for you, that's all."

"Oh, very well," he said, looking at the mass of dirty plates, cups and bowls that scattered the work surface. "Why don't you leave the dishes? You could do them later if you like. There's so much mess in here, I don't think it's going to make a difference, do you?"

"Okay," I said. "Can I get you anything before I go into my room?"

He looked thoughtful for a moment, holding out his glass for a refill of the wine. As I poured the dark, almost black, liquid into his glass, he moved his hand so that it brushed against mine and smiled. I wasn't sure how much more of this kind of behavior I could stand, but I didn't say anything.

"I'll be waiting for you," he said as I walked out of the kitchen.

In my room I looked over my writing. The story centered on a young man named Richard, who could not accept that his girl-friend, Emma, had ended their relationship. I described the boy standing outside Emma's flat, watching her windows, unable to understand why he had been rejected. Memories of their time to-gether infuse him with a kind of ecstatic happiness, and he be-comes so possessed by the past that he believes he and Emma are still together. He goes back to his new, empty flat, picks up some shopping on the way and cooks a delicious supper. He sets the table for two, and during dinner he talks to the space across from him as if it were occupied by his girlfriend. He makes a toast and raises his glass to Emma, the perfect woman he would always love, who would, in his mind at least, forever remain unchanged and untouchable.

I found Crace in the drawing room, his eyes closed, his brow furrowed. When he heard me walk into the room, he opened his eyes, smiled and told me to sit on the chair opposite him.

"Make yourself comfortable and then you can begin," he said, obviously amused.

I coughed and explained that the story was just a fragment of what I hoped would form a larger work. Tentatively, I started to read. At various points I looked up to see Crace listening carefully to my words, occasionally nodding his head in appreciation, agree-ment, recognition or merely force of habit. I'm not sure how long I read, perhaps a quarter of an hour or so, but by the time I reached the end of the story, the part where Richard sits down to dinner and addresses his fantasy girlfriend, I noticed that Crace had tears in his eyes. When I finished, he looked so moved that he couldn't speak.

"Sorry," he said, waving his hand in front of his face. "That . . . well . . . that was beautiful. Beautiful."

"I'm afraid it still needs a bit of work," I said, astonished and embarrassed by his reaction.

"No, no, I think it was just perfect."

"Of course, I'd appreciate any criticism, anything you think I needed to change or alter."

"You mustn't change a word," he said. "No, not a single word."

"Thank you, Gordon. That means a great deal to me."

"Not at all, my dear boy. It really was very well drawn. You have a great talent for invention."

⊬⟞⟝⊢

Over the course of the next few days, I carried on with my duties, getting the Francesco de' Lodovici woodcut fitted with a new piece of glass and rehanging it on the wall, straightening the rest of the pictures that Crace's former employee had disturbed, cleaning the kitchen of dirty pots and pans and tidying the drawing room. As I worked, I rehearsed the scene in which I finally confronted Crace with the evidence about his past. I imagined myself walking into the drawing room, where Crace was reading, and asking him to listen to me; I had something important that I wanted to say. He would look up without interest initially, but then, when he heard the contents of my speech, panic would infect his eyes. I ran through our conversation over and over, and in my imagination I acted out my lines using different intonations, emphases and punctuation. I would pause for a few moments, watching Crace's face for a flicker of emotion, after I let it be known that I had obtained Chris's suicide note. Yes, that would add greater dramatic effect. That would work splendidly.

It was important to present myself in a persuasive, confident manner; after all, I didn't want Crace to twist my words. But there was no way he could absolve himself of guilt on this occasion. I had it all in black and white, the truth of the written word.

Timing, choosing the right moment, was important. Before confronting him, I wanted to try and lull him into a false sense of security, so I did everything according to his instructions, careful not to upset or antagonize him in any way. I ignored his occasional bursts of rudeness, his impolite dismissal of questions and inquiries, and endured his pathetic attempts to flirt with me. When he "accidentally" brushed against me, the jut of his ribcage pressing against me as he tried to squeeze by me in a corner of the kitchen, I closed my eyes and imagined that I was somewhere else. Since my return, his interest in me had heightened to a level that I would describe as near-obsession. The act of leaving the palazzo to get the glass fitted on the Francesco de' Lodovici woodcut, for example, had almost reduced him to tears. But after I promised to be as quick as I could and presented him with the alternative—hanging the picture back on the wall in its damaged state—he relented. Often I would catch him looking in my direction, a dreamlike expression on his face, living out some fragment of memory from the past.

One evening after Crace had told me he was retiring for the night, I ran a hot bath. I eased myself down under the water and closed my eyes. I heard the murmur of my heartbeat like an uncertain drum in the distance. I stayed under the water for some time; I'm not sure exactly how long, but I do remember the sense of freedom I felt in that dark place, deprived of my senses. Before the water started to cool, I soaped and rinsed myself, climbed out of the bath and had just started to dry my body when I saw the handle of the bathroom door slowly beginning to turn. I realized I had forgotten to lock it—Crace, after all, had already wished me good night—but as I quickly reached out to slide the bar across the space between the latch and the frame, the door began to open. I secured the towel around my waist, but Crace was already in the room before he asked whether he could come in. He apologized, but he had an urgent need to pee, he said. He was still fully dressed in the pair of bright orange corduroys, white shirt and light brown tweed jacket he had been wearing all day. Obviously, he had decided not to go to bed after all. His eyes gazed upon my chest, running up and down my torso as if he were about to feast on my flesh.

"I'll leave you to it," I said, feeling my face redden.

"There's no need to leave on my account," he said. "After all, we are all boys together, aren't we?"

"No, honestly, Gordon, it's fine," I said, leaving the room as he started to unzip his trousers.

As I stood in the corridor, I could hear him relieving himself. A few moments later he called my name, saying that the bathroom was free. He waited in the doorway, knowing that I would have to brush by him. I smiled, hoping that he would move, but he remained fixed to the spot.

"You know, it's extraordinary, isn't it?" he said.

"Excuse me?"

"You and me. Here and now."

"I don't quite follow, sorry."

"It was almost like it was meant to be, don't you think? I mean, everything you've done for me since you arrived here, all your kindnesses and careful attention to detail. You saw how I fell apart when you went away for a week or so. Terribly pathetic on my part, I realize, but your influence has been life changing, it really has."

"I'm pleased that you're happy."

"Oh, yes. Happier than I have been for years."

I stepped toward him so as to suggest that he stand away from the door, but he did not move, so I jumped nervously from foot to foot in a mock attempt to keep warm.

"How inexcusably insensitive of me. You're still wet; you must be freezing. You must get dressed at once. What was I thinking?"

He turned sideways in the doorway so as to offer a space by which I could pass him. Holding the corner of my towel with one hand and bending my head slightly forward so I wouldn't meet his eyes, I passed by him, half expecting to feel the touch of his hand on the base of my back. Although he let me walk by him without assault, once I was inside the bathroom he continued to stand in the doorway with a curious expression on his face. I willed him to shut the door and go away, but he carried on looking at me as if he were testing my reaction. What did he want me to do—let him watch me as I finished drying myself? The idea was abhorrent to me, enough to turn my stomach. My face reddened again, anger pulsing inside me, and I felt my wrist beginning to ache from the intensity with which I gripped my towel. I had to concentrate to keep my hand where it was as I was afraid of what I might do. But just then, in the instant before I lost control, Crace shifted his body and stepped back.

"You mustn't let me keep you," he said. "Look at you, you poor thing, you're shivering. We don't want you to catch your death, do we?"

As soon as he walked across the corridor and into his bedroom, I slammed the door and collapsed, shaking, onto the edge of the bath. I couldn't allow myself to think about what had very nearly happened. I proceeded to dry my body, wiping myself clean of the drops of water that spotted my skin, and as I dressed I tried to convince myself that this was merely another example of Crace's eccentric behavior. But the way he looked at me when he was standing in that doorway. It was not so much an expression of desire as one of expectation.

⊹══⊰⊱══⊹

In the dream I was in my parents' house, only the corridors seemed to stretch on forever and the building had a lot more rooms. I was running, searching their home for something, but I was uncertain what it was I was looking for, although I was sure that I would recognize it when I found it. I climbed the stairs, which felt as though they were melting away beneath me, but when I stretched out my foot to step onto the landing, instead of rising upward I felt myself falling for what seemed like hundreds of feet through darkness until I landed in the corridor outside my teenage bedroom. From outside I heard music playing, a CD I knew I had bought but couldn't place. I turned the handle of the door and stepped inside to see the figure of a boy sitting on the bed with his back to me. He was wearing the same black trousers, blue blazer and white shirt that made up the school uniform and, because of this, I took him to be one of my friends from my year. But, curiously, I didn't know his name. I took a step closer to the bed, but as I reached out to touch the curve of his cheek and he began to turn his head toward me to reveal himself, I felt something brush against me in the exact same spot on my own face.

I opened my eyes and sat bolt upright, certain that whatever had touched me was not confined to a dream. Outside my room I was sure I could hear footsteps disappearing down the corridor. I rubbed my eyes as I tried to look into the darkness of my room, gradually making out the curved frame at the foot of my bed, the shape of the shutters by the window, the line of the desk and the mound of my rucksack in the corner. I tried to listen for more signs of Crace, but all I heard was water lapping outside the palazzo. I checked my watch by the bed. It was 3:26 AM.

It had only been a matter of hours since Crace had surprised me in the bathroom. Now he had taken to stealing into my room in the middle of the night. I ran my fingers over my cheek to the spot that I was convinced he had just touched, somehow believing that it might feel different or that he had left a trace of himself behind. The nerve endings still tingled with the memory, almost as if Crace's hand still lingered over my skin.

I pushed myself out of bed and, as quietly as I could, walked over to the door, which was slightly ajar. I was convinced that I had shut it properly when I had entered the room earlier. I opened the door and stepped into the dark corridor and, running my hands along the wall, felt my way along to the portego. Moonlight streamed into the hall from the window overlooking the canal, casting its eerie silver sheen onto the pictures and etchings. I eased my way down the corridor but stopped outside Crace's quarters. I was certain I could hear him inside. I was about to turn around and trace my way back to my bedroom when I heard Crace's door opening and a shaft of light slashed into the darkness.

"Adam? Is that you?" said Crace, standing in his doorway.

"Yes," I whispered.

"What on earth are you doing?"

"I've just been to use the bathroom."

"Oh, you gave me a terrible fright. I heard someone lurking outside and thought it must be that awful boy again."

"No, it's only me," I said, pretending to yawn.

"I couldn't sleep," said Crace, walking out of his room and opening the bathroom door. "I need to get some pills. Now, where are they? I know they're in here somewhere."

I turned down the corridor and started to head back to my room when I heard Crace call my name.

"Would you mind helping me?" he said with a note of desperation in his voice. "I can't find the fuckers. What is it with all this stuff? Where the hell are they?"

In the bathroom he had pulled out all the contents of the medicine cabinet—plasters, empty tubes of hemorrhoid cream, nail clippers, a few sterilized wipes, and dark plastic bottles containing old drugs—and thrown them into the sink where he rummaged about among the mess, occasionally tossing items over his shoulder as he dismissed them from his search.

"Gordon, here, let me," I said, easing my way by him. "Look, why don't you go and try to lie down and I'll find the tablets and bring them to you."

"Would you? That would be very kind. I don't know what's the matter with me. I suppose I haven't been the same since . . . well, you know."

He raised his thin, almost invisible eyebrows in a gesture of acknowledgment and mutual understanding, but the manic glint in his eyes and his rictus smile unsettled me.

"Which tablets are you looking for? What's the name of them?"

"I think they're diazepam."

"You go back to bed and I'll be with you in a couple of minutes."

His eyes lingered on my face before he turned around and walked back into his room. I searched my way through the bottles of old cough medicine and calamine lotion, tubs of decongestant and dozens of different pharmaceuticals until I found the pills he was looking for. I set them to one side and then placed everything else back into the cabinet. As I closed it, I caught a glimpse of myself—or was it Chris?—in its mirrored surface.

In the kitchen I filled a glass full of water and returned to Crace's bedroom with the pills. He was sitting in his elaborate bed, surrounded by the red velvet curtains, his head resting on a pillow propped up on the ivory headboard. His bedside light cast strange shadows about the alcove and over the figure of the Madonna.

"What would I ever do without you?"

It was a refrain he had repeated several times to me since I had arrived back at the palazzo. I gave him the sleeping pills and the glass of water.

"Thank you, my dear, thank you," he said, his thin tongue flicking over his lips.

The loose flesh on his scrawny neck quivered as he swallowed the tablets. He reached out and placed his hand over mine, clasping it in silent appreciation, where it stayed until I could no longer bear the feel of his skin next to mine.

"Here, let me plump up this pillow for you," I said, reaching out. "We'll get you nice and comfortable so you can have a good sleep."

Whether it was from the drug itself or a psychological effect brought about by merely swallowing the pills, Crace's eyes began to flutter. He tried to engage in snatches of conversation so as to fight the impulse to sleep, but eventually he could no longer resist. I pulled together the thick curtains that shrouded his bed, sealing him into his velvet cocoon, and was about to turn off his bedside light when Crace sighed deeply. I leaned forward and pulled back a little of the thick fabric to hear him whisper the name "Chris." I left him in the dark, dreaming of the past.

┼══════┼

As I walked out of my room each morning, I felt as though I were stepping onto a stage, ready to perform a certain part in front of Crace. Each day I had to tell myself that it wasn't for much longer; if only I could endure a few more weeks with him, then I would be in a position where I was in ultimate control, free to tell his story in any way I saw fit, able to mold his history according to a pattern I had conceived. The pressure to behave in a certain way, appearing to be constantly courteous and ever obliging, caused my genuine feelings of dislike and disgust to intensify. My only outlet was my notebook, which I took out of its hiding place at the end of each day and used as a means to purge myself of my increasingly poisonous emotions. It became a receptacle of all that was dark in myself.

Occasionally Crace would catch me brooding. He would ask me whether I was all right, and I would have to look down so as not to let him see the hatred in my eyes. I was a good actor, though, able in an instant to lighten my mood and flash him a winning smile. I could always explain my seemingly distant demeanor with the fact that I was having problems with my book. "Writer's block," I would say, and he would nod knowingly. He advised me to keep a notebook in which I entered my day-to-day thoughts and observations. That was always a good way, he had found, of keeping the creative juices flowing. But nothing in the world would make him want to publish again, he added; he would rather die than see his name on the front of a book.

Now that I knew the circumstances surrounding his decision to give up writing, I had to admit that, despite the almost visceral repulsion I felt toward him, I admired the fact that he had never been driven to change his mind. I wondered if he knew about the death of Chris's mother? After all, her existence—and Chris's note to her telling her what to do in the event of Crace seeking publication of *The Music Teacher*—was the one big obstacle preventing the release of his second novel. I suppose Shaw posed a small risk, as he knew about the existence of the book, but now that I had bought his silence I doubted he would do anything. Ultimately, I was the one who held all the cards, the one with the power to shape Crace's future. I was the teller of his story, his ventriloquist, his biographer.

Sitting up in bed, writing in my notebook, I listened as the rain lashed against the window. After a delicious supper of *linguine di mare,* Crace and I had done a spot of reading in the drawing room, and then at eleven o'clock, with the storm already raging over Venice, he had asked me to get him his customary glass of water and two sleeping pills. Although I had suggested that he see a doctor, he had refused. He couldn't bear the thought of a stranger examining him, he said, poking around his body like an unwanted intruder. He had told me that he had quite a stash of pills he had hoarded over the years that should keep him going for some time to come. I wondered why he had gone to the bother of amassing the tablets. The most likely reason, the only motivation I could discern, was a knowledge that one day he might feel compelled to take his own life.

Since my arrival back at the palazzo, his dependence on me seemed complete. From first thing in the morning, when I made his breakfast and stood by him as he got dressed, through the day, when I would read to him or sit by him as he talked about his art collection, to the evening, when I would help him take off his clothes and assist him as he climbed into bed, he demanded that I stay with him. Leaving him for a matter of minutes to get some food from the local shop induced spells of anxiety, which, if not allayed by soothing words and reassurances of a quick reappearance, resulted in hysteria, while the only time I got to myself—when I could write in my notebook—was after he had gone to sleep.

That night after I had given him the sleeping pills, he retired to bed. He must have been asleep for two hours when I heard a series of disjointed, unintelligible shouts coming from his room. Had Crace's old employee returned? I hid my notebook under my pillow and, wearing only a vest and shorts, ran down the corridor and into the portego. I switched on the lights in the grand hall, illuminating the vast space, but there was no sign of an intruder. The sound, a frightened, animalistic cry, continued to come from Crace's bedroom. I gently knocked on his door, but as there was no answer except for the terrible moaning that continued to echo down the corridor, I entered the room. In the darkness I saw Crace writhing in his bed, kicking and hitting the surrounding velvet curtains as he thrashed out with his legs and arms. It was obvious he was having a nightmare.

"Gordon, Gordon, wake up," I said, walking into the alcove.

I opened the dark red curtains and switched on his bedside light, but the nightmare still gripped him.

"Gordon," I said, reaching out to touch his bony shoulder through his cotton nightshirt. "Gordon?"

He arched his back, pain etched deeply into his face, and woke with a jump.

"Oh, thank God," he said, rubbing his eyes. "I was having the most awful dream."

He sat up in bed and looked at me with a dazed, confused expression on his face.

"Just thinking about it unsettles me," he said, shivering. "Oh, it was horrible and so realistic. I went out for a walk, something that, in itself, filled me with fear, and if that was not bad enough, I came back to find that . . . that . . . you were dead."

Tears clouded his eyes as he relived the dream.

"You were sitting there at the kitchen table with your head slumped forward. I thought at first you were asleep and I came over to try and wake you. But you didn't move. You felt cold to the touch. I couldn't take it in. I kept trying to shake you, but you didn't stir."

"That does sound horrible," I said, trying to calm him down. "But it was only a dream. Look, I'm here, alive and well."

He took hold of my hand, and I felt his skin, both cold and clammy, rub against mine.

"Yes, yes, you're here. You'll never leave, will you? My Chris, you'll never leave. Nothing will separate us now."

He leaned forward and embraced me, his hands twining themselves around my neck. I felt his finger stroking the back of my neck, tracing its way down to my shoulder blade. His other hand snaked its way down my arm, massaging my triceps, before it moved on and came to rest on my leg.

"Gordon," I said, gently. "It's not Chris; it's Adam. I'm *Adam*."

He started to whisper Chris's name over and over again, and I felt the occasional flick of his tongue brush against my ear.

"Gordon," I said more sternly. "Wake up. It's Adam."

As his fingers started to worm their way up my leg toward my crotch, I took hold of his shoulders and pushed him away from me.

"Stop it, Gordon. Stop it!"

He blinked a couple of times, as if waking from a dream, and then, as he realized what he had done, covered his face with his hands. His long fingers looked like those from a Quattrocento painting.

"Adam, will you ever forgive me? Oh, what a fool I've made of myself."

"Don't worry about it," I said. "You were obviously having a nightmare."

"Yes, I was—an awful, awful dream. I can't apologize enough. Oh God, you'll hate me now, think me no better than a dirty old man."

"I don't think anything of the kind. Please, Gordon, don't worry—"

"I hope I won't drive you away," he said, taking hold of his nightshirt and twisting it with his hands. "I wouldn't blame you if you did leave. It was absolutely unforgivable behavior. Inexcusable."

"Honestly, Gordon. Let's just forget it ever happened."

"God, I'm never going to get to sleep now," he said, biting his nails. "Would you mind awfully getting me two more tablets?"

"Is that wise? You've already taken two."

"No, it will be fine. Otherwise I'm going to be up all night, worrying, playing the whole thing out in my mind over and over again."

"Well, if you are sure."

"Yes, I'm sure."

I got the pills and some more water for Crace. As he tipped the tablets into his mouth, he turned to me and, with a look of genuine affection, thanked me.

"I should sleep like the dead now, shouldn't I?" he said, resting his head back on the pillow.

I left him and returned to my room, the noise of thunder rumbling in the distance.

Back in my room I couldn't sleep. The feel of Crace's fingers on my neck and on my legs, working their way up my thighs, continued to burn into me. The fear of what he might have done next unsettled me, and a thousand elaborate, equally disturbing, scenarios ran through my mind. I realized that I couldn't continue as I was, and I made up my mind that the next day I would present him with my evidence. I would give him an ultimatum, a choice between cooperation and exposure. Of course, I would have to prepare myself for a degree of unpleasantness, but that would be better than the alternative. At least with this solution I would have, as they say, a certain amount of closure. I would be the one in control.

Lightning flashed outside my window, splitting the night sky. With each strike I became more and more anxious, as if the electrical storm were somehow wired into my central nervous system. Before trying to go to sleep, I had placed my notebook back in its hiding place under the floor by my desk, but I felt an overwhelming urge to look through it. Still wearing just my vest and shorts, I got out of bed and walked across the room. I took out the chisel from my desk drawer, where it was hidden under a pile of old newspapers, and used it to ease up the edge of the panel. Inside was my little literary treasure trove, the papers that I hoped would bring me fame, perhaps even fortune. I dusted off the layer of dirt that had settled over the bag and unwrapped the package. I flicked through my notebook, amazed that I had managed to write so many words about my time with Crace. I really had done quite a sterling job. But when I reread Chris's suicide note, I remembered that there was one thing missing—a copy of *The Music Teacher*. If I could only track that down, then I would have located the final piece of evidence. If I got my hands on the unpublished manuscript, then my case against Crace would be so much stronger.

As I remembered Crace's words to me when I had left him in the bedroom—how he was going to sleep like the dead—I knew that I would have to take the opportunity. I quickly pushed all the papers and my notebook back into the bags and placed them under the floor. I put the chisel into the drawer and under the newspapers, and picked up my small pen torch and dropped it into the pocket of my shorts. Thunder roared outside, shaking the foundations of the palazzo, and a wall of rain lashed against the window. If Crace could sleep through a storm as ferocious as this, then he really was dead to the world.

I opened my door and walked down the dark corridor into the portego. I stopped at the entrance to the next corridor, the one that led to Crace's quarters, and then again outside his bedroom, listening for movement, but could not hear a thing. I pushed open the door into his bedroom and stepped onto the terrazzo. I had to be certain that Crace really was asleep before I proceeded any further, so as I moved into the alcove that housed his bed, I coughed, quietly at first and then more loudly. But all I heard from inside his velvet canopy was the sound of breathing and the occasional guttural snore. I pulled back the curtain and peeked inside to see Crace lying in a fetal position, his mouth open, a bubble of spit at the corner of his lips. Although his lids were closed, his eyes continued to move under the skin at a rapid pace, a sign that he was in the deepest of sleeps. I closed the curtains and left Crace dreaming.

I walked across the room and opened the door to his study. I took out my pen torch and shone it into the darkness. Illuminated by the pocket of light I saw the face of the terrapin ink pot staring out of the gloom and then the various objects standing on Crace's cabinet of curiosities: the slipware flask shaped like a scallop shell; the range of fine vases; the miniatures in their velvet frames; the white marble relief of Mucius Scaevola; the triangular perfume burner with its winged figures; the brass candlesticks and the bowl showing Ganymede being abducted by an eagle, a representation of Zeus. The rich, red, fabric-lined walls looked like they were covered in blood.

I searched the cabinet first, running my fingers along the spaces between the mass of objects and down the back of the shelving for any sign of an envelope or package, but there was nothing. I looked around the room at the piles of books, some of which, despite my best efforts, were still arranged in unstable towers. I knelt down by some oversize volumes that Crace had placed in one of the far corners of the study. I lifted each one off the pile, quickly flicking through the pages so that I could see the space behind them, but again there was no sign of Crace's book. Although I had already looked through his desk soon after arriving at the palazzo and had found no trace of a manuscript, I began to search that too. After all, I couldn't rule out the possibility that Crace may have secreted the typescript in another part of the palazzo before moving it to his desk in the last few weeks. One thing I had learned during the course of my research was that you had to be thorough. Assumptions were dangerous things.

I opened the small drawers at the top of the desk and found the tiny gold keys and the buff-colored envelope that still contained the lock of flaxen hair, which I now knew probably belonged to Chris. But at the back of the drawer was another, larger envelope, one I hadn't seen before. I pulled it out and shone my torch inside it to see another lock of hair, similar in color to Chris's but not quite so brittle in texture. I remembered the iciness of what I had taken to be Crace's fingers on my face while I slept, but now it seemed more likely that what I had felt was the press of cold metal scissors against my skin, scissors he had used to cut the hair from my head. As I turned over the envelope, a rash of goose bumps prickled the skin at the base of my neck. Written on the back of the envelope was a phrase in Italian that seemed vaguely familiar. It was in Crace's handwriting.

"*Io son colei che ognuno al mondo brama, perché per me dopo la morte vive,*" it read.

At that moment I heard a noise behind me. A slash of light burned into the room. I turned around. Crace was standing at the door, wearing a nightshirt and a dressing gown. He was holding a gun.

"Found something interesting?" he said.

"Gordon—it's not like you think, I'm—"

"You're what? I know very well what you're doing."

"I was just trying to find—"

"It's no use, Adam. Stop lying for once, will you?"

He took a step toward me and raised the gun, using both hands to bring it up to eye level.

"*E se vitio o virtude opera trama,*" he said, his voice rich and mellifluous.

"What are you saying?"

"Just completing what you had started to read, that's all. An Allegory of Fame. Quite appropriate, don't you think, in the circumstances? I'd remember this if I were you. It might prove useful . . . *Tal che a le spoglie o al degno imperio arrive . . .* "

Although his weak arms trembled as he tried to hold the gun steady, his eyes shone with a steely, focused determination, almost a passion. I couldn't take it in. He was actually going to shoot me.

"Per quello infamia son per questa Fama . . . "

If I waited one more moment, I knew he would press the trigger.

"E a colui per me solo si ascrive . . . "

Without a second thought, I launched myself forward with all my strength, letting the torch drop from me. I crashed into him, and we both collapsed onto the Persian rug. I heard the gun hit the floor with a dull thud. Crace started to scramble for the weapon, thrashing about with his sinewy limbs in a frenzied manner. I jumped up and started to scan the room for any sign of the gun, sweeping my hands over the floor as I did so.

"I'm going to kill you, you bastard," Crace screeched from behind me.

Frantically I looked around me and finally spotted the weapon beneath the cabinet of curiosities, its mother-of-pearl sheen glinting in the darkness. I lunged forward, my chest skidding and chafing along the rug, as I reached for the gun. As I stretched out to grab the weapon, I felt something tugging at my feet. It was Crace, suddenly possessed with more strength than I had ever witnessed before. He jerked me backward, clawing at the skin around my shins.

As I tried to reach for the gun, only a foot or so away from the ends of my fingers, the muscles in my back trembled and my shoulder felt as though it was dislocating from its socket. If I could only free myself from Crace's grip, I could almost touch it. Wrenching one of my legs out of his hands, I kicked out backward, hitting Crace squarely in the face. Suddenly I could move. I scuttled forward like some kind of creature from the depths of the ocean, grabbed the gun and spun around so that I lay on my back. Crace came toward me, holding a paper knife that he had found on his desk. As I grappled with the gun, trying to stop my hands from shaking, he brought the knife down hard, stabbing it deep into the top of my right foot. I cried out in pain as he wriggled the blunt-edged blade into me. I heard the sound of the knife cutting through my skin and I had to stop myself from retching. The gun, with its iridescent surface, slipped about in my hands like a fish, but as I tried to steady it, Crace pulled the paper knife out of my foot. I screamed in pain.

"Don't be such a baby," he said, raising the blood-soaked blade above his head and stepping nearer to my prostrate body.

With my good foot, I kicked him in the groin. His face creased with pain and he fell forward as though all the air had been forced out of his body. Using a nearby chair as a support, I lifted myself upward and dragged my injured foot over to the desk. As I moved I left a trail of blood behind me.

Crace, still gasping for breath, turned toward me, his eyes glinting maniacally. He lifted the knife above his head and moved a step closer to me.

"Gordon . . . Gordon—"

"Don't say anything."

"But . . . Gordon . . . stop . . . think—"

"You fucking viper in the nest."

"Please . . . Gordon . . . stop—"

I had no choice. I pressed the trigger, the explosion reverberating inside me. The first bullet hit the cabinet, smashing the bowl with its figures of Ganymede and Zeus into a thousands pieces and shattering the scallop-shaped slipware flask. I shot again, badly, the bullet destroying the perfume burner and the white marble relief of Mucius Scaevola before smashing the marble urn on the chest where Crace had hidden the gun. He turned his head to assess the damage and then continued in his steady progression toward me.

"E a colui per me solo si ascrive," he said, resuming his recitation of the quotation. *"Del Biasmo il suono ond'a costei si dona de la gloria le palme e la corona.* Even though I translated it for you once before, let me try and help you. After all, I understand that this may not be the most conducive of settings in which to work out the translation. 'I am she whom everyone in the world longs for, because through me they live after death.'"

He took another step nearer.

"'And if vice or virtue operates so as to obtain plunder or honorable empire, I am infamy for the former and for the latter fame,'" he said.

"Gordon . . . step back. You know I don't want to do this."

My palms were wet with sweat and my fingers were shaking.

"Really? Are you sure? Hasn't it always been your greatest desire, your secret wish, to kill people?"

"Gordon—"

"'Vice has only blame from me while virtue has glory, palms and crown.'"

Just as he intoned the last word of the quotation—and was now almost near enough to reach out and touch me—I pressed the trigger again, this time aiming the gun directly at him. The tension that had built up inside me over the last few months found perfect release in that one moment. The bullet hit his chest, near his heart. Crace fell backward, his face transformed not so much by agony but by what I can only describe as love. As he staggered like a drunken man desperate to find his footing, he clutched at anything around him, grabbing the back of a chair and the edge of the door frame before finally holding on to the cabinet of his treasures, most of them now smashed into pieces. He looked at me and past me, smiled, and then pulled down the cabinet, and all its objects, on top of himself. A stain of blood began to spread itself across the front of his nightshirt like a sinister bloom. I bent down over him, cleaning the debris from his body.

"Gordon . . . I'm sorry," I said, dropping the gun onto the floor.

He looked directly into my eyes with an expression of gratitude, his mouth forming itself into a word he never said. Blood sprouted on his lips and bubbled over down his chin before his head dropped to one side. He was dead.

I looked at the scene of devastation around me, the floor littered with shards of broken pottery and slivers of glass, the air thick with the smell of the gun. Blood continued to seep out of Crace, pooling below him—a body drowning in dark water.

I tried to stand up, but the pain in my foot crippled me. I held on to the corner of the cabinet and raised myself upward. Blood trickled out of the wound in my foot, a nasty little cherry red mouth, mixing with Crace's on the floor. I already felt faint and nauseous, but now I trembled so badly that every movement I made, no matter how small, seemed to spawn a kind of underlying counterpoint, a vibrational echo that made my whole body shake. I dragged myself out of the study, through Crace's bedroom and into the bathroom, leaving a trail of blood behind me. Using my hands, themselves covered in scratches and cuts, I lifted my right leg into the bath and turned on the cold tap. Pain stung deep inside me as the wound came in contact with the water, and I had to grip the side of the cold bath to stop myself from screaming out. The water turned red as I cleaned the blood from my foot.

After I finished washing it, I grabbed a white hand towel from the rail and pressed it down onto the wound, wrapping it around my ankle and securing it with a safety pin I had found in the medicine cabinet. I tried to walk by shifting most of the weight onto my left foot. My first step was agony and I almost doubled up in pain, but somehow I managed to hobble out of the bathroom and into the portego. Through the windows I could still see the lightning fissuring through the sky, and I heard the sound of thunder over the city, the noise sending shock waves through the water.

In the grand hall I stopped by Battista del Moro's *An Allegory of Fame*. I peered closely at the figure of Fame standing high above the representations of vice and virtue, under which was written the verse that Crace had quoted to me. What had he said? That I would need to remember something about the etching? I recalled our first conversation about the picture and how he had mentioned that Fame seemed more intrigued by the satyr of vice than the feminine ideal of virtue. As I examined it, I noticed that there was something sticking out from behind the bottom right-hand side of the frame. It was the corner of an envelope. I pulled it out and saw that Crace had written my name on the front. Inside was a sheet of white paper, blank except for one cryptic line, also in Crace's handwriting: "If you want to find the manuscript, first seek out the sunshine muse."

What on earth did that mean? Was Crace playing some kind of game? And why would he want to help me find the unpublished book that had effectively ruined his writing career? In my head I ran through our various conversations we had had over the past few months. The sunshine muse. I limped down the portego looking at the windows, trying to remember what the hall looked like during the day when light streamed into the space. Did the clue suggest I should look in one particular place that was

struck by the rays of the sun? The figure of the muse suggested inspiration, but did that mean I should search out the spot in which
Crace felt creatively invigorated? I walked back to his bedroom
and into his study. The shock of him lying there, his limbs spread
out at odd angles on the floor, nearly turned my stomach.

I searched through Crace's bedside cabinet but came across
nothing except a dirty dried tissue and a pile of books. I hobbled
back into the portego and was just about to turn into the drawing
room when it came to me. How could I have been so stupid? I
turned around and scanned the wall for the Francesco de'
Lodovici woodcut, the *Triomphi di Carlo*. The clue had been staring me in the face all along—the figure of the poet kneeling before
his patron, the inspirational figure of his muse portrayed as a sun
shining above him. As I lifted the frame from the wall, another
letter dropped onto the floor.

Again it was addressed to me, again in Crace's handwriting. I
tore open the envelope, almost ripping the letter inside, and read
the sentence Crace had written: "You are one step nearer. Answer
this: who wrote that a prisoner in the Sala del Tormento 'sustaineth so great torments that his joints are for the time loosed
and pulled asunder?'"

I knew immediately what Crace was referring to. It was the
book that he had been reading on my very first day at the palazzo,
the one that had made him laugh, the one about the man who had
visited Venice a few centuries ago and who had claimed to have
introduced the fork to England. But what was it called? I couldn't
believe I had forgotten the title. Fuck. I could see Crace sitting in
his chair with two books covered in red leather, their spines embossed with gold leaf. But what was the name? In frustration, I
hit out at the wall, smashing my fist into the glass that covered
one of the etchings. Then I remembered that I had written about

that day in my notebook. I was sure I would have mentioned the title in my journal.

I moved as fast as I could, my foot still smarting, toward my room. Inside, I turned on the lights, pulled open the drawer of my desk and took out the chisel. I dropped onto my knees and wrenched up the wooden floor panel. I split open the plastic bags, tearing into them with a fury, and grabbed my notebook from inside. I flicked through the pages, the words dancing before my eyes, until I reached the beginning of my time with Crace. I scanned the entries, searching for the day, jumping past records of our conversations, details about my life before I came to Venice and dreams of what might happen after I had left, until I found what I was looking for. I had indeed written down the name of the book. The author was Thomas Coryat and the title was *Coryat's Crudities*.

I turned and, as quickly as I could, stumbled down the corridor, through the portego and into the drawing room. Since arriving at the palazzo, I had arranged the books neatly on the shelves, so I knew that it shouldn't take me too long to locate the volume. I ran my fingers down the spines of the books, remembering how dusty they had been when I had first started to sort them out. By my recollection the volume I wanted should be on the first shelf near Crace's collection of books on Venice, along with Ruskin's *The Stones of Venice,* W. D. Howells's *Venetian Life, The Letters of Lady Mary Wortley Montagu,* and Aretino's *Ragionamenti.* But it was nowhere to be seen. I checked the titles, making sure it had not slipped behind one of the other volumes, and then looked down the entire shelf, a feeling of panic rising within me. I told myself that I had to keep calm. Perhaps he had placed it in a different part of the room. I picked up the library steps and, my foot still throbbing with pain, climbed onto them. I stretched up and looked along the shelves but could not see the name. I moved the steps farther toward the other end of the library, but again there was nothing.

I heard a crack of thunder crash above the palazzo. The titles of the books danced in front of my eyes until I could no longer focus. I swept my hand along the shelf, dislodging a whole set of books and sending them flying onto the floor, the impact causing the glass shards of the chandelier to shiver and ring above me. I thrashed out again and again, clearing most of the shelves of their books, tearing off spines and ripping out pages. I felt consumed by anger, a murderous rage. By the time I had finished, I had reduced Crace's fine collection of books to a chaotic heap, a pyramid of loose paper, creased leather and twisted spines.

Feeling weak and sick, I pushed my way through the chaotic pile of broken books. I cleared off some torn pages that lay on Crace's chair and sat down, my head in my hands. What on earth was Crace trying to do? What kind of sick game was he playing, even now when he lay dead? I took some deep breaths and tried to think. I knew the volume wasn't in his bedroom or his study, and I had checked all the shelves in the drawing room. Where else was there to look? There weren't any books in the kitchen, the portego or the bathroom. The only place I hadn't searched—in fact, the only part of the palazzo that I had never stepped into, apart from the flooded lower quarters—was the floor above. Now that Crace was dead, I could explore it for the first time.

I left the drawing room and stood by the entrance to the apartments, by the internal staircase that led to the next floor. Dragging my injured foot, I slowly climbed the stairs, listening to the wailing of the wind outside. At the top there was an old, thin door, its surface mottled by woodworm, secured by a small padlock. I pulled at the lock, trying to wrench it open. It wouldn't budge. In frustration, I ran at the door, using all the power of my shoulder, channeling the pain in my foot and anger I felt toward Crace. The wood began to splinter, but the lock remained fixed. Taking a deep breath, I launched myself at the door again, gritting my teeth as the pain consumed me. I heard the sound of the padlock hitting the floor as the door banged against the wall.

The vast space was dark and, as Crace had said, completely empty. I felt around the wall for a light switch, my hands swathed in cobwebs, and finally found one. A single bulb hanging from the middle of the room flickered for an instant before fading away, plunging the space back into darkness. Fuck. I would have to go back down to the study to retrieve my torch.

I retraced my steps, lowering myself gently down the staircase, and edged along the portego and back through the bedroom to the study. Crace lay there, his skin now a ghostly white, the blood around him beginning to darken. I stepped over the debris and found my torch nestling by the desk. I picked it up, wiped it as if it was covered in blood or the fingerprints of a guilty man, and made my way back up to the empty floor.

I shone the torch into the darkness, illuminating nothing except for bare walls, cracked plaster and dirt. As the light hit the far corner by the window overlooking the canal, I heard a scuttling sound, the noise of rats running to safety. I walked forward into the emptiness, feeling the brush of spiderwebs on my face, scanning the room for the book. Then something seemed to glint above me. I raised my torch to the ceiling and saw an elaborate octagon of gold leaf, still luminescent despite the buildup of years of grime, surrounded by what looked like folds of decaying skin and the disembodied heads of dozens of baby boys. I stepped backward, unsettled and confused by what I had just seen, and as I did so, I fell over something on the floor. I dropped my torch and suddenly found myself encased in blackness. The memory of what had happened in Dorset flashed into my mind. The velvet darkness. The sharp edges of the rock in the palm of my hand. Lavinia's bloodied face, her skin studded with jewels of glass.

I heard the rats, suddenly liberated by the lack of light, scuttle across the floor toward me. I scrambled around in the dust, stretching out into the darkness to find my torch. I reached out and felt something. It was moving.

I kicked out in the direction of the rat. As I did so, I felt something near my feet. I stretched my hand out slowly, fearful that I might touch one of the creatures again, and pushed my way through a mass of powdery dirt. I felt something cylindrical. It was my torch. I picked it up and shone it over the surface of the floor. The rats dispersed quickly into the dark corners of the room, which looked more like a vast underground tomb than a former living space situated at the top of a grand palazzo. As the torch light pierced through the gloom, I spotted something on the floor. I eased myself up, another wave of nausea threatening to consume me. I bit on my lip and pushed myself forward. I realized, as I got closer, that the object was a book. I picked it up. It was *Coryat's Crudities*. The satisfaction I felt on finding the volume was erased by an overwhelming sense of dread. For a moment I considered dropping the book on the floor, leaving it to decay among the filth and the rats, and escaping the palazzo before it was too late, but I realized that this was impossible. I had to know. I had to find Crace's manuscript.

As I hobbled back toward the staircase, I shone the torch onto the ceiling. The sight that had unsettled me—the seemingly infinite number of babies' heads—was actually nothing more than an old stucco velarium, the decoration formed to make it look like a vast piece of fabric supported by winged male infants. I took a deep breath and limped toward the door. Slowly, I descended the stairs, each step sending stabs of pain up my leg.

At the bottom of the staircase I brushed the dust from my body and sat down. I opened the book. Sandwiched between two of the leaf-thin pages was another note, this time a much longer one. Again, it was written in Crace's spidery handwriting.

Dear Adam,

First of all, thank you for what you have done. It's a blessed release. Life had lost all its sparkle, and I've been thinking how best to go for quite some time. Suicide always strikes me as a little banal, don't you think? Murder, however, is a lot more interesting. If you forgive the bad joke, there's nothing like going out with a bang.

I must also congratulate you on your resourcefulness, which is, frankly, much more than I had ever expected from you. What a sleuth you've been to get this far, to find this letter. You are really quite the little detective, aren't you? Who would have thought you could unearth so much about me? But I suppose some of your methods are, how shall I say it, a little unconventional.

Unfortunately, you were not clever enough, my dear boy. I became aware of your little "project" soon after you moved in here. Did you really think I could be that blind? I knew about those letters, the ones from Lavinia Maddon and Shaw, a long time before you even set foot in this palazzo. They were a little test for you, one that I'm sorry to say you failed. And as for all those silly stunts, such as the one when you tried to get the key for the letter box from me, well, I don't know what you must have been thinking. I may be old, my eyesight is not what it was, but I am far from stupid. Of course, I was terribly disappointed in you, extremely angry, and even considered getting rid of you. But then I thought, why not have a little fun with you instead? And how could I dismiss you, you who reminded me so much of my golden boy, Chris?

The first time I saw you, when you came to deliver your letter, I thought a ghost had emerged from the canals to haunt me. That or I was going mad. I had to make sure. And when you came for the interview, there was no mistaking it. The similarity was just too striking to ignore and so, as I told you, I had to get rid of the boy I had previously employed.

He did not, however, come back to demand money from me. That was a little poetic license on my part. I simply threw the Francesco de' Lodovici onto the floor, stamped on it with my shoe and cut my hands with the glass. Of course it hurt a little, but it was nothing but a few surface grazes. And all that with my back—when you had to help me undress and bathe—well, it was just an elaborate put-on, one I must say I rather enjoyed. In fact, the whole thing has been a sham, including my nightmare.

Did you really think I could find you attractive in any way? You are a pretty boy, you certainly do look like him, but you're not that special and certainly not in the same league as Chris. There's something about your personality that's a little odd; let's just leave it at that, shall we? However, I must congratulate you on the way you dispensed with the enterprising Ms. Maddon. You know my opinion of biographers. I'd say she got her just des-

erts, wouldn't you? But if you want to make it as a real novelist, I have two pieces of advice for you. One: you're going to have to learn how to be a lot more observant. I didn't take those sleeping pills that you gave me tonight. In fact, I've never really needed them. I pretended to swallow them, and when you left me alone I wrapped them in a little piece of loo paper and flushed them away. Two: if you ever go on a trip to the shops or the post office again (which I very much doubt you'll be doing, at least in the near future), make sure to hide your notebook in a place where peeking eyes can't find it. Oh, and if you do insist on fashioning a hiding place under the floor, you must make an effort to check it more regularly.

It's a shame, as we could have had such a happy future together if you hadn't started on your so-called biography. But having said that, I don't regret a thing. I think it's all turned out for the best, as they say.

For the record, I want you to know one thing. Despite what you might have heard from Levenson, I loved all those boys at the school in my own way. But my relationship with Chris didn't start out like that. He was different from the others. There was no need to persuade him. In fact, he was the one who initiated it. He loved me you see, loved me like none of the others could have.

There's no need to tell you that his death destroyed me. I'm not going to give you the satisfaction of telling you exactly how it affected me, but let's just say I was never the same again. Of course, after I discovered what had happened I couldn't publish the book. In fact, I couldn't stand the sight of it, so I burnt it. As I watched the pages disappear into the flames and turn to ash I felt a sense of purging, a punishment, if you like. Subsequently, I found I couldn't write a thing. Not a word. That's what guilt does, you see, as you may soon find out yourself.

Now I'm afraid you've got to do a little more work if you want to find the manuscript that you are looking for. Love looks not with the eyes but with the mind. Think about it.

> *Yours,*
> *Gordon Crace*

The note fell from my hands onto the floor. I felt weak, drained of energy, near to fainting. The bastard, the fucking bastard. Feeling the rage rise within me, I stretched out my arm and pulled off the pictures from the walls of the portego, smashing the glass of the etchings and breaking the frames. I stumbled into the drawing room and threw a table light into the mirror above the fireplace. I saw myself shattered into a thousand pieces. I picked up one of the books lying on the floor and tore it apart, sending the pages flying into the air. I wrenched an oil painting from the wall and punched my hand through its canvas. I moved into the kitchen and turned over the table and threw a chair against the window. As the glass cracked, I felt the wind from outside whip around the room. I hobbled across the portego into Crace's bedroom. I pulled down the curtains from his bed, knocked over his bedside table and ripped apart his pillows, sending feathers cascading through the air. I couldn't bear to see the Madonna looking so serenely down at me. I forced the painting down from the wall and smashed it over my knee.

By the time I reached the study, I was exhausted, my anger almost spent. I saw Crace's pathetic form lying on the floor, and although I wanted to beat him into a pulp, I felt tears running down my face. I dropped to my knees and sobbed over his body, images and snatches of conversation from our months together playing through my mind. I'm not sure how long I stayed there by his corpse, but as I came to my senses one question continued to worm its way through my mind. If he really had destroyed *The Music Teacher*, what manuscript was he talking about? Also, I couldn't forget the last line of Crace's note. Was he referring to my own situation with Eliza or the fictional one I had created and read to him? Was Crace telling me to look for the answer to the clue inside my own notebook?

Wiping the tears from my eyes, I dragged myself out of the study and back to my bedroom. I picked up my journal, feeling sick at the sight of it, despising every word I had written. I resisted the urge to tear out every page and flicked to the entries where I had written about my relationship with Eliza and then to the sketch about Richard and his growing obsession with his ex-girlfriend, Emma. I read through the accounts, the one real, the other fictional, but I couldn't find anything. What a waste of fucking time the whole thing had been! But just as I was about to throw the notebook across the room, I remembered something Crace had said to me. I turned the pages back to the beginning of the journal, where I had written about tricking Crace into giving me the key to the letter box. As we had walked down to the courtyard, he had gestured toward the cupid that stood on the top of the Corinthian column and said that comment about how love looks not with the eyes but with the mind.

I pushed myself upward and out down the corridor. I weaved my way past the shards of glass, the broken canvases and the

splintered frames and through the portego to the top of the stairs.
I stepped outside into the rain, the night sky still illuminated by
flashes of lightning. I eased myself down the stairs, using the
metal banister as a support, and toward the statue. Attached to its
head by a large elastic band was a plastic bag. I saw an image of
Lavinia, her head bloodied. I was back there, on that dark night. I
had just killed her, the feel of the rock smashing into her head still
fresh in the memory of my skin. I had placed the bag over her
head so as not to get the blood on my clothes. I had turned around,
but when I looked back, shining the torch in her direction, her lips
were still moving underneath the surface of the plastic, making a
series of silent, unknowable words.

I stood there in the courtyard, letting the rain wash down my
face and over my body, stinging the scratches that covered my skin.
I hoped the water would cleanse me of my sins, help me forget the
past. It didn't. I grabbed the package, snapping the elastic band,
and made my way back up the stairs into the portego. Even though
I was soaking, I didn't wait to dry myself. I tore through the bag to
find another envelope. I took out the short note, now splattered
with drops of water from my hands and face, and read it.

Dear Adam,

*My, you were observant, weren't you? Did you write
down everything I said? I feel honored you found me of
such interest. I hope I haven't disappointed you in any
way.*

*Now, just one last thing before I leave you to your
thoughts. You'll find a copy of the book hidden on my
corpse. It will be nice for me to think of you touching me
even after my death. And you never know—you may
actually find that you enjoy it.*

Contrary to what you might think, I have been quite busy. I did most of the writing at night in bed, scribbling away in an old notebook. The copying out was rather a bore, and I only just managed to finish it. But I didn't want to leave without providing you with a little reading matter; after all, where I suspect you are going, you might need something to alleviate the boredom.

Hopefully the material is so strong that my publishers won't mind the primitive method of presentation. I gave the book to Lucia to post when you were out. So, you see, she did come in useful after all.

I can't thank you enough for all you've done. Your help has been invaluable. I think you'll find you make a fascinating character.

> *Good-bye,*
> *Gordon Crace*

I let the letter drop onto the floor and ran back to the study. As I turned into the corridor, I slipped. I looked down at my foot. The blood from my wound had soaked through the towel, which was now a mass of red. I raised myself upward, screaming and cursing, leaving a bloody snail-like trail behind me.

Yet the pain from my foot was nothing compared to the sense of panic inside, a plague of locusts trapped in my ribcage. I couldn't breathe. My lungs were drowning. I felt like I was going to swallow my tongue.

Crace's lizard eyes stared blankly out of his ghastly white face, his thin lips curved into a slight smile as if he were determined to have the last laugh. Feeling repelled by the idea of searching his dead body for the book, I steadied myself by the chest. But then my legs gave way and I collapsed by Crace. Underneath me I felt the sticky viscosity of his darkening blood clinging to my skin. Closing my eyes, I pressed my hands down onto his nightshirt and began to feel his skeletal corpse for any signs of the hidden manuscript. The blood from his wound stained my palms and, as I searched, I left another trail across him. Slipping my hands underneath his slight frame, I turned him over and repeated the process on the back of his body, feeling the sharp bones jutting out of his thin, cold skin. As I traced my fingers down toward the bottom of his spine, I felt something hard and rectangular under his nightshirt. I pushed my hand under the fabric.

Pulling back the nightshirt, I saw a black, cloth-bound book strapped to the base of his back. I pulled the elastic, snapping it. Here was the lost manuscript that I had been looking for. I turned to the first page where the words *The Lying Tongue* had been written in Crace's spidery handwriting. As I started to read, spots of blood from my hands dropped onto the paper. A terrible fear gripped me. Its main character was called Adam. It was my story. They were my words.

acknowledgments

I could not have written this book without the support and love of those around me, especially my parents and family. Thanks, too, must go to my ever enthusiastic agent and friend, Clare Alexander, whose insight and judgment is second to none, and to all the staff at Gillon Aitken, in particular Sally Riley, Lesley Thorne and Justin Gowers.

I would like to thank the whole team at Canongate Books in the United Kingdom, especially my wonderful editor Dan Franklin, and first class publisher Jamie Byng. In the United States I owe a great deal to everyone at Atria Books and Simon & Schuster, in particular to my editor Peter Borland and his assistant Nick Simonds, designer Jaime Putorti and publisher Judith Curr.

Thanks to Gavanndra Hodge, who read an early draft of this novel, and to Christopher Fletcher, Susan Shaw, Peter Parker, Jonathan Gathorne-Hardy, Mary Greene, Victoria Millar, Mike Jones, Frances Wilson, Christopher Stocks, Charles Darwent, Salvatore Grigoli and Ewa Gizowska. Thank you, too, to Marcus Field—you know how much you mean to me.

This is a work of the imagination, but a number of sources have proved invaluable, including:

K. Andrews. *Catalogue of Italian Drawings,* two volumes. Cambridge: National Gallery of Scotland, 1968.

P. Aretino. *Selected Letters,* tr. George Bull. London: Penguin Books, 1976.

B. Berenson. *The Venetian Painters of the Renaissance,* 3rd ed. London: 1907.

M. Garrett. *Traveller's Literary Companion to Italy.* Brighton: In Print Pub., 1998.

M. Garrett. *Venice: A Cultural and Literary Companion.* Oxford: Signal Books, 2001.

M. Grundy. *Venice: An Anthology Guide.* London: Lund Humphries Publishers, 1980.

P. Humfrey, T. Clifford, A. Weston-Lewis and M. Bury. *The Age of Titian: Venetian Renaissance Art from Scottish Collections.* Edinburgh: National Galleries of Scotland, 2004.

G. Mazzariol and A. Dorigato. *Venetian Palazzi.* Cologne: Evergreen/Benedict Taschen Verlag, 1998.

J. Newman and N. Pevsner. *The Buildings of England: Dorset.* London: Penguin Books, 1972.

B. Skinner, Andrew Wilson and the Hopetoun Collection, *Country Life,* 15 August 1968, pp. 370–372.

J. Steer. *Venetian Painting.* London: Thames and Hudson, 1907, reprinted 1970.

G. Vasari. *The Lives of the Artists,* tr. George Bull. Penguin, 1971.